Moonflower Madness

"The wedding will take place here, of course," her aunt was saying. "As soon as Henry arrives. I shall get in touch with the shipping office in Shanghai and make the necessary bookings for you aboard the *Eastern Queen*. It will be something to look forward to, will it not?"

"Yes, Aunt Honoria," Gianette said dutifully, but she wasn't thinking of the *Eastern Queen* or the long sea journey back to England. She was thinking of the mountains and valleys of Kansu. Of the journey she intended to take, alone in the wake of Lord Rendlesham and Zachary Cartwright.

Margaret Pemberton is the bestselling author of numerous novels published on both sides of the Atlantic. Married with five children, she is the former chairman of the Romantic Novelists' Association and lives in London.

Moonflower Madness

Margaret Pemberton

A Woman's Weekly Paperback
MOONFLOWER MADNESS

First published in Great Britain 1993
by Severn House Publishers Ltd
This edition published 1995
by Woman's Weekly
in association with Mandarin Paperbacks
an imprint of Reed Books Limited
Michelin House, 81 Fulham Road, London SW3 6RB
and Auckland, Melbourne, Singapore and Toronto

Copyright © Margaret Pemberton 1993
The author has asserted her moral rights

A CIP catalogue record for this title
is available from the British Library
ISBN 1 86056 085 7

Printed and bound in Great Britain by
BPC Paperbacks Ltd
A member of
The British Printing Company Ltd

For Natasha Christina

CHAPTER ONE

The British Residency in Chung King was ablaze with flowers. Yellow jasmine climbed the walls, honeysuckle tumbled down the steps of the entrance, white anemones with lamp-black centres surged from terracotta pots, deep drowned-purple pansies vied for space with drifts of golden fabaria. Beyond a tangle of aged roses the broad, glittering curve of the Yang-tze River could be glimpsed, surging on and down to the distant sugarloaf gorges of Ichang.

Gianetta Hollis sighed and pushed a glossy black tendril of hair away from her face. The garden she sat in was supremely beautiful. The light had the pearl-like translucence peculiar to China, the air was heavy with scent and the only sound to be heard was the gentle tinkling of pagoda bells. And she was bored. Unspeakably, unimaginably bored.

She had been in China for nearly a year and apart from the week's voyage by steamer up the Yang-tze from Shanghai to Ichang and the thrilling, perilous five-week journey by junk through the gorges and ravines that separated Ichang from Chung King, she had seen nothing of the country. Nothing at all.

She sighed again, this time with rising impatience. It really was ridiculous for her aunt to be so over-protective of Serena and herself. It was five years now since murderous rebels had rampaged through the country vowing to kill every foreigner on Chinese soil. Her aunt and uncle had been living in Peking and for fifty-five terrifying days had been besieged, with over a hundred

1

other Europeans, inside the Legation Quarter. They had held the rebels at bay with great cost of life until, at last, an international rescue force had marched into the city and relieved them.

It was an experience her aunt would never forget. Although the country was now calm again, she would not allow her daughter or her niece to venture beyond the Residency compound into the narrow crowded streets of Chung King or the wild, unexplored countryside beyond.

To Gianetta's chagrin, their only journeys were to the nearby Anglican Mission, and even then they were obliged to travel by sedan-chair and under heavy protective escort. It was not what Gianetta had imagined when she had dreamed of China. She had envisaged exotic vistas; horseback rides into the foothills of mysterious mountains; magical walks through the courtyards of ancient temples; adventure, danger, excitement. Instead she was obliged to spend her days in a monotony as unrelieved as the one she had left behind at Sutton Hall, her aunt and uncle's family home in Lincolnshire. Her pleasures were now, as then, circumscribed by Serena's pleasures.

If Serena wanted to go on a picnic or an expedition to a local beauty spot, then of course such expeditions were arranged. If Serena wished to ride, suitable horses and grooms were speedily found. If Serena wished to take up the fascinating new pastime of photography, then the very latest whole-plate camera was purchased for her use. Unfortunately for Gianetta, it was very rare that Serena expressed the wish to do anything as exciting as ride or experiment with photography. She was easy-tempered, sweet-natured and unimaginative. As Gianetta's aunt was often heard to say with relief, Serena was as dissimilar to her cousin as chalk from cheese.

Gianetta kicked a smooth white pebble away with the toe of a neatly-booted foot and watched as a lizard scurried away, seeking fresh cover. What her aunt said was true. She and Serena *were* dissimilar in temperament, but that was only to be expected. Serena was totally English and had been brought up in the calm atmosphere of the Lincolnshire fens. She, Gianetta, was half-Italian and had, for the first twelve years of her life, been brought up in the exciting, mercurial atmosphere of the Villa Simione, overlooking Lake Garda.

Her father, Edward Hollis, had embarked on a Grand Tour in 1887 and had travelled no further than Florence when he had fallen in love not only with the Duomo, the church of Santa Croce and the slow-moving waters of the Arno, but also with the bewitching and incomparably beautiful Lucrezia Segatti.

It had not been a love affair looked fondly on by either family. The Hollises had been appalled at the thought of Italian blood sullying their ancient family tree. The Segattis had been equally aghast at the prospect of their high-born daughter throwing herself away on an Englishman with only a minor title. Both families had agreed on one thing only. There would be no marriage. It was then that Edward Hollis had shown his true mettle. He had ridden at night from his *penzione* in Florence to the Segatti's family villa and he had urged Lucrezia to climb down from her room and elope with him.

The result had been a marriage that the Hollises had eventually accepted only grudgingly, the Segattis not at all. Twelve years later, an unrepentant Lucrezia had succumbed to tuberculosis. Her heartbroken husband, riding too recklessly in an effort to assuage his grief, had been thrown from his horse and had never recovered consciousness.

Gianetta, aged eleven, had been obliged to accept the offer of a home in England with a cousin she had never seen.

All in all it had not been so very dreadful. She had not been beaten or starved, but she had hated the cold, flat greyness of the Lincolnshire fens and the cheerlessness of a house which, during her aunt and uncle's long absences in China, was inhabited only

3

by Serena, Serena's governess, and an army of servants.

It was Serena who had made it bearable. She had been overjoyed at having her loneliness relieved by Gianetta's arrival, and greeted her as if she were a long-lost sister. Five years later, at Gianetta's urging, Serena had written to her parents asking if, accompanied by Gianetta, she could travel out to join them. The reply, to Serena's nervous apprehension and Gianetta's ebullient delight, had been in the affirmative.

They had sailed from Gravesend aboard the SS *Eastern Queen*, chaperoned as far as Hong Kong by Sir Archibald and Lady Plaxtol, old friends of the Hollises, returning to China after a year's furlough. Also accompanying them was their son Henry, a pleasant-faced, mild-mannered young man who had recently been ordained into the Church of England. In Hong Kong they had said goodbye to the Plaxtols, continuing their journey to Shanghai under the protective eye of the ship's captain.

Shanghai had been all that Gianetta had dreamed it would be. The narrow streets were crowded with Chinamen, their hair worn in long single pigtails down their backs. Rope-dancers span and twirled, pedlars cried their wares, jugglers and acrobats vied for attention with storytellers and scribes. Gianetta had sighed with rapture at the strangeness of it all, oblivious to the heat, and the stench of garlic, tobacco and stale, unwashed bodies.

Her rapture had been short-lived. Her uncle who had met them off the boat, had no intention of delaying his return to Chung King by spending unnecessary time in Shanghai. At seven the next morning they had boarded the steamer that was to take them to Ichang. A week later, they had transferred from the steamer to the junk for the long, laborious last stage of their journey up the Yang-tze to Chung King.

Since then, to Gianetta's chagrin, there had been no exploratory excursions into the surrounding countryside. For her, China was the carefully tended grounds of the Residency. It did not help that Serena was happy to accept this restriction. With a gesture of impatience, Gianetta flicked a fluttering butterfly away with her hand and rose to her feet. For all the excitement she was experiencing, she might just as well have stayed in Lincolnshire. At least there she had been able to go for long, unaccompanied walks. Here, there was no outlet for her frustrations and she was rapidly beginning to feel as if she were in an exotic, flower-filled prison.

"Gianetta! Gianetta!"

She turned her head as Serena, in a high-necked white lace blouse and an ankle-length turquoise skirt, ran lightly down the shallow stone steps towards her.

"What do you think? We are to have visitors this evening. A Mr Zachary Cartwright, who Papa says is a very famous botanist, and his cousin, Lord Rendlesham."

Serena's corn-coloured hair was brushed away from her face in a sleek chignon, her grey-green eyes alight with pleasure at being the bearer of such agreeable news.

Gianetta frowned, determined not to be shaken out of her despondency so easily. Lord Rendlesham was eighty. She knew, because his birthday had been announced not long ago in *The Times*. His friends would no doubt be equally aged and uninteresting. All her uncle's dinner guests were.

"Is that the only reason for your good humour?" she asked, her eyes going to the tell-tale envelope protruding slightly from the pocket of Serena's skirt.

Serena laughed and linked her arm as they began to walk back towards the house.

"No," she said, a light blush touching her cheeks. "I received another letter from Henry Plaxtol this morning. He is returning to England very soon, but is visiting Ichtang and Chung King before he does so."

"And is that such wonderful news?" Gianetta asked unimpressed.

The blush in Serena's cheeks deepened. "Yes," she said, unconcealed happiness in her voice. "It is for me."

Gianetta stood still on the flower-edged path and stared at her in disbelief. "You can't possibly be in love with him!" she said incredulously. "He's a clergyman!"

"I know," Serena said, with all the serenity of her name, "but he is an only son and Sir Archibald is a very old friend of Papa's. I think he and Mama would be quite pleased if . . . if anything should come of our friendship."

Gianetta felt the blood drain from her face. If Serena married Henry, then she would return to England. What would happen to her if she did so? She couldn't imagine for a moment that her aunt would invite her to stay on in Chung King, and if she didn't, what were the alternatives? A return to Sutton Hall, this time without the benefit of Serena's companionship? Or even worse, a life as a lovingly tolerated guest in Serena's marital home, for Serena was sure to invite her to live with her. The prospect filled her with horror. Dearly as she loved Serena, she could not bear the thought of living always in her shadow, a voyeur of her happiness, her only practical role that of aunt to Serena's children.

"Come along," Serena said good-naturedly, taking no offence at Gianetta's lack of enthusiasm for her news. "The Chinese artist Mama has engaged for our art lessons has arrived. He looks terribly nice. Very small and very nimble."

Gianetta's interest was aroused. The tutor had been engaged to instruct them in the art of Chinese flower painting, and she had already determined to ask him if he would also give them instruction in landscape painting. If he did so, then her aunt would surely have to give permission for them to journey a little way out of Chung King, so that they could study and paint some suitable views.

"Mr Li is waiting for you in the drawing-room," her Aunt Honoria said, as they entered the Residency's cool shade.

She was a tall, statuesque woman who possessed none of her daughter's grace or beauty. As if to compensate

6

for these deficiencies, she took great pride in always doing her duty, no matter how disagreeable that duty might be. It was wifely duty that kept her in China, a country she hated, and it was family duty that had obliged her to give a home to Gianetta. She had no sense of humour and seldom smiled. The fact that she was at the moment looking extremely pleased with herself, as if she had just received news which had given her great satisfaction, filled Gianetta with foreboding. On a nearby desk top, an envelope identical to the envelope that Serena had received lay open and empty. Her foreboding deepened. Henry Plaxtol had not only written to Serena, he had written to her parents as well. And if her aunt's demeanour was anything to go by, his communication had been well received.

"Has Serena told you we are having guests to dine this evening?" her aunt asked, giving Gianetta the rare benefit of her attention. "Mr Zachary Cartwright is one of England's leading botanists. Queen Victoria consulted him frequently and I have it on very good authority that, since her death, he has continued in royal favour. He has been a guest of King Edward's at both Sandringham and Balmoral."

Gianetta strove to look suitably impressed and must have succeeded, for her aunt now turned her attention towards Serena. "Papa is at present on a visit to the Chinese consulate, but when he returns, both he and I would like to have a word with you." She smiled and patted her daughter's arm with maternal tenderness. "Alone and in Papa's study if you please, Serena."

The flush that had touched Serena's cheeks in the garden now coloured them once again.

"Yes, Mama," she said, her happiness so transparent that Gianetta hated herself for her own, horrified reaction to her aunt's words,

How on *earth* could Serena be in love with a nonentity like Henry Plaxtol? It didn't seem possible. True, they had spent long periods of time in each other's company aboard the *Eastern Queen*, but she had assumed that that had been mere politeness on Serena's part. She looked across at her cousin and at the hot tide of colour in her cheeks, and was forced to accept that it had *not* been politeness. Unbeknown to her, Serena had fallen in love, and it was a love story that was apparently going to have a happy ending. For Serena, but not for herself. She thought of her own future if Serena married; of Sutton Hall and the damp Lincolnshire fens. She shuddered. Somehow, somewhere, there must be an alternative for her, but as she went into the sun-filled room with Serena to meet Mr Li, try as she might, she could not think of one.

The art class temporarily took her mind off her problem. She had always excelled at drawing and was fascinated by the delicacy and precision of Chinese painting. To enable him to judge their talent, Mr Li asked them to sketch a rose that was standing in a porcelain vase on a small enamelled table. Serena's execution was, as he had imagined it would be, competent but uninspired. Gianetta's filled him with stunned surprise.

In only a few spare lines she had caught the overblown lushness of the rose to perfection, and the anatomical details of petal, leaf and calyx were pleasingly correct.

"I shall come again," he said, bowing his head as he took his leave of them, "I shall come again at the end of the week."

"When you come again, Mr Li, could you instruct us in landscape painting?" Gianetta asked. "Something in the style of Kuan T'ung or Wang-Hui?"

Mr Li blinked. He had had the privilege of teaching art to the English daughters of consuls and merchants in Peking and Shanghai as well as Chung King, but he had never before taught anyone who had the slightest knowledge or, he suspected, interest in his country's art or artists.

"I have seen a copy of Wang-Hui's *The Colours of Mount T'ai-hang* in a book," Gianetta continued winningly, "and I think it very beautiful."

8

He beamed at her. "Indeed it is, Miss Hollis, very beautiful," he said warmly.

"Perhaps we could attempt something similar?" Gianetta continued. "From above Chung King there must be many splendid views of the river."

Mr Li nodded his head. "Many, many," he agreed. "Chung King has a number of wonderful views."

"Then I will tell Lady Hollis that you recommend we journey out into the hills for our next lesson," Gianetta said, well satisfied with the results she had achieved. "There is no need to worry about bearers, Mr Li. There are plenty here, on the Residency staff."

Mr Li bowed again. She was unusual, this dark-haired English girl. There was no condescension in her voice when she spoke to him, no superiority in her manner. He had not met such an English girl before, and his heart warmed towards her.

"We will paint landscapes in the manner of the ancients," he said in his almost flawless English. "Landscapes that will pierce the heart and startle the eye." With that amazing promise, he took his leave of them.

"What an incredible little man," Serena exclaimed, laughing. "Do you think Mama will give permission for us to go up into the hills?"

"I don't know," Gianetta said truthfully, "but we can at least try. Nuns must have more freedom of movement than we do. Do you know that we haven't been *anywhere*, apart from the Anglican Mission, for eight *months*."

"But as far as Mama is concerned there is nowhere for us to go," Serena said with sweet reasonableness. "Chung King is the most remote outpost that any consul can be posted to. There are no other diplomats stationed here, no European families in residence, no-one for us to pay visits to. Believe me, Gianetta, Mama and Papa hate it almost as much as you do, but Mama says that it is a posting that has to be endured. It is only until the end of the year. Then Papa will be relieved of his duties and his next posting

9

will be somewhere far more congenial. Kabul perhaps, or Delhi."

"But I don't hate Chung King!" Gianetta cried passionately. "I love it. I love the temples and pagodas and the plum blossom and the junks on the river. What I hate is only being able to see these things from a distance. I want to *visit* the temples. I want to walk out on the hills beneath the plum trees. I want to *enjoy* China, not be protected from it!"

Dark tendrils of hair had escaped from her upswept hairstyle and clung softly against her cheeks. Serena regarded her affectionately. Her mother had often been heard to say, though not in Gianetta's hearing, that it was a pity Gianetta was not more *English* in her colouring, and that she had not Serena's height and consequent grace. It was true that when they had attended balls together she, Serena, had always attracted the most attention from gentlemen admirers. But she had always modestly assumed that to be because of Gianetta's well known lack of all inheritance, or any prospect of one.

Gianetta's violet-blue, wide-set, black-lashed eyes, met Serena's. Her full mouth widened in an apologetic smile. "I'm sorry, Serena. I'm being an awful bore. It's just that I find it all so frustrating. It would be the same if we were in Kabul or Delhi. We still wouldn't be able to leave the house and gardens. There are times when I truly wish I had been born a man."

Serena gurgled with delight at her ridiculousness. "You sound like one of those ladies who admire Mrs Pankhurst!"

"I am." Gianetta retorted darkly.

Serena's amusement deepened. If and when they returned to England she could quite imagine Gianetta with cropped hair, proudly marching to win votes for women. "When do you intend asking Mama's permission for our painting expedition?" she asked, tactfully changing the subject.

"Now," Gianetta said resolutely.

As she moved purposefully towards the door, Serena

said musingly, "I wonder what time the junks from Ichang will dock? I heard Mama give instructions that they were to be met by every sedan-chair and bearer available. Mr Cartwright and Lord Rendlesham are to travel into parts of China that no European has ever ventured into before. The equipment they have brought with them must be prodigious."

Gianetta hesitated at the door, looking at Serena with interest. It had not occurred to her that Mr Cartwright and Lord Rendlesham would be doing anything more than journeying from Shanghai to Chung King by river and, after a short rest, making the return journey in the same manner.

"I don't see how Lord Rendlesham will be able to travel further than the Residency," she said candidly. "He's ages old. The only equipment he and Mr Cartwright will have with them will be foot-warmers and bath-chairs."

Serena had burst out laughing and Gianetta had left her and gone in search of her aunt. Her aunt had not been available. She was at her desk, writing copious letters to acquaintances in Peking and friends in England, and had given instructions that she was not to be disturbed.

The long afternoon wore on. Shortly after three o'clock, Gianetta heard the sedan-chairs and bearers leaving the rear of the Residency on their way down to the river. The level of the Yang-tze changed dramatically according to the seasons, and long stone staircases led down from the bank to the present level of the water. If, as Serena had said, Mr Cartwright and Lord Rendlesham had brought extensive equipment with them, then unloading and then transferring it up the steep stone steps would take a long while.

She wandered out into the garden with her sketch-pad, and was absorbed in capturing the lines of a delicately shaped terracotta pot with peonies spilling down from it, when she heard the noise of the sedan-chairs returning. She ignored the commotion, having no curiosity at all about either Lord Rendlesham or his companion. It

11

seemed to her that every Englishman who visited China did so only in order to find fault with it. Lord Rendlesham and Mr Zachary Cartwright would be no different. She didn't care if she met them at all.

She looked down at her sketch-pad with satisfaction. She had captured the clean, pure lines of the flowers and the jar. The next thing she was going to do was to approach her aunt again. If she could look forward to an escape from the Residency, however temporary, then she would be able to survive the boredom of dinner that evening with her uncle's guests.

Her aunt looked at her coldly. "No, Gianetta. You most certainly can *not* indulge in an unnecessary expedition into the countryside. Mr Li has been engaged to instruct yourself and Serena in the art of Chinese flower painting. There are plenty of flowers in the garden which can be painted. The kind of venture that you are suggesting is quite out of the question."

"But it would be a simple expedition to arrange, and Mr Li thinks it most necessary . . ." she persisted desperately.

Her aunt silenced her with a steely eye. "I think you have made a mistake. I am quite sure that Mr Li does *not* consider it necessary at all. I want to hear no more about it. And now, if you will excuse me, I have an appointment with your uncle."

She swept from the room without a backward glance, her lips tightly set, her jawline implacable.

Gianetta clenched her fists and fought the temptation to pick up the nearest ornament to hand and throw it in her aunt's wake. As she struggled for self-control she saw Serena descend the last few steps of the staircase and cross the hall towards the study her mother had just entered. The family *tête-à-tête* was about to begin, and Gianetta was sure she knew what subject was under discussion.

Filled with a sense of approaching doom, she made her way slowly towards the stairs. Dinner would be served in little over an hour. Her aunt would expect her to fulfil her role as dutiful niece, and to listen with polite interest to the boring ramblings of her guests.

Gianetta's Chinese maid was already filling up her bath with enormous jugs of water. She opened her closet doors, wondering which of her gowns, nearly all of them originally Serena's, she would wear. Listlessly she plucked a lemon Crêpe de Chine dress from a hanger. It had a high-boned neck and long sleeves, tight at the wrist and then flounced so that they extended over her well-shaped hands, drawing attention to them.

"Your bath ready now, Missy," the maid said dutifully, and Gianetta thanked her, wondering if she was perhaps drawing too many conclusions from too little evidence. Serena had not actually said that Henry Plaxtol had asked her to marry him, or that she would accept him if he did so. Her aunt had said nothing to indicate that the meeting in the study was about Serena's marital future. And yet . . . and yet . . .

She sank into the fragrant water.

What else could the *tête-à-tête* be about? Two letters had arrived from Henry on the same day, and since their arrival her aunt's eyes had held an unmistakable gleam. Wedding bells were in the air, and they certainly were not for herself. All the young men she had met so far had seemed far more attracted to Serena's fair, English-rose prettiness than they were to her own dark vibrancy.

So . . . Henry had asked for Serena's hand in marriage and, because he was his father's sole heir, her aunt and uncle had been only too happy to give his request their blessing.

Gianetta wriggled her toes moodily in the water. Why, oh why, hadn't her Italian grandparents become reconciled with her mother? If they had done so, her own position would be far different. She would in all likelihood be living with them in Italy, not facing a future as a permanent house guest of Serena's, or a lonely existence in a cold, draughty house in the Lincolnshire fens. She towelled herself dry, hoping vehemently that

13

Serena would have more sense than to accept Henry Plaxtol's proposal, and knowing that a quiet-spoken vicar with ample independent means was exactly the kind of husband Serena would choose.

By the time she had dressed and re-done her hair she knew that she was late. Not late for dinner, that would be a *faux pas* even she would not dare to commit, but late for pre-dinner drinks with her uncle and aunt and their guests in the main drawing-room.

The Chinese boy her aunt had trained as a footman and who wore a striking livery of her own design, opened the drawing-room doors for her and she stepped inside, registering with immediate alarm her aunt's rare good humour.

"Ah, there you are, Gianetta. Please allow me to introduce Lord Rendlesham to you." She turned to the compactly built gentleman standing behind her, half-obliterated from view by her Junoesque proportions. "Lord Rendlesham, my niece, Miss Gianetta Hollis. Gianetta, Lord Rendlesham, a very *distinguished* member of the Royal Geographical Society *and* the Royal Botanical Society, Kew."

Gianetta accepted his proffered hand, her eyes wide with shock. He was in his middle thirties, with thickly curling auburn hair and a smile that was easy and engaging.

"I'm delighted to meet you, Miss Hollis," he said. There was a hint of suppressed amusement in his voice, as if he were aware that he was not at all what she had expected.

"Mr Cartwright has been unavoidably detained," her aunt was saying to her. "Some difficulty with the transporting of equipment from the riverside to the Residency. We are delaying dinner until his arrival."

Gianetta's amazement increased. To delay dinner was unprecedented. Lord Rendlesham and his companion were obviously far more important than she had imagined.

"Lady Hollis tells me that Serena and yourself are having lessons in Chinese flower painting," Lord Rendlesham

14

was saying to her. "As a botanist, I wish I had a little more talent myself in that direction."

Gianetta made a polite answering remark but her attention was focussed on Serena, who was standing a few feet away from them, next to her father and the Chinese Viceroy. Was she imagining it, or was Serena glowing with an inner radiance? If only she could catch her eye then she would know if her suspicions were correct, but Serena infuriatingly kept her gaze upon her father, who was explaining to her the difference between a botanist and a naturalist.

"I had a very pretty collection of dried flowers when I was a girl," her aunt was saying. "Such an *edifying* occupation, I always think."

"Yes, I am sure it must have been, Lady Hollis," Lord Rendlesham murmured. Seeing the good humour in his voice and the laughter in his eyes, Gianetta decided that she liked him very much. The evening was not going to be boring, after all.

"And what is to be your final destination?" her uncle asked, turning towards Lord Rendlesham. "It might just be possible to travel further west by junk to Luchow, but the junk would have to be manually hauled from the river bank, as they have to be through the Ichang gorges."

"We are going north, Sir Arthur, not west," Lord Rendlesham said, and her uncle's eyebrows flew high in surprise.

"Impossible," he said decisively. "There are no more consulates to offer protection, and the area is for the most part uncharted."

"Nevertheless, that is the direction we intend to take," Lord Rendlesham said easily. "We hope to reach the northern province of Kansu and to search for plants along the western border with Tibet."

If he had said he intended searching for plants on the surface of the moon, Gianetta's uncle could not have looked more astonished.

15

"But my good man!" he protested apoplectically, "Such a journey is physically impossible! You surely haven't forgotten what happened to Margery when he made a similar attempt?"

"No, indeed I haven't," Lord Rendlesham said, unruffled. "But that was nearly thirty years ago and I don't anticipate that we shall meet with the same fate."

"Who was Margery?" Serena asked her mother in a whisper.

"A gentleman directly responsible for *our* being in Chung King," her mother said, her voice low so that she would not be overheard by the Viceroy. "He attempted to cross into one of China's more remote provinces from Burma. He was most cruelly murdered by the local people, and the British government insisted on an agreement with the Chinese that such a thing would not happen again. It is for that reason that Papa is in Chung King, to ensure that the agreement is kept and that British travellers are not molested."

"But how on earth can Papa ensure such a thing?" Serena asked in bewilderment. "He never travels out into the countryside . . ."

"Serena!" The tone of her mother's voice silenced Serena instantly.

Lady Hollis turned to her guest and forced a smile. "I think I have just heard someone entering by the main door. Mr Cartwright must have arrived."

Gianetta was aware that Serena's remark had vastly entertained Lord Rendlesham and wondered if his friend, now audibly approaching, was equally good-humoured.

"I was very sorry to hear of your father's death," Lady Hollis was now saying to him. "I knew him very well, as you know, and always thought him a most remarkable person."

Lord Rendlesham accepted her condolences, and as he did so the drawing-room doors were flung open to admit a tall, broad shouldered young man.

"Mr Ca't'ight, Ma'am," the Chinese footman said, but

16

he went unheard. Mr Cartwright was already making his own introductions.

Even though she was no longer expecting to see an old man, Gianetta felt a slam of shock at Mr Cartwright's youth. He was even younger than Lord Rendlesham, no more than twenty-six or twenty-seven. Dazedly, she wondered how such a young man could have earned himself such a prestigious professional reputation. He was shaking hands with Lady Hollis and turning towards Serena, and Gianetta's second realization was how excessively good looking he was.

His colouring was as dark as her own. Blue-black hair tumbled low over strongly marked brows. His nose was straight, his jaw firm, his mouth finely chiselled, and when he moved, he did so with the ease and grace of an athlete.

Her uncle was introducing him. "Mr Cartwright, my niece, Miss Gianetta Hollis."

The eyes beneath the demonically winged brows were as dark as she had expected them to be, the deep brown irises flecked with gold. His well-shaped mouth was not softened by laughterlines as Lord Rendlesham's was. Instead there was an abrasive, uncompromising look to his handsome features that indicated he was not a man it would be wise to trifle with.

His eyes were preoccupied as they were introduced and then his attention returned immediately to Serena. Gianetta knew, with amusement, that Serena's fairytale blonde beauty had worked its magic yet again.

"Let us go in to dinner," her aunt said, determined that it should be delayed no longer. "Lord Rendlesham, would you be so kind as to escort Serena? And Mr Cartwright, if you would escort Gianetta. We are only a small party but I'm sure you will find the Viceroy's comments on your proposed expedition extremely interesting."

The Viceroy had already made it known that he had given permission for Lord Rendlesham and his companion to journey through his province. Gianetta had a shrewd

17

idea that, even if he had refused, it would have made no difference to Mr Cartwright. He was a man who would not take no for an answer, even from a Viceroy.

Conversation at dinner, as Lord Rendlesham explained to his host exactly what it was he and Mr Cartwright hoped to achieve on their expedition, was so fascinating that Gianetta forgot about her fear that Serena had become engaged to Henry Plaxtol.

It transpired that Lord Rendlesham had never been to China before but that Zachary Cartwright had previously travelled in Western Hupeh. There he had heard rumours of blue Moonflowers growing in the more northerly province of Kansu.

"Oh!" Serena breathed. "How romantic! Is that why you are in China, Mr Cartwright? To find a blue Moonflower?"

Zachary Cartwright had taken little part in the conversation so far, allowing Lord Rendlesham to answer most of his host's questions. Now, as Serena fixed her gaze wonderingly upon him, he leaned forward slightly, saying with a depth of feeling that sent a tingle down Gianetta's spine, "To find the blue Moonflower and to find hundreds of other plants that are, as yet, unknown in Europe."

"But why do you do it?" Serena's father asked in bewilderment. "What sense is there in risking life and limb, and suffering untold hardship, all for the sake of a flower?"

Zachary Cartwright's eyes blazed. "I do it because my search takes me into country where no Englishman has ever ventured. I do it because the beauty and majesty of the mountains and valleys that I explore have not yet been violated by civilisation. I do it because I can imagine nothing more wonderful than discovering an unknown flower and bringing the seed of that flower back to England, enabling hundreds of thousands of people to enjoy its beauty."

Sir Arthur cleared his throat, embarrassed by his guest's

18

intensity. "Yes, I can see that that might be a jolly fine thing to do," he said, quite obviously not seeing at all.

Gianetta's fingers curled into her palms. It was *not* a jolly fine thing to do. It was a *wonderful* thing to do. A magical thing to do. To search for flowers that no European had ever seen! To journey into valleys into which no European had ever ventured! The blood pounded in her temples at the very thought.

Lady Hollis was rising to her feet, indicating that the gentlemen should be left with their port. Gianetta and Serena followed her out of the dining-room and into the lamp-lit drawing-room.

"And now, Gianetta," her aunt said with unconcealed satisfaction as the footman closed the *portières* behind them. "I have news which I am sure will please you as much as it does me."

Gianetta's eyes flew from her aunt's to Serena's. Serena smiled radiantly and slipped her hand into hers.

"Henry has written to Papa, requesting permission to ask for my hand in marriage," she said happily, "and Mama and Papa have given his request their blessing."

Gianetta knew that instead of looking overjoyed at the news, she looked horrified. She struggled to alter the expression on her face, saying, in a strangled voice, "I hope you will be very happy, Serena."

"Of course, this means that Serena will be returning to England," her aunt said, her eyes carefully avoiding Gianetta's. "I'm sure you will agree that it would be impractical for you to stay on in China in those circumstances, Gianetta, and so I will make arrangements for you to travel home with Serena and Henry."

"I want you to live with us," Serena said, lovingly squeezing her cousin's hand. "I know that Henry will not mind. He is so very kind, and he would hate the idea of you living alone at Sutton Hall as much as I do."

Gianetta tried to speak and couldn't. It was as if the floor were shelving away beneath her feet. No doubt Henry Plaxtol *was* kind, but she didn't want his kindness.

She didn't want to live with him and Serena. She certainly didn't want to live in Lincolnshire again. She wanted to live life her own way, as Lord Rendlesham and Zachary Cartwright lived theirs. She wanted to travel out into the wilds of unexplored China. She wanted to see scenes no English girl had ever seen before. She wanted to find blue Moonflowers.

"The wedding will take place here, of course," her aunt was saying. "As soon as Henry arrives. I shall get in touch with the shipping office in Shanghai and make the necessary bookings for you aboard the *Eastern Queen*. It will be something to look forward to, will it not?"

"Yes, Aunt Honoria," Gianetta said dutifully, but she wasn't thinking of the *Eastern Queen* or the long sea journey back to England. She was thinking of the mountains and valleys of Kansu. Of the journey she intended to take, alone, in the wake of Lord Rendlesham and Zachary Cartwright.

CHAPTER TWO

When her uncle and his guests rejoined them in the drawing-room, Gianetta found it hard not to betray her rising excitement. Where Lord Rendlesham and Mr Cartwright were going, she was also going. The knowledge made her head swim and the blood sing along her veins. As the conversation returned to the expedition and the reasons for it, her mind whirled feverishly, busy making plans.

"The general object of our mission is to collect seeds and plants of an ornamental and useful kind," Lord Rendlesham was saying, in the easy manner which she found so appealing. "They must, of course, be plants that are not already in cultivation in England. We also hope to obtain, for the Royal Horticultural Society, information on the methods of Chinese gardening and agriculture.'

As she listened to him, Gianetta knew that she would feel perfectly safe with him, no matter how lonely and wild the surroundings in which they found themselves. She cast a covert look across at Zachary Cartwright. She certainly wouldn't feel quite so comfortable with Mr Cartwright. He really had a most forbidding manner. The conversation at the dinner table had obviously bored him and, apart from the time when he had responded to Serena's questions, he had taken almost no part in it at all. Even now he was not sitting with his friend and the Viceroy, but was moving restlessly around the room, inspecting the books on the shelves, his open indifference to his host and hostess bordering almost on insolence.

Sensing someone's gaze on him he turned his head.

His eyes met Gianetta's and, for a heart-stopping second before she could drag her gaze away, held. She saw surprise flash through the dark depths of his eyes followed immediately by an ill-concealed mental shrug of dismissal.

That the dismissal was because it was she and not Serena he had surprised looking at him was obvious, as was his mortifying assumption that her gaze had been one of admiration. Furious at herself for giving so false an impression, she moved so that her shoulders were set firmly against him and, with an effort, returned her attention to Lord Rendlesham.

"Some provinces of China, those that are easily approached by sea, have of course already been thoroughly explored," he was saying to her uncle. "The problem is that the provinces in question all have tropical or sub-tropical climates, and the flora found there will not grow happily in England. Our objective is to find unknown plants growing in a temperate zone. Plants that will flourish in English gardens."

She would have to follow them at a distance for two or three days, possibly longer. If she caught up with them too soon they would simply have her escorted straight back to Chung King. She would have to wait until the distance they had travelled was so great that they would have no option but to allow her to continue with them.

"And does Kansu have a temperate zone?" her aunt was asking with polite interest.

Lord Rendlesham grinned. "Oh yes. Weatherwise, Kansu is influenced by the high plateau of Tibet. The plants we find there will live very happily in northern Europe."

Gianetta listened to him avidly. She would have to bring clothes that were both serviceable for travelling, suitable for wear now and warm enough for the colder climate of Kansu. It wouldn't be an easy task, especially as she could only take what could be easily carried on a mule or a donkey.

Mr Zachary Cartwright had finished his perusal of her uncle's books and was sitting in a chair to the left of the Viceroy. Gianetta kept her eyes steadfastly away from his, aware, nevertheless, that his own attention was once more focussed upon Serena.

"It was Zac who fired my imagination and tempted me into accompanying him," Lord Rendlesham was saying frankly. "Compared to his, my botanical knowledge is nil."

Her uncle politely said he was sure that couldn't be true, but Zachary Cartwright made no attempt to correct his friend's statement. Gianetta wondered if other people, apart from Lord Rendlesham, referred to him as Zac. Certainly the name suited his hard masculinity far better than the more biblical Zachary.

"I still think you should spend longer in Chung King before departing on such a hazardous venture," her aunt was saying to Lord Rendlesham.

Gianetta suppressed a smile. If her aunt had deigned to look in Zachary Cartwright's direction she would have seen the way he was looking at Serena and wouldn't, then, have been so keen for him to prolong his visit.

Lord Rendlesham smiled. "I would have liked to stay here for several weeks, but if we are to avoid the summer rains we must leave immediately. Our equipment merely has to be repacked on to the mules we have hired, and that is being done at this very moment."

Gianetta felt a slam of shock that left her almost breathless.

"When . . . when do you intend to leave?" she asked. She had thought it would not be until the end of the week. Possibly not until the beginning of the week following.

"Tomorrow at dawn," Lord Rendlesham said, and as he spoke to her there was sincere regret in his voice. He would have liked to have stayed longer. Gianetta Hollis had a dark, magical quality about her that aroused him deeply. He saw her eyes widen. Eyes so startlingly violet against her night-black hair that their beauty took his breath away. He wondered what her ancestry was. Her eyes, and the creamy whiteness of her skin, were obviously the legacy of her English father, but her mother must have been Irish, or Italian perhaps, to account for the glossy darkness of her brows and lashes and the unbelievable blue-black lustre of her hair.

"Oh!" For one devastating moment, Gianetta was certain that all her plans were in vain, and then she knew that time made no difference. She needed only a mule, some provisions, and detailed knowledge of the route Lord Rendlesham and Mr Cartwright were to take. The mule could easily be borrowed from the Residency stables, and so could the provisions, from the Residency kitchens. The only item she lacked was information.

"How far do you hope to travel on your first day?" she asked.

He smiled, his warm blue eyes crinkling attractively at the corners. "I'm afraid you will have to ask Zac that question. He has far more knowledge than I have about how far we might be expected to travel in one day."

Unwillingly Gianetta transferred her attention to Mr Cartwright. "How far do you expect to travel tomorrow, Mr Cartwright?" she asked coolly.

He gave a barely discernible shrug of his broad shoulders. "Possibly to Fu-tu Kwan," he said laconically.

She had heard of Fu-tu Kwan. It was a small, walled town some fifteen miles to the north.

"And then, after Fu-tu Kwan?" she asked with studied carelessness.

Again there was a slight lifting of his shoulders. "It isn't possible to say with any certainty. Kaingpeh maybe, or Lingtao."

"I do not understand why you t'avel by 'oad and not 'iver," the Viceroy said, breaking his self-imposed silence. "It much easie' to t'avel by 'iver."

"If the plants we find on our way to Fu-tu Kwan are disappointing, then we will alter our plans and travel the rest of the way, as far as Peng, by river," Zachary

24

Cartwright said, and Gianetta was intrigued to note that there was a pleasant courtesy in his manner towards the elderly Chinaman that had been lacking in his previous, brief conversation with her uncle and aunt.

"You speak Manda'in?" the Viceroy asked him suddenly, leaning towards him, his robe of brocaded silk shimmering in the lamplight.

Zachary Cartwright nodded. "Yes, Your Excellency. And Cantonese." There was no boastfulness in his voice. It was merely a statement of fact.

"Then you will have no p'oblems in Szechuan or Kansu," the Viceroy said. "It is only people who have no love of Chinese cultu'e or unde'standing of the Chinese people, who have p'oblems."

His eyes flicked momentarily towards Lord Rendlesham and then towards his host. Although his face was impassive, Gianetta was sure that both gentlemen fell into the Viceroy's category of men who had no deep understanding of his country.

"I cannot envy you the inns you will have to stay in *en route* to Kansu," her aunt said to Lord Rendlesham with a shiver of distaste. "I am sure that the Viceroy will be in agreement with me when I say that the local inns leave much to be desired."

She was being polite. The local inns were lice-infested horrors no European willingly entered.

Gianetta felt her stomach muscles tighten. She had not thought about where she would sleep at night. The inns were not only lice-infested, they were rat-infested as well. They possessed no fresh water and had no sanitary arrangements.

"We shall very seldom be using inns," Lord Rendlesham said reassuringly. "So far, unless we have been on board a boat, we have slept out in the open."

"Umph," Gianetta's uncle grunted disapprovingly. "Healthier certainly, but not very safe. This isn't Lincolnshire. There are bandits and robbers by the score. And on the river there are pirates." He pursed his lips. "I wouldn't give much for your chances unless you are heavily armed and the Chinese accompanying you are one hundred per cent trustworthy."

"The men I have engaged are all trustworthy," Zachary Cartwright said, the underlying steel in his voice repudiating the unsaid suggestion that they might not be.

Gianetta's uncle looked disbelieving, but good manners and the Viceroy's presence prevented him from pursuing the subject.

The grandfather clock that had been laboriously transported from Lincolnshire to Chung King began to chime ten o'clock. Lady Hollis rose to her feet.

"Goodnight, gentlemen. I doubt that I will see you again in the morning, but you have my very best wishes for your journey."

She turned to the Viceroy and wished him a courteous goodnight. Gianetta and Serena hastily rose to their feet to say their own goodnights and to follow their aunt, as she swept from the room.

As Gianetta followed her aunt up the wide staircase, she was aware that Lord Rendlesham had been disconcerted by their sudden leave-taking. His regret that he had not been able to talk to her further was obvious. A smile quirked the corner of her mouth. They would soon have plenty of time to talk to each other. All the time in the world.

"If the noise of Lord Rendlesham's and Mr Cartwright's departure disturbs you in the morning, please ignore it," her aunt said as they reached the broad landing from which the bedrooms led off. "I do not want either of you downstairs saying goodbye to them at such an hour. You would only be in the way."

"Yes, Mama," said Serena, her thoughts too full of Henry to care about Lord Rendlesham's and Mr Cartwright's dawn departure.

Her aunt took Gianetta's silence as being equally agreeable and, after receiving a dutiful kiss on the cheek from each of them, retired to her room.

"Goodness, I thought the evening would never come to an end," Serena said as they entered their own room and she threw herself face down on her bed. "Mama wanted to tell Lord Rendlesham and Mr Cartwright of my engagement to Henry, but Papa said that she must not announce it publicly until it has appeared in *The Times*." She giggled. "By the time it has done so, Henry and I will already be married!"

Gianetta was no longer interested in Serena's engagement to Henry Plaxtol. She was trying to make up her mind whether or not it would be safe to take Serena into her confidence.

"You will be my bridesmaid, won't you, Gianetta?" Serena continued dreamily, "and you will live with us after we are married, won't you?"

Gianetta withdrew a large carpet-bag from the bottom of her *armoire* saying affectionately, "You're assuming rather a lot, Serena. How can you be so sure that Henry will want to have a cousin-in-law living under his roof?"

"Because if he didn't, he would not be the sort of person I would wish to marry," Serena said simply. "And he is."

Gianetta smiled, amused by her confidence. "I think you're probably right, Serena, and I'm sure you and Henry will be blissfully happy together. But I will not be living with you. I couldn't. I should feel as if I had turned into an old maid overnight."

"Don't be silly . . ." Serena began good-humouredly. Then she saw the carpet-bag. "Gianetta! What on earth are you doing?"

Gianetta lifted an ankle-length skirt and a lace-trimmed blouse from a hanger. All along, deep inside her, she had known that she could not leave without taking Serena into her confidence. Now the moment for confession had come. She tried to think of words that would persuade Serena that what she was about to do was both sensible and sane, and failed to find any. She said starkly, "I'm going to go with Lord Rendlesham and Mr Cartwright to Kansu."

27

"You're going to *what*?" Serena rolled off her stomach and sat bolt upright.

"I'm going to go with Lord Rendlesham and Mr Cartwright to Kansu," Gianetta repeated, folding the blouse and skirt neatly and placing them in the bottom of the carpet-bag.

Serena swung her legs from the bed and ran across to her, seizing her arm. "Gianetta, you can't be serious! Even you would not do something so dangerous and rash!"

Gianetta surveyed a pale pink chiffon dress and regretfully left it on its hanger. Pink chiffon would not be suitable either for travelling or keeping warm. She packed another skirt, a blouse with trimmings of fluted muslin and a bolero cut in the fashion of a boy's Eton jacket.

"They will not take you with them, Gianetta! It would ruin their reputations!"

Gianetta turned away from the *armoire* and gently removed Serena's hand from her arm. "I know that, Serena, and so I am not going to ask them to take me with them, nor am I going to make any attempt to go with them. I am going to follow them at a distance. When they have travelled so far that to return would be impractical, then I will catch up with them."

"Gianetta! You *cannot!*" Serena said, her eyes ablaze with urgency. "You *cannot* travel across China with two men you barely know! It's impossible!"

"Then it shouldn't be impossible," Gianetta said crossly. "Both Lord Rendlesham and Mr Cartwright are gentlemen. If it's my virtue you are thinking of, it's going to be no more at risk than it would be in Lincolnshire."

"You can't know that. Lord Rendlesham looks very honourable and kind, but we know nothing of Mr Cartwright except that he is a respected botanist. He doesn't look to me at all the sort of man a woman would be safe with on her own, and certainly not in the wilds of China."

Privately, Gianetta was in agreement with her, but she

28

wasn't going to be on her own with Zachary Cartwright. She was going to be with him and Lord Rendlesham and she was sure that she could trust Lord Rendlesham completely.

"Listen to me, Serena," she said, taking Serena's hands and holding them tightly in her own. "This is something I *must* do. Much as I love you, I can't face the thought of returning to England and living with you and Henry as if I were a maiden aunt. Neither can I face the thought of living alone in that mausoleum of a house in Lincolnshire. And there's no reason that I should have to. It's 1905, not 1805. Lots of women are now living their lives exactly as they want to and I'm going to be one of them. I want to see China and I'm going to see China. All I want from you is your promise that you won't tell your mother or father what I intend to do."

"But I *must!*" Serena insisted, her face pale. "If I don't, and anything should happen to you, it would be my fault and I would never forgive myself."

"Nothing is going to happen to me," Gianetta said spiritedly, "except that I'm going to enjoy myself hugely. Now, do I have your promise, Serena? If I do, then *I* promise *you* that when this expedition is over I will return quite contentedly to England and live with you and Henry. That is, if you still want me to."

"Oh, but of course I will still want you to!"

"Then do you promise?" Gianetta said ruthlessly, "Because if you don't I shall probably never speak to you again."

"But will you be safe?" Serena asked, terrified.

"Of course I'll be safe," Gianetta said, knowing that the battle was as good as won. "Now stop crying and help me to decide what I should take with me. Lord Rendlesham said Kansu had a temperate climate, which means that it will be much cooler than it is here. Do you think I could borrow a couple of your winter camisoles?"

The colour began to edge back into Serena's cheeks. She had been too busy thinking about Henry to pay

29

much attention to the conversation that had taken place in the drawing-room. She had only the haziest idea of where Kansu was and how far away. Now she suddenly became convinced that Gianetta was behaving so recklessly because Lord Rendlesham had indicated to her that he had fallen head over heels in love with her, that he wanted to elope with her, just as Gianetta's parents had eloped. The whole enterprise suddenly seemed no longer insane but extremely romantic. "Yes, of course you can," she said eagerly, "and would you like to borrow my kid gloves as well?"

Gianetta accepted, relieved that Serena had so easily and naively come to terms with what she was about to do. When the few clothes she was taking with her had been packed in her bag, she turned her attention towards provisions.

"I shall need enough food for at least two days, maybe three. I will leave a letter with you, for your mother, asking her to deduct the cost of whatever I take from my allowance."

"You can't go down to the kitchens now," Serena said practically. "They will be locked."

Gianetta's well-shaped brows pulled together in a little frown and then she shrugged. "It doesn't matter. I can't set off too soon after Lord Rendlesham and Mr Cartwright or they will see me. If they leave at dawn and I leave about nine o'clock, it will put plenty of distance between us and also give me heaps of time to raid the kitchens."

Serena yawned, unbuttoned her skirt and stepped out of it. "I can't see how you are going to be *able* to leave, not with a donkey and a carpet-bag and half a week's groceries." She slipped her arms out of her blouse and laid it over a chair.

"Don't you think someone will see you, and find it a little odd?"

"I don't intend to be seen," Gianetta said, wondering how on earth she was going to be able to avoid it. As

Serena pulled her nightdress over her head and climbed into bed, Gianetta tried to think how it could be managed, and failed. She began to undress. She was tired and she needed to sleep. After she had slept she would be able to think more clearly.

She turned out the lamp, sliding into bed, wondering with a knot of excitement in her stomach what Lord Rendlesham's reaction would be when he knew she was to be part of his expedition to Kansu. She closed her eyes, but it wasn't Lord Rendlesham's face that burned against the fizzing dark of her eyelids. It was the hard-boned, abrasively masculine face of his companion, and she knew with a shiver of apprehension that there would be no pleasure in *his* eyes when next they met. The knowledge filled her with unexpected desolation and she curled her fingers tight into her palms. She wouldn't think of him. He didn't matter. It was Lord Rendlesham who mattered and she was sure that *he* would understand her reasons for joining them, and that he would applaud them.

The next morning, even before it was light, she was woken by the muffled sound of mules being herded together in the courtyard at the Residency's rear. She lay quite still, savouring the thrill of expectation that rippled through her. Lord Rendlesham and Mr Cartwright were preparing to leave, and in a few short hours she would be following them. There would be no more boredom, no more long, tedious hours spent confined in the Residency gardens. And, sadly, no further flower painting lessons with Mr Li. It was her only regret. She lay for a further few minutes, utterly convinced of the rightness of what she was about to do, then she swung her feet quietly to the floor and began to dress, taking care not to disturb Serena.

The cavalcade assembling in the chill dawn light was, for China, surprisingly small. From one of the rear windows she could see Lord Rendlesham, dashing in khaki jodhpurs and jacket and knee-high riding-boots. He was standing beside his mount, a strong-looking pony. She

31

could see another, darker pony, tossing its head friskily nearby. A string of ten mules carried the baggage, and though there were dozens of Chinese scurrying to and fro, only five, in shabby quilted breeches and jackets, looked as if they were dressed for travel.

She stood discreetly at the side of the window watching the expedition, *her* expedition, preparing to depart.

Although her aunt had asked her not to come down and say goodbye to Lord Rendlesham and Mr Cartwright, she felt no guilt. She had not given her word, and anyway she was not saying goodbye to them. She was merely watching.

There was a sudden flurry of movement around the door immediately below her window. Seconds later Zachary Cartwright stepped into view, flamboyantly dressed in Chinese riding boots cuffed with black velvet. His breeches were pale grey, his jacket a darker grey, and a white linen shirt was gashed open at his throat, revealing strong chest muscles and a hint of tightly curling, crisp dark hair.

A hot, unidentifiable sensation flooded through her and she averted her head swiftly. There was a go-to-hell attitude about Zachary Cartwright that both aroused and disturbed her. At dinner the previous evening, Gianetta had been instantly aware that his bored, restless politeness was a veneer, beneath which was a man who didn't give a damn for polite society. As the evening had progressed she had become convinced that he didn't give a damn about anyone or anything; that he lived life exactly as he pleased. She had become aware of something else, too. That though she could find nothing likeable about him, she was inexplicably drawn towards him.

He mounted the dark coloured pony with agile ease and the Chinese servants coaxed the mules into an orderly string behind him. Lord Rendlesham mounted his pony and her uncle went up to him, bidding him a last goodbye. She saw him turn towards Zachary Cartwright, but whatever he said, it was brief. Cartwright had not endeared himself to the consul the previous evening.

Gianetta's uncle stepped back, raising his hand in a gesture of final farewell and Zachary Cartwright led the small expedition out of the Residency courtyard and into the narrow, earth-beaten streets beyond.

Gianetta remained at the window even when they were out of sight, straining her ears until the sound of hooves could be heard no longer. She knew which way they were going. They were going to leave the city by the north gate. Mentally she travelled with them, down the Pai-hsiang kai, the Street of the White Elephant, the main business street of the city, containing many fine two-storeyed buildings, the homes of bankers and merchants. When they reached the end of the Street of the White Elephant and the homes of the rich, the upper town would be behind them. They would pass out of the north gate, descending the plateau on which Chung King was built by traversing a winding staircase of one hundred and fifty shallow stone steps. The ponies and mules, chosen in preference to horses because they were so much more sure-footed, would pick their way downwards with practised ease.

The exit from the north gate was the same exit that she and Serena had taken on their rare visits to the Anglican Mission. She knew that Zachary Cartwright and Lord Rendlesham would have to ride in single file because of the shops and booths that pressed in on either side. At the bottom the shops and booths would be left behind, the steps leading out on to a cornice road shaded by fine old banyan trees. The swirling waters of the river would be on their left, the steep, treeless hills on their right. Then they would turn off the cornice road into the hills. Before the morning was very much older, she would follow in their wake.

Gianetta turned away from the window. She had to pack some provisions and she had to borrow and saddle a pony from the stables. The provisions would be easy, the pony less so.

Her uncle was a keen polo player, and the stables at the Residency's rear were large. In the pale light of

33

early dawn she eyed the strong, sleek polo ponies and knew that if she took one of them she would never be forgiven, not ever. There were plenty of mules, looking mildly surprised at being disturbed so early in the day, but having seen that both Lord Rendlesham's and Zachary Cartwright's mounts had been ponies, she thought it best that her own mount should be a pony as well.

Gianetta looked regretfully back towards the polo ponies and a couple of them began to whinny and toss their heads fretfully. She turned away from them. They were superbly fit but they were also highly strung. A highly strung pony would be a handicap, not an asset.

An unblinking eye held hers. In a stall at the very end of the stable a small Chinese pony was regarding her with bright interest. She hurried up to it and it moved towards her, blowing softly onto her hand through velvety nostrils.

"Oh, you darling," Gianetta whispered, opening the door of his stall and stepping in beside him. He was small and shaggy and unkempt. He was also toughly built and endearingly friendly.

"Would you like to travel to Kansu?" she said to him softly, running her hand down the rough coat of his neck. "Would you like to search for blue Moonflowers?"

He exhaled warm air and nuzzled her. "Then we'll go," she said, pleasure welling up inside her. She gave him another loving pat and stepped outside his box, saying to one of the Chinese stable boys, "Would you saddle him up for me, please? I want to go for a ride on him." Her eyes sparkled. "A *long* ride!"

"Yes, missee." The stable boy nodded. He had not understood all that she had said but he had caught the gist of it. The English lady wanted the pony saddled and she wanted to ride him. It was none of his affair if she wanted to do so unaccompanied. English ladies were not sensible beings. Everyone knew that. He took down a wooden *miao-tse* saddle from a hook. It was covered with heavy lacquer and topped with a wadded quilt. When he had finished adjusting the saddle, he put a collar of bells around the pony's neck, so that pedestrians would be warned of the pony's approach and step aside. The pony shook his head impatiently, eager to be off, and the bells jingled.

The stable boy wondered where the English lady intended riding. The two English gentlemen who had just left were rumoured to be riding north to Kansu and Tibet. Tibet was the roof of the world, so far away and so inaccessible that no-one he knew and no-one his father or his father's father had known, had ever been there. Perhaps the English girl thought that she, too, would ride to the roof of the world. He giggled to himself at the idiocy of such an idea and continued with his morning tasks, filling the polo ponies' mangers with fresh hay.

Gianetta made her way quickly back to her bedroom, taking care to be seen by as few of the servants as possible. Serena was still asleep, her blonde curls vulnerably tousled. Gianetta hesitated. She wanted to wake Serena and say goodbye to her but she was frightened that in the cold light of day Serena might no longer view her adventure as romantic but see it as insane, and insist on telling her mother about it.

The early morning sunlight flooded through the chinks in the closed shutters, spilling into dappled patches of gold on the floor. Gianetta turned away from Serena's bed. She couldn't wake her. The risks were too great. She sat at her dressing-table and wrote a letter to her aunt and another to Serena. Then, her heart beating fast and light, she picked up her carpet-bag of clothes and provisions and, with one last regretful look towards the still sleeping Serena, she tiptoed quietly out of the room.

It was nearly eight o'clock and there were far more servants around than there had been earlier. They looked at her impassively as she walked out of the Residency and across to the stables. None of them spoke much English and she knew none of them would take it upon themselves to report her early morning departure to either her aunt or her uncle. To see nothing and to hear nothing was a great Chinese ability.

Gianetta stepped into the stables, the smell of horse strong and warm. She walked quickly past the stalls until she came to the end one. The little Chinese pony eyed her eagerly. She put down her bag, opened the door of his stall and gazed at the saddle with defeat. It had never occurred to her that it wouldn't be an English side-saddle.

"Drat!" she said, giving vent to the worst expletive she knew. "*Now* what are we going to do?"

The pony nuzzled its neck towards her in an encouraging manner. She patted him, frowning thoughtfully. She could ask the stable boy to re-saddle him with an English saddle, or she could change her skirt for something that would enable her to ride more easily. One of the Chinese girls who worked in the Residency kitchen was crossing the top end of the stables. She was wearing the garments that were a household uniform. A blue, lightly quilted high-necked jacket over narrow fitting trousers. If Gianetta wore the same, and if she let down her waist-length hair and plaited it in a queue, then not only would she be able to travel with greater ease, but she would be safer, for from a distance she would look Chinese, not foreign.

"I'll be back in a minute," she said to the pony and, leaving her carpet-bag on the floor at his feet, she ran towards the servant's quarters.

"I want the servant's linen-room," she said breathlessly to a startled house-boy. "Can you tell me where it is?"

"Nothing for missy in se'vant's linen 'oom," he said, backing away from her as if she had taken leave of her senses.

"That is for me to decide," Gianetta said with school-ma'am crispness. "Now come along, show me where it is."

She had no way of knowing whether she would find clean garments as well as dirty ones in the linen room, but knowing how particular her aunt was about the cleanliness

36

and neatness of her household staff, she was reasonably optimistic.

The house-boy, certain that this lightning inspection of the linen-room meant trouble, stood apprehensively to one side as she opened the door he indicated.

"Thank you," she said, stepping inside and giving thanks for her aunt's meticulous housekeeping. Large baskets held dirty linen. Shelf upon shelf held newly-washed and freshly-pressed clean linen. She scrambled out of her skirt and into a pair of surprisingly comfortable trousers. Then, aware that she could never hope to make her way back to the stables without being seen, she pulled her ankle-length skirt over the top of her trousers and donned one of the Chinese jackets.

It was now after eight-thirty and she knew that, with every passing minute, the chances of running into her uncle or aunt were increasing. Quickly she hurried once more out of the Residency and across the courtyard to the stables. There was no-one about, not even the stable-boy. Even so, she was going to take no chances. She would lead the pony by the rein until they were clear of the Residency grounds. Then, in a suitable place where she would not attract attention, she would discard her skirt.

"Are you ready?" she said to the impatient pony. "I'm not going to mount you yet. I'm going to lead you out of the courtyard and into the street."

He hurrumphed agreeably and she wondered what his name was. There was no name on the door of his stall and she had to be able to call him something.

"Would you mind being called Ben?" she asked him.

He looked like a Ben. Friendly and dependable. He hurrumphed again, brown eyes gleaming, and with a furiously beating heart she led him out of his stall and towards the Residency gates and the road beyond.

CHAPTER THREE

The gates leading from the Residency into the street were flanked by thick bushes and banyan trees, and it was here that Gianetta quickly took off her skirt, rolling it up and stuffing it into her already full carpet-bag. She felt strange in the trousers and mandarin-necked jacket, as if she were about to go to a fancy dress party. A little soft round hat, the kind that most Chinese wore, bulged in the pocket of the jacket. She took it out, hesitating. Until she changed her hair style, no matter how Chinese her dress, she would still never be mistaken for a Chinese. Hesitating no longer, she hurriedly took the pins from her hair, shaking her head so that her heavy, waist-length hair tumbled loose and free. Then, with nimble dexterity, she plaited it into a long, single pigtail, securing it with a piece of thread from her jacket.

"Right," she said exultantly to Ben, placing the little blue cap on top of her head. "Now we really are ready to go."

She swung herself up into the wooden saddle, anchoring her carpet-bag firmly to the pommel. Ben tossed his head, gave himself a little shake and then, as she touched him lightly with her heels, set off down the dust-blown road at a purposeful trot.

It was a strange experience to be outside the Residency grounds without the protection of sedan-chair and servants. For a fleeting moment, panic assailed her and then was banished, never to return. This was what she had longed for from the moment she had set foot on Chinese soil. The noise and clamour and colour assailing her were the *real* China. The China she had been protected from for far too long.

Chung King was built on a high, rocky peninsula and the Upper Town, where the Residency was situated, was the highest point of all, standing on a sandstone plateau with breathtaking views of the broadly flowing Yang-tze and the pale, tawny hills beyond.

As the homes of the rich were left behind, the streets grew narrower and even more crowded. Families squatted by the roadside, pecking at their morning meal with chopsticks; lacquered ducks as flat as pancakes hung from shops that were little more than holes in the walls; hawkers cried their wares, loping along with heavy containers of food dangling at both ends of bending bamboo poles that arched across their shoulders; elderly women hobbled on feet that had once been cruelly bound; pedlars shouted their wares, donkeys and mules jostled for right of way with sedan-chairs.

Ben trotted on unperturbed by the crush and the noise and Gianetta rode with her eyes firmly downwards, terrified that one of her uncle's envoys would be in the street and would recognise her, that perhaps even her uncle himself would pass her in his sedan-chair.

The steps began and she tightened her grip on Ben's rein. He descended without hesitation, only pricking his ears and checking slightly when he had to confront a camel that was making its way, heavily burdened, up to the town from the riverside wharf.

The walls surrounding the base of the town came into view. The north gate was open, the smell from the river strong and pungent. No-one had challenged her. In a city thronged with dozens of different races; Mongolians, Manchurians, merchants from Turkestan, she had gone unnoticed. The bells on Ben's collar jingled merrily as he trotted out through the gate and on to the broad causeway beyond. The river was on their left-hand side, innumerable eddies, like the curls and whorls of Chinese characters, rippling its glittering smooth surface.

Gianetta leaned forward and patted Ben's neck. The first hurdle had been overcome. They were out of the city and on the open road; soon they would be in the hills. She began to hum to herself and then to sing an Italian folk-song that she had often heard her mother sing. It brought back childhood memories of Italy, of Lake Garda glittering beneath the summer sun, of hillsides dark with cypress trees, of the distant snow-capped peaks of the Alps. No snow-capped peaks confronted her now, only gently rolling golden hills, their upper slopes occasionally wooded with walnut and chestnut trees, their lower slopes thick with honeysuckle and larkspur.

In less than half a mile she had left the Yang-tze and the stone causeway behind her and was following the beaten track north to Fu-tu Kwan. She wondered how far behind Lord Rendlesham and Zachary Cartwright she was. There was no sign of them ahead of her. Nothing but the hills and the woods and a bird singing.

At lunchtime she stopped to give Ben a rest and to have a picnic of bread and cheese. She wondered again what Lord Rendlesham would say when she caught up with him. She remembered the way his blue eyes crinkled at the corners when he laughed, the easy-going tolerance in his voice. Her heart began to beat in slow, thick strokes. Every instinct she possessed told her that he would be pleased to see her, that he would be delighted at the prospect of having her as a companion on his journey to Kansu.

With a quick, sharp gesture she brushed breadcrumbs from her Chinese blue jacket. She must not start thinking of how delightful a companion he would be. She wasn't riding in his wake because she had fallen violently in love with him. She was riding in his wake because she was sure that he was kind and honourable and because she wanted to travel far into the heart of China in search of blue Moonflowers.

She coaxed Ben away from the short, sweet grass he was enjoying. Though she had no intention of catching up with them today, she knew that she would feel easier in her mind if she could see them in the distance before nightfall. The sun was high in the sky now, and hot. The little round hat she was wearing offered no shade and very little protection from the heat. She thought longingly of the wide-brimmed sunhat she had left behind her at the Residency. Perhaps Lord Rendlesham or Zachary Cartwright would have a spare hat with them that she could borrow. If not, then she would have to buy one of the broad-brimmed straw hats worn by the peasants in the fields.

The hills closed round her on every side, but the track continued, clear and well-defined. Occasionally other travellers passed her, on their way to Chung King, but she always lowered her head at their approach, keeping her eyes fixed firmly on the pommel of her saddle. Ben had long since settled down to a steady walk and needed so little guidance from her that once or twice she closed her eyes, falling into a light doze.

The sun was just beginning to lose its heat, the vivid blue of the sky smoking towards dusk, when she saw Lord Rendlesham and Zachary Cartwright ahead of her. She had ridden high up the side of one hill and was just cresting it. Down the far side, nearly at the foot, were two well-recognised figures on ponies, a string of mules and a clutch of Chinamen in their wake, the walls of Fu-tu Kwan two miles or so ahead of them.

She reined Ben to a hasty halt. If they saw her from that distance they would automatically assume her to be Chinese, but she knew that Zachary Cartwright carried strong field-glasses amongst his equipment and she didn't want to run the risk of him training them on her.

The hillside was heavily wooded and she stayed beneath the shade of the trees, watching as Zachary Cartwright led his party towards Fu-tu Kwan. She wondered if they would make camp before the town or beyond it. The countryside was wild and open and she was chillingly aware of how vulnerable a small camp, with little protection, would be. As she faced the prospect of camping out alone, with no protection whatsoever, Gianetta was fiercely tempted to dig her heels into Ben's sides and spur him on so that he would catch up with the riders ahead. She fought back the temptation, knowing what would happen if she did so.

Zachary Cartwright was only a day's ride from Chung King. A lost day would not disrupt his plans irrevocably. He would insist that she was returned to Chung King and would no doubt carry out the task himself. She kept her hands motionless on the reins. No, she would not ride after them and catch up with them just because dusk was approaching. She would follow the plan she had set herself. She would wait another two or three days, until Zachary Cartwright was so far away from Chung King that not even her arrival would tempt him to return.

She didn't move from the trees until the horsemen ahead of her were so far away they were barely visible. Only then did she urge Ben into movement, grateful for the sure-footed way he descended the steep track. Wherever she stopped for the night, before Fu-tu Kwan or beyond, she would need fresh water and grazing for him. She knew that the Kialing river, one of the Yang-tze's largest tributaries, was near at hand. Several times through the day she had caught glimpses of it. Although it wasn't, at the moment, visible she knew that it couldn't be more than half a mile away. If the riders ahead of her made camp at a stream that did not run down towards where she stood, then she would make for the banks of the Kialing.

The light was growing muted as the walls of Fu-tu Kwan drew nearer, the white and dusty glare of day merging into the rose and purple of evening. The small figures ahead of her showed no signs of halting. It was obvious that Zachary Cartwright intended entering the town and, presumably, leaving it before nightfall.

Dusk had fallen by the time she reached the main gate. It was only a small town, not remotely as grand as Chung King, and the stench that reached her nostrils from the overcrowded streets and insanitary housing made her retch.

"Come along, Ben," she said to the tired pony. "Let's leave these streets behind as soon as we can."

Ben plodded on stoically, carefully negotiating the rubbish in his way, the open, running sewers. There was no discernible main street through the town, only a maze of alleyways and ginnels, each one dirtier and narrower than the one before.

"Come on, Ben," Gianetta repeated, overcome by tiredness. "Let's get out of here."

A tattered beggar leered at her from a doorway and then, with no warning, lunged towards her, grabbing her saddle with black, grimy hands.

"Go away! Go away!" she shouted furiously, digging her heels hard into Ben's side.

Deformed hands grabbed her jacket, closed on her legs. For a hideous moment she thought that Ben was too exhausted to summon up any remaining strength and make a gallop for it. Then, as she felt herself being pulled from the saddle, he gave a great buck with his hindquarters and, with a snort from his nostrils, surged into a headlong gallop. Pedlars and hawkers scrambled out of his way. Women screamed, hobbling to safety. The beggars gave chase for fifty yards or more and then fell back with high-pitched screams of manic laughter.

Gianetta was half-sprawled over Ben's neck as he charged down first one muddy dirty alleyway and then another. She had lost all sense of direction, but Ben seemed to have no doubt about which way to go. They dodged under poles of washing jutting out like flags from windows, they jumped over pools of stagnant waste, they raced on heedlessly and unhesitatingly, out of the warren of streets, through the town gate that was just about to be closed and into the blessed clean air and relative safety of the countryside beyond.

"Oh, you angel!" Gianetta panted as soon as she was

able to push herself back into a sitting position in the saddle and tug restrainingly on the reins. "It's all right now. You can slow down. They won't come after us, the city gate is closing."

Ben slowed to a canter and then to a trot. His flanks were heaving, his nostrils foam-flecked. She reined him in, patting his side, looking around her in the rapidly deepening twilight. There was no sign of Lord Rendlesham or Zachary Cartwright. She had no way of knowing if they were on the road ahead of her or if they had remained in the town.

Behind her the city gate had closed. No-one would be allowed in and no-one would be allowed to leave until dawn.

"If Lord Rendlesham is ahead of us, he won't be far," she said to Ben. "He'll be getting ready to camp for the night, and that's what we have to do."

Ben gave an agreeing hurrumph.

"We have to find water and grazing before it gets too dark to see."

It was already nearly too dark to see and there was no promise of a moon.

"Come on," she said encouragingly. "This way. The river flows to the left of the town. It can't be far."

She urged him into an unwilling walk, straining her ears for the sound of water. It came, just as she was about to give up hope. She reined Ben to a halt, slipping off his back and running forward to where the Kialing surged silkily and glossily southwards.

"We have our camp-site, Ben," she said, her voice determinedly cheery.

She walked back to the pony, looking around her. In the darkness, the town could no longer be seen. There was no glow of a fire that might have signalled Lord Rendlesham's camp.

"But that also means that there are no beggars' or robbers' camps," she said, forcing herself to take comfort from the isolation and not to allow it to dispirit her. She

44

unsaddled Ben and rubbed him down with the wadded saddle quilt. The darkness was deep and menacing and full of terrifying sounds, small animals hunting and being hunted; squirrels perhaps, or hares. She tried to think what other animals might be roaming in the darkness. Leopards were said to inhabit the hills. What if a leopard came down to the river bank for a drink? At what distance would it be able to scent human flesh?

"Stop it!" she said to herself sharply as fear bubbled up in her throat. "There isn't going to be a leopard! There isn't going to be anything!"

Something slithered past her in the grass and she pressed the back of her hand to her mouth, silencing a scream. "Oh God," she whispered. "Why didn't I realise it would be like this? Why didn't I bring a gun? A knife! *Anything*!"

Ben, serenely unperturbed, was drinking his fill from the river. She took comfort from his serenity. If there was danger, then Ben would sense it and warn her. She pulled her quilt from her carpet-bag and wrapped it around herself. She must sleep. If she didn't sleep then she wouldn't have her wits about her in the morning, and she might not locate Lord Rendlesham and Zachary Cartwright ever again.

Determinedly she closed her eyes, but not until Ben moved close beside her, comforting her with the sound of his breathing and the heat from his body, did she fall into a restless sleep.

When she awoke it was dawn, and she was cold and damp and stiff. A pair of goldfinches, bright as butterflies, were wrangling in a nearby shrub. The shrub was grey with yellow flowers that she had never seen before. She wondered if perhaps she ought to cut a sprig and put it in her carpet-bag. It might be one of the rare species that Lord Rendlesham was searching for.

She stood up painfully and stretched. It was morning and she had survived the night. There had been no unwelcome visitors. Gianetta laughed with joy, gave Ben a good morning pat and walked down to the river to wash her face. What she saw there made her blood run cold. There were markings in the soft sand of the river bank. Animal markings. She had no idea to what animal they belonged, but something had drunk from the river during the night. Something wild; something that had been only yards away from her.

Slowly she bent down, splashing her face with water. She wouldn't camp alone again. There were too many risks. She would wait until Lord Rendlesham and Zachary Cartwright were camped and then ride up and confront them. Zachary Cartwright would not want to spend two days returning to the point where she had joined them. He would be furious with her, but he would have no choice but to allow her to stay with them. And she would be able to count on Lord Rendlesham's support. Of that she was sure.

She breakfasted on bread and cheese, while Ben murched at the grass that grew lushly by the side of the river. Then, with the sun still edging over the horizon, they set off at a gentle trot in search of Lord Rendlesham and Zachary Cartwright.

When it was almost noon and she still hadn't found them, Gianetta began to think Lord Rendlesham's party was still in Fu-tu Kwan and that she would have to return there. She was just pausing, debating what to do, when a cloud of dust on the road ahead of her shimmered and dissolved, revealing a small group of ponies, mules and men.

"There they are!" she said exultantly to Ben. "Now all we have to do is to keep them in sight until nightfall."

The going was more arduous than it had been the previous day; there were many gullies which Ben scrambled up and down gallantly; often, the road disintegrated altogether, leaving small chasms which he jumped with nimble dexterity. There were more flowers, too, than there had been the on the way from Chung King to Fu-tu Kwan: harebell poppies fluttering their petals like purple banners; pale lilac anemones with indigo hearts; carnations – their scent thick as smoke in the strong afternoon sunlight. She had taken a cutting of the grey shrub with the little yellow flower and wrapped the stem in a handkerchief soaked in water. Even if the plant was unbelievably common, she knew that Lord Rendlesham would not laugh at her but would appreciate her interest. And she was indifferent to what Zachary Cartwright might say or think.

By late afternoon, the hills were not so steep or so wooded and Ben was able to walk with greater ease, the bells on his collar tinkling merrily.

She wondered when and where Lord Rendlesham would make camp. They had passed several impoverished villages where children had run out, laughing and pointing at her strange round eyes, but none of the villages had been large enough to have possessed an inn. If her suspicions were correct, and Lord Rendlesham and Zachary Cartwright had stayed in an inn the previous night, they would not be able to find the same sort of accommodation for the coming night. No walled town was visible on the horizon, only bare, lion-coloured hills and, to the left, the bright, glittering sweep of the Kialing.

As dusk approached, she felt the muscles in her stomach tighten. A score of times she had mentally imagined what Lord Rendlesham's and Zachary Cartwright's reactions would be when she rode up and confronted them. Now, in an hour or so, perhaps even less, she would find out if any of her imaginings had been even remotely correct.

The party made camp just as the first stars were beginning to sprinkle the sky. She reined Ben in, watching from a distance. She would wait until they were settled, until the Chinese accompanying them had made something for them to eat, then she would ride out into the open. A small animal screeched in the undergrowth and she shivered, determined that, whatever happened, she would not spend another night alone, in the open.

Half an hour passed and a wisp of blue smoke rose from the camp-site. They were having their evening meal. Her mouth watered. She wondered what it was. Whatever it was, it would be preferable to stale bread and hard cheese.

"Another five minutes," she whispered to Ben, a pulse in her throat beginning to beat fast and light. "Just another five minutes and then we'll join them."

She counted out the time and then, excitement rising up in her until she thought she would burst with it, she touched Ben's flanks lightly with her heels and set off at a gallop towards her unsuspecting quarry.

They had pitched camp on the banks of the Kialing. Gianetta could see the shapes of the Chinese moving backwards and forwards in the firelight as they tended the food they were cooking, their quilted jackets and narrow trousers identical to her own. The ponies and mules were loosely tethered and she could see a tall, broad-shouldered figure removing something from one of the saddle-bags. The other remaining figure was sitting in a canvas chair, one leg across a knee, head bent, writing intently.

The small tableau was almost instantly disrupted. She heard cries of alarm from the Chinese, saw the seated figure leap to his feet, grabbing the rifle that had been lying on the ground at his side, saw the figure by the saddle-bags spin round, pistol in hand.

"Don't shoot!" she cried out in sudden alarm, as she galloped out of the twilight towards them. "It's not a bandit! It's me! Gianetta Hollis!"

Her pigtail bounced on her back, the little round hat, emblem of a house-servant, slipping precariously down over one eye. She heard Zachary Cartwright's deep, dark voice utter an incredulous, "What the devil . . ." and then she was among them, reining Ben in, slithering down from his lathered back.

"It's me," she said again unnecessarily, smiling around

at them with far more confidence than she felt, "Is there anything good for dinner?"

Zachary Cartwright covered the ground between them in one swift stride and seized her shoulders. "What the bloody *hell*" he snarled viciously, "do you think you are doing?"

Gianetta was aware that such expletives existed, but she had never imagined that she would hear them uttered so threateningly, or that when they were they would be directed at herself.

"Kindly remove your hands from my person," she said icily, and then turned towards Lord Rendlesham who, as leader of the party, was surely the only person to whom she was answerable. He was standing to one side looking strangely ineffectual, his pistol still in his hand, his good-natured face bewildered.

"If I could talk to you for a moment in private . . ." she began, trying to sound as dignified as the situation would allow. Zachary Cartwright still held her tightly and was showing no signs of releasing her.

"But, Miss Hollis . . ." Lord Rendlesham said dazedly. "I don't understand . . . Your clothes . . . Why are you dressed in such a peculiar manner? Who are you with? Where are your companions?"

Gianetta had been manhandled for long enough by Zachary Cartwright. She kicked him viciously in the shin and at the same time tried to twist herself free of his grip. She failed. He merely gave an expletive even worse than those she had already heard and dug his fingers even harder into her shoulders.

"I am dressed like this because I thought I would be safer," she said, directing her attention solely towards Lord Rendlesham and trying to sound level-headed and practical. "And I'm not with anyone. I rode here alone."

"*Then you can ride back alone!*" Zachary Cartwright rasped savagely. "Of all the stupid, empty-headed, *insane* things to do! Don't you know that you could have been killed? Don't you know that there are leopards in the hills

49

that come down at night to raid pigs from the village sties? Don't you know that there are half-starved beggars and bandits who would have killed you for your pony without a second thought?"

He released his hold of her so suddenly and contemptuously that she stumbled. "And if you *had* come to grief, don't you realise who would have been held responsible? *We* would have!"

His brows were pulled together satanically, his black eyes blazing. "We would have been accused of luring you from home with God knows what kind of intentions. Our expedition would have been ruined and your uncle's colleagues in the diplomatic service would have made it impossible for us to mount another. All because you have fallen victim to a foolish infatuation."

"How *dare* you?" Gianetta was nearly robbed of speech. "How *dare* you suggest that I rode out here because . . . because . . ." She was aware of Lord Rendlesham standing only feet away from them, and her cheeks burned at the memory of how she had thought it would be pleasant to be his companion on the long, lonely journey to Kansu.

"And so you follow me here," Zachary Cartwright was thundering, "and now days have to be wasted in returning you to Chung King and heaven knows how many more days wasted in explanations to your uncle!"

It was dark now and the only light was from the fire, which continued to burn and crackle, sending golden-blue tongues of flame skywards.

"Follow *you*?" she gasped incredulously. She remembered her curiosity about him when she had been at the Residency, the way she had gazed speculatively at him in the drawing-room when she thought he was unaware of her doing so, the way he had spun round and taken her by surprise, and the assumption she had seen in his near-black eyes, that her gaze had been one of admiration.

Rage and mortification swept hard on the heels of her

incredulity. "Follow *you*?" she repeated, panting. "Why, I wouldn't follow *you* anywhere, Mr Cartwright! Not even out of a room! Certainly not to the furthermost parts of China!"

There came the sound of a quickly stifled laugh and Lord Rendlesham stepped forward. "Why *did* you follow us, Miss Hollis?" he asked, amused curiosity replacing his earlier stunned bewilderment.

Gratefully Gianetta turned towards him. "I came because . . ." She paused. How could she tell him in a few words that she had come because of Serena's impending marriage and the change it would make to her own way of life, because of the tedium of life in the Hollis' home in Lincolnshire, because of the horror she felt at the alternative prospect of living on Serena's charity. She had come because she longed to live her own life independently, she ached to see the real China, the China that existed beyond the high, confining walls of the British Residency. She had come because, above all, she wanted to search for exotic flowers, flowers that had never bloomed in England. Flowers that she could help introduce into English gardens.

"I want to be a plant-hunter," she said at last, succinctly. "I want to find blue Moonflowers."

"God's teeth!" Zachary Cartwright exploded. "This isn't a pleasant botanical outing in St James's Park! This is a scientific expedition and there is no place for a woman on it. Especially a woman who is inexperienced, under-age and who has no more brains in her head than a bird." In the flickering firelight the harsh, abrasive lines of his face were taut and threatening.

Lord Rendlesham ignored his seething companion. "Does the Consul know where you are and what your intentions were when you left?"

"Yes, I left a letter . . ."

Zachary Cartwright swore again, savagely. "You'd think if the man had an iota of commonsense he would have caught up with her before she even left the city.

51

As it is, with luck we'll meet up with whoever he's sent after her and not have to return every step of the way to Chung King."

"I'm not going back," Gianetta said defiantly.

"You damned well are!" Zachary Cartwright thundered.

"Does she have to?" Lord Rendlesham asked pleasantly.

Zachary Cartwright wheeled on him. "Of course she has to. You heard what I said to her a few minutes ago. Unless she's returned, our personal reputations will be ruined both here *and* in England. She can't be a day over seventeen . . ."

"Eighteen," Gianetta corrected.

". . . and she's the Consul's niece," Zachary continued, taking no notice of her interruption. "Can you imagine the hue and cry she's left behind her?"

"As I am only the Consul's niece and not his daughter, and as he's always found me an inconvenience to take care of, he might not much mind that I've decided to live an independent life," Gianetta said practically.

A smile quirked the corners of Lord Rendlesham's well-shaped mouth. "I cannot imagine you being an inconvenience to anyone," he said gallantly. "You are obviously very tired. Don't let Zac bully you any more. We can discuss your return to Chung King later. For the moment you need a rest and something to eat. We were just about to have some lemon chicken," and he took her gently by the arm and led her away from Zachary Cartwright and towards the fire.

The Chinese, who had been staring wide-eyed at the altercation between the two European gentlemen and the English missy bizarrely garbed in Chinese dress, hurriedly resumed their culinary duties.

"Thank you very much, Lord Rendlesham," Gianetta said, her heart beginning to beat a little less furiously. "There really is no need for me to be returned to Chung King. If you would just let me explain . . ."

52

"You can't keep calling me Lord Rendlesham, out here in the wilds of nowhere," he said, smiling down at her, the corners of his eyes crinkling attractively. "My name is Charles."

She found herself smiling back at him. "If we are to be so informal, then you must use my Christian name also."

"Gianetta is a very pretty name," he said, sitting her down in the canvas chair that Zachary Cartwright had been sitting in when she had ridden up to them. "Is it Italian?"

She nodded. "Yes, my mother came from Florence, though when I was a child we lived further north. On the shores of Lake Garda."

"And are your parents still there?" he enquired, fetching another collapsible chair and setting it down alongside hers.

"No," she said, looking with interest at the plant-collecting box that lay on the ground at the side of her chair and the notebook, covered with strong, bold handwriting, that Zachary Cartwright had thrown down on her approach. Lord Rendlesham waited expectantly. "They're both dead," she said briefly, and did not see the slight lift of Zachary Cartwright's brows as he looked across at her, an indefinable expression in his near-black eyes.

She rose to her feet suddenly. "I'm sorry, Lord Rendlesham . . . Charles. I can't sit down and eat yet. Ben will be tired, too, and I haven't seen to him yet."

"Ben?" He stood up with her, looking puzzled. "I thought you had ridden here alone?"

"My pony," she said with a tired smile. "I don't know what his real name is, but I've christened him Ben and he's quite, quite wonderful."

She walked out of the circle of firelight and across to where Ben was standing, still saddled and patient.

"There's nice grass for you, and fresh water," she said, patting him lovingly. "And tonight we'll both

53

have some company. It won't be as frightening as last night was."

"I'll take his saddle off for you," Zachary Cartwright's deep, dark voice said from behind her. "Those *miao-tse* saddles are heavy."

She whipped her head round, hoping that he hadn't overheard her admission of fear.

"I can manage," she said stiffly. "I've managed quite well for two days now."

He took no notice of her, unsaddling Ben and slackening his bit, unbuckling an end of the rein and tying it to a nearby sapling so that he could graze.

"If you have, you've been lucky," he said curtly. "China isn't a country where it's safe for anyone to travel alone not even a Chinese."

"I think you're wrong," she said coldly, trying not to remember the gang of beggars in Fu-tu Kwan who had almost pulled her from Ben's back. "The Chinese are just as courteous and hospitable as anyone else."

His brow quirked and she looked away from him swiftly, hating the discomfiture he aroused in her.

"I quite agree with you that they are an amazingly courteous nation. They quite often carry hospitality to incredible lengths, but realities have to be faced and the reality is that the countryside is vast, poverty-stricken and infested with beggars and brigands."

What he was saying was true, but she had no intention of admitting it. Picking up the quilted cloth that had been on the saddle, she began to rub Ben down. He watched her silently for a minute or two and then said, his voice oddly gentle, "You have to go back, you know."

Her fingers tightened on the cloth. "I do *not* have to go back," she said fiercely, keeping her back to him. "If I go back I shall be sent to England and in England I shall have to live in a mausoleum of a house with no-one for company but servants."

"Is that where you lived before you came to China?" he asked, and there was genuine interest in his voice.

54

"Yes." She continued rubbing Ben down. "My aunt always travels with my uncle, and until a few months ago it was customary for Serena to remain in England in the care of her governess. When my parents died I was obliged to join her." She paused for a moment, stroking Ben's neck, saying with touching candour, "Serena never minded the arrangement very much because she has never been used to anything else, but I hated it. The house is in Lincolnshire," she added, as if it explained everything.

Zachary Cartwright's unsmiling mouth twitched suspiciously at the corners. "Yes," he said sympathetically. "Lincolnshire must have been rather dull after Lake Garda."

All through their conversation she had had her back towards him. She was just about to turn to him and tell him confidingly how *extremely* dull Lincolnshire had been after Lake Garda, when she remembered to whom she was talking. Her chin lifted defiantly. "And so you see, Mr Cartwright, I shall *not* return to Chung King or to England. I am going to Kansu."

The moment of near-camaraderie was lost. His mouth hardened. "Not with me, you aren't," he said with all his old fury.

She swung around to him, facing him fully, refusing to be intimidated by his almost overpowering masculinity. "You are not the only member of the expedition to Kansu, Mr Cartwright. Lord Rendlesham may very well have other ideas."

The fire was some distance from them but, in the flickering light that it gave, her small high breasts were clearly defined beneath her jacket and her softly rounded hips were anything but male in the frugally cut Chinese trousers.

"Yes, and I can imagine what some of them are," he said darkly. "You are returning to Chung King tomorrow. I'm going to take you there myself."

Her eyes flashed furiously. "We'll see about that," she said between clenched teeth, striding past him and back towards the circle of fire and Lord Rendlesham. She placed herself firmly in front of him.

"Lord Rendlesham . . . Charles . . . I am formally asking you that I may be allowed to join your expedition to Kansu. I can be very useful." She tried desperately to think in what way she could be useful. "I can help find flowers. I've already found one that I've never seen before. It's in my saddle-bag. I can paint the flowers that we see. I am a very good and accurate artist. I can . . ."

Charles raised a hand protestingly. "Please, Gianetta. I am sure that you could be very useful indeed, but the decision is not mine to make."

She looked at him blankly and he said apologetically, "The expedition is not *my* expedition, Gianetta. It's Zac's. I am merely an invited amateur. I can make no decisions as to who may join us, or where we are to go. All those decisions are Zac's."

"So you see, Miss Hollis," a dark, smugly satisfied voice said from behind her. "You *will* be returning to Chung King after all."

She dug her nails into the palms of her hands and lifted her head a fraction higher. "At least you can have a look at the flower that I brought with me," she said, still speaking to Charles. "It's very pretty." Her voice was suspiciously thick. "I've never seen one like it before," and she turned away from him, running into the concealing darkness towards Ben and her saddle-bag.

Neither man attempted to follow her and it was several minutes before she returned. When she did so her eyes were overly bright, but her voice was once again normal. She handed the cutting she had taken to Charles. "Have you any idea what it is?"

He took it from her and to her relief did not laugh. "I'm not sure. It looks a little like a potentilla. What do you think, Zac?"

Zachary Cartwright lifted the cutting from the damp handkerchief around its stem and laid it flat on the palm

56

of his hand. "It's a Potentilla Veitchii" he said with sharp interest. "Where did you find it? Were there many of them?"

She shook her head, disappointed that he had known immediately what it was and that it was obviously very common. "It was growing near the river where I camped last night. There was only one bush. I didn't see any others."

"You should have had the sense to take a root cutting . . ." he began angrily.

She had had enough of his anger and his contempt. "Why should I?" she flared, interrupting him. "I'm not a member of your expedition, as you have so rightly pointed out. And if it's only a common old Potentilla Veitchii, what does it matter?"

"Potentilla Veitchii isn't common," he snapped back at her. "It's usually to be found in the far west, on the borders with Burma. I've never come across it so far east before."

She forgot her fury at his bad temper and her crushing disappointment at having to return to Chung King. "Really?" she said, her face brightening. "You mean I've actually found something interesting? Something rare?"

"Yes, which makes your negligence in not taking a root cutting, and not knowing exactly where you found it, even more reprehensible."

"I can draw the cutting for you," she said, refusing to be browbeaten. "Do you have pencils and a sketch-book?"

"We're a scientific expedition," he retorted. "Of course we have pencils and a sketch-book."

In the light from the leaping flames, with his thick black hair tumbling low over his brow and his winged brows drawn together demonically, he looked so like a storybook picture of Lucifer that she burst out laughing.

"What is so funny?" he asked, startled.

"You are," she said, still laughing. "You look exactly like Lucifer!"

Charles hooted with laughter. "She's right, Zac. I can't

imagine why I never saw the likeness before," he took Gianetta's arm. "Come on. Stop wrangling with Zac and let's eat. I'm starving."

As he propelled Gianetta once more towards one of the canvas chairs he said, still smiling, "You know, I've finally realised why you and Zac are like cat and dog. Seeing the two of you there together, you looked exactly like brother and sister. You have the same kind of hair, so black it's almost blue, and there's something else similar about the two of you that I can't quite put my finger on. Whatever it is, it explains a lot. People who look alike *never* get on and brothers and sisters certainly don't. I fight like the very devil with mine."

Gianetta didn't see how she could take being likened to Zachary Cartwright as a compliment, but Charles obviously didn't mean to be insulting and she said a little stiffly, "It isn't always true that it is opposites that attract. Serena has just become engaged to Henry Plaxtol and both he and Serena are very alike, especially in their tastes."

This time it was Charles' turn to quirk an eyebrow. "Has she indeed? That will take the wind from Zac's sails. He was quite bowled over by her and looking forward to seeing her again."

She had known that Zachary Cartwright had been much taken with Serena, but it hadn't occurred to her that he had intended pursuing his interest. The knowledge gave her an uncomfortable sensation that she couldn't identify. It was almost as if a fist had been slammed hard into her solar plexus. She said crisply, "Mr Cartwright isn't at all the sort of man to appeal to Serena. She is very gentle and placid; he would terrify her half to death."

Charles laughed. "Yes, he would. He terrifies me half to death and I've known him all my life."

The Chinese had begun to serve the chicken. Zachary Cartwright was sitting on the ground, his legs crossed Indian fashion, and as he was well within earshot she decided not to ask Charles how it was that he had known Zachary Cartwright for so long.

The chicken was tender, deliciously flavoured and very welcome after her tedious diet of bread and cheese. Even though Zachary Cartwright was still adamant that she couldn't remain with them, there was an atmosphere of camaraderie that evening, as they sat around the fire, that Gianetta was never to forget. When the dinner had been eaten and the dishes cleared away, Zachary had picked up his discarded notepad and, still sitting Indian-fashion on the ground, had continued to write up his notes, including the details of her potentilla.

Charles had put the cutting into a little jar of water and placed it on the small, collapsible table. Gianetta had begun to sketch it, noting every tiny detail of the stem and leaves and promising that in the morning she would draw another, when the petals were open. Charles had sat at her side while she had worked, chatting about how much he had enjoyed the voyage up the Yang-tse, through the Ichang gorge, and of how he was hoping that they would not only reach the border of Tibet, but actually cross over and into it.

At one point the ponies became restless and Zachary rose to his feet, with the panther-like grace that characterized all his movements, to calm them. While he was out of ear-shot, Gianetta asked Charles, "How is it that you have known Zachary Cartwright all your life?"

He leaned back in his canvas chair. "Zac's father was one of my father's closest friends. He was killed fighting alongside General Gordon at Khartoum. Zac was seven. His mother died soon after. From then on, Zac lived with us. It was difficult for him, I think, though he never admitted it. Although his family tree goes back even further than my own, there wasn't much family fortune left by the time his father died and while I went off to Eton, Zac went to the local grammar school. He won a scholarship to Cambridge and it was there that he became a passionate naturalist."

He grinned. "I couldn't understand what he saw in it at the beginning, but he soon made me see that the subject wasn't as boring as I had originally thought and before very long I was as hooked as he was, though never as knowledgeable. He didn't come back to live with my family after Cambridge. He went straight to London, to Kew, and two years later he was off on his first expedition."

"Where did he go?" Gianetta asked, intrigued.

"The Himalayas. He's one of the very few Englishmen to have ever stood on the snows of the mountain reputed to be the highest in the world."

Zachary Cartwright walked back towards them and said brusquely, "It's nearly midnight and I want to make an early start in the morning."

"All right," Charles said, taking the hint and rising to his feet. "What sleeping arrangements do we make for Gianetta?"

"We don't make any," Zachary Cartwright said, his lean, bronzed face harsh and uncompromising. "She sleeps as she slept last night, in whatever it was she thought fit to bring with her."

He turned away from them, walking down into the darkness towards the river. A few minutes later they could hear the sound of him diving into the water for a midnight bathe.

"What did you . . . er . . . sleep in last night?" Charles asked her, a trifle uncomfortably.

"A quilt that I brought with me. It was perfectly satisfactory," she added, trying not to remember how stiff and cold she had felt when she had woken in the morning.

"Have my sleeping-bag tonight," he said generously. "I'll ferret out some of the spare blankets that we've brought with us."

He led her across to where his sleeping-bag was laid out on the ground. "I'm afraid we're not taking advantage of the tents we've brought with us," he said apologetically.

60

"It isn't worth putting them up for one-night stops, especially when the weather is so mild."

"I don't mind," she said truthfully. The comfort of the glowing fire and the knowledge that both Zachary Cartwright and Charles were armed, were all the luxuries she craved.

Another sleeping-bag was lying uncomfortably close to the one Charles was offering her. She averted her eyes from it quickly. The camp fire had been banked for the night, only an occasional flame shooting skywards. The Chinese were sitting on the ground a little distance away, their knees pulled up to their chins, blankets around their shoulders. She paused hesitantly. There was nowhere secluded where she could take off her jacket and trousers. She would have to sleep with them on.

As if reading her thoughts, Charles said with a hint of laughter in his voice, "At least you won't have to travel back to Chung King in your Chinese regalia. You do have European clothes with you, don't you?"

"Oh yes, but I think I actually rather prefer these clothes for riding in. They're very comfortable."

"They're not very suitable," he said, his voice thickening slightly. "Not for someone as beautiful as you."

Gianetta stood very still. In the velvety darkness she could barely make out the figures of the dozing Chinese. From the river there still came the sound of Zachary Cartwright cavorting like a water buffalo.

"You are very, very beautiful, Gianetta," Charles whispered, touching her face tenderly with his hand. "I thought so when I first saw you at the Residency and I think so now, even though you are dressed like a boy."

At his touch she had started to tremble slightly. "Thank you," she said hoarsely, "and now I think that perhaps I should . . ."

"Not yet," he said, and drawing her purposefully into his arms he lowered his head to hers, kissing her with passionate intensity.

61

CHAPTER FOUR

Charles Gianetta action was so unexpected, the feel of his lips on hers so disturbing and shocking that for a stunned moment couldn't move. Then, as his hands bent her in fiercely against the hard length of his body and his mouth parted hers, his tongue plunging deep in a manner she had never even suspected existed, she gathered her scattered wits and pushed against his chest with her hands, kicking out at his leg with her booted foot, struggling to twist her head away from his.

His breathing became deeper, and for a moment she thought he was going to take no notice of her protests. Then, as a subconscious part of her brain became aware that the sound of splashing and cavorting from the river had ceased, he released her abruptly, looking past her into the darkness, his face tightening. Almost immediately his eyes returned to her, and as he looked down at her he gave her a curiously charming, apologetic smile.

"I'm sorry, Gianetta. I'm afraid for a moment I let my heart rule my head. It was foolish of me. There's no offence taken, I hope?"

She sensed, rather than saw, Zachary Cartwright emerging into the dim circle of the light from the dying fire.

"No . . . of course not," she said uncertainly, too confused and bewildered to know whether what she felt *was* offence or not.

He gave a short relieved laugh and tilted her chin upwards lightly with his finger. "You're a very special girl, Gianetta," he said, his voice husky and low. "I'm damned if I'll apologise for the kiss. Only for the circumstances."

Something hot flickered at the back of his eyes. "And when the circumstances are more appropriate, I'll kiss you again, Gianetta, and next time you won't be afraid. I promise."

Zachary Cartwright's voice said curtly from a few yards away from them. "If you've finished saying goodnight to Miss Hollis, perhaps we can all turn in and get some sleep."

The unconcealed sarcasm in his words sent the blood stinging to her cheeks. Charles said blandly, "I've arranged that Gianetta should have my sleeping-bag. I'm going to dig out a couple of blankets from the stores for myself."

"Do that," Zachary said with a rude curtness that only increased Gianetta's discomfort.

Charles knew Zac had seen him kissing Gianetta and was amused that his worldly companion should have reacted so uncharacteristically.

"Goodnight, Gianetta," he said easily and then, as Zac glowered at him, his amusement over the incident began to fade.

He admired Zac greatly and, though he wasn't adverse to arousing his jealousy, he certainly didn't want to become the object of his contempt. He walked away and over to where the stores and provisions were stacked, frowning slightly, almost wishing that the incident had not taken place.

Gianetta's back was still towards Zachary Cartwright, but she was acutely aware of his menacing presence, only feet away from her.

"You have my congratulations," he said tightly, moving forward and whipping his sleeping-bag from the ground next to hers. "You are obviously a lady who is well able to transfer her attentions from one man to another at the slightest provocation."

She sucked in her breath, struggling for speech. "How dare you!" she managed at last. "You cannot really think

63

that you were ever the object of my . . . my *attentions*, as you call them!"

She had spun round towards him, glaring at him, almost spitting the words. He was standing, glowering back at her, the sleeping-bag in his hands, but it wasn't his ferocious expression that disconcerted her even further. It was his semi-nakedness. He still wore his breeches, belted and buckled and snug about his hips, but his torso was bare, his whipcord muscles gleaming with drops of river water. She looked away swiftly, the crimson in her cheeks deepening.

He laughed shortly. "Are the realities of camp life a little more than you bargained for, Miss Hollis? Or had you not imagined bathing and dressing on the long, lonely journey to Kansu?"

"I had not imagined anyone could be as *hateful* and as *rude* as you are!" she hissed between clenched teeth, her fists closing in her unspoken desire to let fly physically at him.

He saw the stiffening of her body, the clenched fists, and laughed again, this time with genuine mirth. "I wouldn't try it if I were you. You would only find yourself being given the sort of good hiding you've obviously lacked in the past," and before she could think of a suitably crushing reply he strode off, leaving her as nearly alone in the darkness as she had been the previous night.

Fighting down tears of weariness and frustration she unlaced her ankle-high boots, tugging them off and then, unable with decency to undress further, she clambered into the comforting warmth of the sleeping-bag. It smelled disturbingly male. There was the same faint aroma of cologne and cigar smoke that had surrounded her when Charles had so unaccountably and shockingly kissed her.

Her cheeks still burned, her humiliation so great she wondered if she would ever survive it. How could he have done such a thing? She had given him no encouragement. It was he who, she had believed, would protect her from

64

any unwelcome advances. Instead, on the very first night that she had joined them, he had acted in a way that made it almost impossible for her to continue with her plans.

Almost, she thought determinedly, but not quite. He *had* apologised. Or she thought he had. When she tried to remember his exact words she wasn't quite so sure. She had been so appalled at the thought that Zachary Cartwright might have seen what had happened, might be overhearing, that she had caught only the sense of what Charles had said to her, not each word.

She lay in the dark, listening to the ponies and mules stirring restlessly, the logs on the dying fire shifting and settling. Had he seen? Why did it matter so much if he had? Why did the knowledge that he thought her foolish and criminally flirtatious fill her with such mortification that she wanted to die? How *could* he have believed that because he had caught her looking at him *once* in the drawing-room of the Residency, she was so besotted that she would have followed him out of Chung King and into the wilderness beyond? And that, when he had arrogantly and rudely assured her that she had done so to no purpose, he should believe she had immediately turned her attention towards his companion and that she had *encouraged* Charles to kiss her!

She tossed and turned in the narrow sleeping-bag, hating the discomfort of the clothes she still wore, hating Charles for so stupidly spoiling everything, hating and detesting Zachary Cartwright for his superciliousness, his arrogance, his unbelievable, unforgivable *rudeness*.

When she woke, the sun was already over the horizon and she could hear birds singing and the fire crackling and the low murmur of voices. She pushed herself into a sitting position. The Chinese were busy making breakfast and Zachary Cartwright and Charles were standing at a small table, looking down at the drawing she had left there the previous evening.

"It's damn good," Charles was saying enthusiastically, and Zachary Cartwright nodded in grudging agreement.

Before she should overhear anything else, perhaps not quite so flattering, about herself, Gianetta struggled out of the sleeping-bag, aware that she looked and felt decidedly unkempt.

"Good morning," Charles said, swinging round and smiling engagingly at her.

His manner was so relaxed and at ease that she wondered for a moment if she had dreamed the encounter that had taken place the previous night. Zachary Cartwright looked towards her and, at the memory of what he had overheard and perhaps seen, she knew the encounter had been no dream. He said a brief good morning and turned away, but not before she had seen the withering expression in his eyes as they raked her untidy appearance.

Her Chinese dress, in the light of day, seemed even more bizarre and unflattering than it had done the previous evening. With as much dignity as she could muster, she bypassed the canvas chairs and table and the fire, walking over to Ben and her carpet-bag.

"Good morning, Ben," she said, slipping her arm around his neck and giving him a kiss on his shaggy coat. "They think we're going back, but we're not, Ben. We're not."

Ben nuzzled against her and she patted him again, taking comfort from his unspoken agreement and unswerving loyalty. She bent down, taking a hairbrush from her carpet-bag, looking longingly at the serviceable ankle-length skirts and blouses that she had brought with her. She had not removed the clothes she was wearing since she had left the Residency. More than anything else in the world, she longed to be able to take them off and plunge into the ice-cool freshness of the river. She looked around her, but there were no concealing trees near the river bank.

"It can't be done, Ben," she sighed, standing up, the brush in her hand. "I can't even change into fresh clothes, much less bathe. Especially after last night."

Ever since she had opened her eyes, she had tried not to think about last night. Charles' kiss had bewildered her deeply and she still didn't know what to think about it. She had known, at the Residency, that he had been drawn towards her and attracted by her, but it had never occurred to her that he might be falling in love with her. And if he was? How did she feel about him?

She unplaited her queue, brushing her hair vigorously. She truly didn't know. If the idea had been put to her a day ago, she would have been highly flattered and perhaps thought it the answer to all her problems. After all, the wife of Lord Rendlesham would never have to contemplate living anywhere as boring as Lincolnshire. She would have an elegant country house and a town house in London, and she would be able to accompany her husband on all his adventures.

A few days ago the very thought would have seemed too wonderful to be true. But it wasn't a day ago. Since then, he had kissed her and his kiss had not been welcome. It had shocked and shaken her, though for what reasons she was not quite sure. She did know that she didn't want him to kiss her again, "And that," she said confidingly and practically to Ben, "is not a very convenient thing to wish about a future husband."

By the time she had finished brushing her hair, her buoyancy and determination had returned in full measure. Despite the kiss, and despite Zachary Cartwright's intention of returning her to Chung King, she was not going to go. She was going to become a part of their expedition. She was going to search for blue Moonflowers in Kansu.

When she had washed as much of herself as decency allowed, she walked back towards the camp, her hair tumbling loose and free around her shoulders and down her back. Charles turned towards her, his light blue eyes immediately appreciative.

"You should always wear your hair like that," he said. "It's like a waterfall of night-black silk."

"It's damned impractical," Zachary Cartwright said, his hard dark eyes flicking towards her and then back to the notes he was making.

"I have some pins in my bag," she said defensively. "I shall put it in a chignon, not a queue."

"I should think not," Charles said warmly, removing his jacket from one of the canvas chairs and motioning for her to sit. "There's no need for you to try and look Chinese any longer. Why haven't you changed into European clothes? You said you had brought some with you."

"Because . . ." she hesitated, aware of Zachary Cartwright listening to her with interest. "Because these are more comfortable," she finished lamely.

"Have some breakfast," Charles said, accepting her explanation at face value. "It won't be what you're used to, but it's filling and nourishing."

It was rice with vegetables, followed by a slab of dark chocolate.

It it had been snails and frogs' legs she would have eaten with relish, simply so as not to give Zachary Cartwright another opportunity of pointing out how unsuitable camp life was for a woman. As it was, the rice was filling and hot, and the slab of chocolate was sweet and delicious.

"The drawing you did was exceptional," Charles said, standing a few feet away from her, a tin mug of steaming tea in his hands. "It's very rare for a non-botanist to be so botanically correct. Isn't that so, Zac?"

Zachary Cartwright gave a grunt that could have meant anything and continued with his notes, Gianetta's drawing propped up on the table in front of him.

"Zac wants you to show him exactly where you camped the night before last, and where you found the potentilla," Charles continued, blandly ignoring the fact that his two companions were obviously barely on speaking terms.

"But that would mean delaying your journey by another day," she protested, surprised. "Is the flower really so important?"

"The flower won't cause us any delay," Zachary Cartwright said tersely. "It is *you* who are causing the delay, Miss Hollis. You can point out the place where you camped when we trace your steps back to Chung King. We shall be setting off in half an hour."

He was wearing the dove-grey breeches and knee-high, velvet-cuffed boots that he had been wearing when he had set off from the Residency, but the white linen shirt he had been wearing then had been changed for one of a deep wine-red.

"Wouldn't it perhaps be more suitable if *I* returned Gianetta to Chung King?" Charles said, his voice studiedly casual. "After all, I think I *did* get on with the Consul a little more easily than you did, and explaining to him that Gianetta left Chung King and followed us without our knowledge isn't going to be easy. He might take it better from me than from you."

"Are you not both returning to Chung King?" Gianetta asked, forgetting for the moment that she had still no intention that *anyone* should return there.

"No," Charles turned towards her, with a frank grin. "Zac intends that I should remain here, with the Chinese, while he rides alone with you to Chung King."

"It will be quicker that way," Zachary said briefly, his dark head still bent over the notes he was making. "There's no sense in the pack mules trailing all that way and back for nothing."

"None at all," Charles agreed easily. "And no reason for *you* to face the Consul's wrath, when *I* can bring the pressure of my name to bear and when he will, rightly or wrongly, believe our innocence a little more readily from me than he would from you."

Gianetta felt her nerves begin to throb. She still had no intention of being returned to Chung King, though she still hadn't a plan for how it could be avoided. But if the worst came to the worst and she *was* returned, she knew with devastating certainty that she didn't want to return with Charles as her sole companion.

Zachary Cartwright had put his pencil down and had turned to look at her. She knew by the expression in his narrow eyes that he also knew why Charles had suggested that he escort her, and that he believed her to be eager that he do so.

"No, Charles," he said curtly, rising to his feet. "I am taking Miss Hollis back to Chung King. You will remain here with the stores and provisions."

It was such a direct order that even despite her relief, Gianetta was shocked. She saw a faint flush touch Charles' cheeks, and his jaw clenched.

"Very well," he said shortly, and Gianetta knew that though he was taking great care not to sound it, inwardly he was furiously angry. "I'm going for a walk," he said, not looking at either of them, but slamming his empty tin mug down on the table and turning abruptly on his heels.

"I have two specimens here that we collected yesterday, Miss Hollis," Zachary Cartwright said, as if the angry exit had never taken place. "Could you perhaps draw them for me in my field book while I make preparations for our journey?"

"Yes," she said, wondering how on earth she could persuade him that the journey was unnecessary; that no great harm would come to either his or Lord Rendlehsam's reputation if she was to continue with them; that she would be a helpful, *useful* member of their expedition, if only he would give her the chance.

He strode away towards the ponies and mules and she picked up his pencil, beginning to draw the two flowers that stood in tiny jars of water on the desk. She wouldn't go back. She *wouldn't*. But how on earth was she going to be able to stay?

Ten minutes later there came an agonized shout, and then a roaring sound as rocks and boulders crashed down into the river. She dropped her pencil, leaping to her feet, looking down-river to where, some fifty or seventy yards away, a great cloud of dust was billowing skywards.

"*It's Charles!*" Zachary shouted, "*The bank has given way!*" He sprinted away from the ponies and down along the river bank to where the cloud of dust was beginning to disperse and settle.

There came another desperate shout, this time for help, and Gianetta began to run in Zachary Cartwright's wake.

The river bank where they had camped had been shallow, and access to the water had been easy. Seventy yards away, at the point Charles had reached on his angry march, the ground rose steeply into a sandstone bank littered with rocks and boulders. He had been scrambling among these, trying to work off his rage at Zachary's humiliating high-handedness, when he had dislodged one. The falling rock had hit and bounced off another and then the whole bank had given way, rocks and boulders and Charles, all tumbling down in a furious cascade into the water.

"Keep your head up!" she heard Zachary shout, and then Charles' tight, frightened voice shouted back, "I can't! I've hurt my arm!"

She ran furiously in Zachary's wake. When he reached the point where the bank had given way, he leapt and slithered down it, hurling himself into the river where Charles was painfully struggling.

By the time she had reached the rock-fall, Zachary was swimming for the bank, hauling a white-faced Charles behind him.

She took the bank as Zachary had done, slithering down it and wading out to help him bring Charles ashore.

"My arm! It's broken!" Charles gasped. "Of all the stupid, nonsensical things to have done!"

There was no disputing his diagnosis. His arm hung, ugly and deformed, the bone of the elbow protruding through the skin.

"I can put a splint on it, but it isn't a straightforward break," Zac panted, taking Charles' weight as they scaled the still-crumbling sandstone.

"It hurts like the very devil!" Charles looked as if he were about to faint. "Will it mend straight, do you think? It won't heal short . . . or odd . . . or anything?"

"I'll tell you when I've had a closer look at it," Zachary said tersely and then, to Gianetta, "The first-aid box is with the stores. It's clearly marked. Run ahead and get it out and opened."

She nodded, taking a last fleeting look at Charles's dripping wet figure. He had begun to shake with shock and, as she sprinted back to the camp, she hoped fervently that there would be some brandy as well as the first-aid box amongst the stores.

The Chinese were standing immobile, the expression on their faces one of alarm.

"There's been an accident," she said briefly. "Can you boil some water and make some tea?"

She wasn't sure if Zachary Cartwright would need boiling water for whatever he was about to do to Charles' arm, but she was certainly in need of a cup of tea.

The first-aid box, with a vivid red cross painted on the lid, was easily found, and by the time Zachary had helped Charles into camp and seated him in one of the canvas chairs, Gianetta had it open and at his side.

"Is there any brandy?" she asked Zachary. "The Chinese are boiling water for tea, but . . ."

"There's brandy in my saddle-bag," Zachary said briefly. "There's no need for tea."

"Oh yes, there is," she retorted spiritedly. "*I* want the tea!"

He looked towards her, his eyebrows raised, a flicker of grudging amusement in his dark eyes. "Yes," he said. "Of course."

To her stunned surprise, she found herself flashing him a smile before she hurried off to search his saddle-bag for the brandy. When she returned, Zachary had removed Charles' shirt, and Charles' face was grey, his jaw clenched against the pain.

"It's a compound fracture," Zachary was saying.

72

"You're going to have to decide whether you want me to do my best with it and continue with the expedition, or whether you want to return to Chung King for proper medical attention."

"What will happen if I stay?" Charles asked, white-lipped.

"It will heal. Healthy bones always do. But it will never be the same as it was before."

"And if I go back to Chung King?"

"Then you'll be able to have the bone set correctly. In three months' time it will be as good as new."

"How will I get back to Chung King? I won't be able to ride."

"You will," Zachary said, taking a sling and bandages out of the first-aid box. Although Charles seemed not to notice, there was a subtle change in the inflection of his voice.

Gianetta looked across at him. Charles was sucking his breath in sharply, clenching his teeth together as Zachary began to bind the arm in a secure sling. He wasn't going to say so, but she knew that he was disappointed in Charles.

If Zachary had fractured his arm she knew he would never, for one moment, have considered calling off the expedition and returning for medical help. Somehow or other, he would have continued. But Charles wasn't Zachary. His commitment to the expedition was not as fierce, or as obsessed. To Charles, the expedition was merely an adventure, an adventure that had gone wrong and that he now wanted to have nothing more to do with.

"Drink the brandy, Charles," Zachary said to him as Gianetta poured a generous measure into one of the tin drinking mugs. "I'm going to bind the sling very firmly against your body. You'll be able to balance and ride with your good arm once the shock has worn off."

Charles downed the brandy, closing his eyes against the pain as Zachary began to bind his arm into position.

73

After a while Charles said, "So we're all going back? We're all going to return to Chung King?"

Zachary secured the broad bandaging with a safety-pin and stood up, looking down at him. "I don't think there's any need," he said at last. "Gianetta has to return, and she might as well do so with you. Two of the Chinese can go with you. I'll carry on as intended and pick up replacement men at the next town."

At the unexpected use of her Christian name, Gianetta's eyes flew open wide. It was the first time he had referred to her as anything but Miss Hollis. She wondered if he was aware of his lapse into familiarity and if so, what had occasioned it. She also wondered how Charles felt at being considered a suitable escort only now that he was disabled.

"Well . . . if you think that would suit," Charles said uncertainly. From the tone of his voice, Gianetta knew that he desperately wanted Zachary to return to Chung King with him, but that pride would not allow him to ask him to do so.

"Yes I do," Zachary said, and the last flicker of hope died in Charles' eyes. "It's only a two-day ride and it isn't over difficult country."

"But will you be able to continue with the expedition by yourself?" Charles asked, a little colour beginning to return to his cheeks.

Zachary grinned. "If I managed in the Himalayas, I can manage in Kansu. The local Chinese are very easy to train as assistant collectors, and they quickly pick up the art of changing drying papers. I shall be able to obtain all the help that I need."

"What are drying papers?" Gianetta asked, interested.

For once he spoke to her without harshness or anger. "When a plant has been collected and the field-notes have been written up, it has to be dried. This is done in presses between blotting paper. With fleshy plants, and in wet weather, the paper has constantly to be changed and dried."

74

"Which would have been one of my tasks," Charles said to her, forcing a ghost of his usual grin. "Even in good weather, the sheets have to be changed at least once a day to make sure that mould hasn't attached itself to the plants, or insects eaten the best specimens."

"And how many plants will there be in the presses at any one time?" Gianetta asked, sipping the tea one of the Chinese had brought across to her.

"Three or four hundred," Zachary said, his mouth tugging into the hint of a smile at her stunned expression. "And though locals can be trained to do a certain amount of the changing, the job of arranging the plants in the press the first time is far too important to be delegated."

"Even to me," Charles said, with a return of his impish humour.

"You don't have the patience." Zachary looked down at him, his hands on his hips. "How do you feel now?"

"Shaky," Charles replied with naked honesty.

Zachary frowned slightly. "The sooner you get to Chung King, the better. I'll have the Chinese sort out enough provisions for you. The next town north is only thirty or thirty-two li away. Once there I'll be able to replace both men and mules."

"When do you think we should make a start?" Charles asked, wincing as he repositioned himself in the canvas chair.

"In about an hour."

Gianetta saw Charles flinch, and her own heart sank. Riding so far with a badly injured arm would not be easy for him. He would need all of her help. Ever since she had first conceived of the idea of travelling to Kansu, she had refused to admit that it might be an impossibility. Now, for the first time, defeat was staring her straight in the face. Charles could not return to Chung King without her. She had to return with him. She had no alternative.

"Would you finish your drawings of the plants we collected yesterday?" Zachary asked her, his hair still glistening with river water, his wine-red linen shirt cling-ing damply to his chest, the whipcord muscles clearly defined.

She nodded. While Charles remained seated, sipping at another glass of medicinal brandy, and Zachary began to sort through the stores, ordering the Chinese to reload the mules, she began once again to draw.

"You don't realise it," Charles said, his voice sharp with pain. "But you've been paid a great compliment. Zac is a very talented artist himself and usually always does his own drawings. I've never known him to allow anyone else to draw for him, especially straight into his field-book."

"It's nice to know he approves of *something* about me," Gianetta said drily, trying to resist the little rush of satisfaction that she felt.

Charles managed a semblance of his old grin. "He is a bit of a bear, isn't he? But take my word for it, his bark is far worse than his bite. My mother tells me he was an exuberant little boy until his parents died. Their deaths must have been a great blow to him."

Gianetta said nothing. She knew exactly how much of a blow it must have been. Like her, he had had to go and live with people who, though kind, had not truly wanted to be burdened with him. He had had to make do with a local grammar-school education when Charles, who had admitted that he didn't have half of Zachary's intelligence or ambition, had been sent away for the most privileged education that money could buy. Yet he had still achieved far more than Charles. She remembered Charles telling her that Zachary had gone up to Cambridge on a scholarship.

"What college was it that he went to?" she asked curiously.

"Christ's," Charles said with a wry grin. "He took honours in the natural science tripos. Very humiliating for me. All I had to show for Oxford was a rowing blue!"

They were laughing together when Zachary strode back

towards them, his previous fleeting flash of good humour nowhere in evidence.

"The mules have been reloaded. You will return with two Chinese and one pack mule. I will take the others."

"Do we need to rob you of the mule?" Charles asked doubtfully. "We shall be in Chung King in two days' time. We don't need much in the way of provisions. What we do need we can carry with us, surely?"

"You're going to have enough problems riding with one arm, without having to cope with extra baggage," Zachary said decisively. "One of the mules, with suitable provisions, goes with you. I've explained to the Chinese what is happening and paid them off. They're both trustworthy men and they'll stay with you until you reach the Residency."

The Chinese were already mounted and waiting expectantly.

"Are we going now?" Gianetta asked, putting down her pencil reluctantly.

Zachary nodded. "The sooner you leave and the sooner Charles' arm is seen to professionally, the better."

Charles rose cautiously to his feet. "This is a damned ignoble way to return," he said bitterly. "Perhaps we'll have better luck next year, Zac. Perhaps we could go to the Himalayas or the upper reaches of Burma?"

"Perhaps," Zachary said non-committedly and Gianetta looked swiftly towards him, suddenly sure that Charles' capitulation to his injury had wrecked any chance of Zac taking him again on a plant hunting expedition.

Filled with an overwhelming sense of despair, Gianetta walked over to Ben and patted him lovingly.

"It's no use, Ben," she said softly. "We have to go back. There'll be no more adventures; no searching for blue Moonflowers."

Ben nuzzled her with his head, understanding only that he was once again about to be ridden, and indicating his pleasure at the fact.

She mounted him and as she did so Zachary helped

77

Charles into his saddle. She heard Charles give a quickly suppressed cry of pain and walked Ben towards him.

"Are you going to be all right?" she asked him anxiously. "Would it be any easier if you rode behind me?"

He shook his head. "No, thanks all the same, Gianetta. I've been riding since before I could walk. I can ride with one arm. Please don't look so worried."

"Whatever you do, don't loosen the bandages binding your arm to your chest," Zachary warned. "As long as they stay firm and your arm stays immobile, you'll have no problem."

"Gianetta will look after me," Charles said with a strained smile. "And don't frown like that, Zac. Her virtue will be safe. I might be able to ride, but if you must know the truth, I feel like the very devil."

For the first time since she had met him, Gianetta saw Zachary Cartwright grin. "You'll be all right. The Chinese can set bones more efficiently than any other nationality on earth."

Charles had walked his pony in front of Gianetta. The two Chinese had fallen into position behind them, with the pack mule on a leading rein. They were ready to leave.

"See you in another ten or twelve months, Zac," Charles said, looking suddenly very young and very vulnerable. "Make sure you bring home something that will knock them cold at Kew." "I'll do my best," Zachary promised. He looked towards her, seemed about to say something and then thought better of it, saying only, "Goodbye, Gianetta. I hope your uncle doesn't give you too hard a time."

For a moment she thought she saw a flicker of sympathy in his near-black eyes, but she couldn't be sure.

"He won't," she said bleakly, with far more confidence than she felt. "Goodbye."

Charles touched his pony's flanks with his heels and began to move off at a steady walk. Zachary stood beside the still burning camp-fire, the collapsible table and chairs nearby incongruous in the vast, bare landscape.

He looked very alone. Very lonely. She turned her head away from him, fixing her eyes firmly on Charles' pony, knowing that if she looked back again the abandonment of her dreams would be too much for her. The tears glittering on her eyelashes would trickle down her cheeks and disgrace her.

Considering the difficulty under which Charles was riding, they made very good time. As dusk approached she was able to recognise the landscape in which she had camped.

"It was just outside Fu-tu Kwan," she said as the town became visible in the distance. "Near the river."

"I don't see how we can hope to find the exact spot where you found your yellow potentilla," Charles said, his face sheened with sweat and exhaustion. "I think we're going to have to disappoint Zac."

Gianetta thought so too. More than once she had thought that Charles had been about to fall from the saddle but the Chinese had ridden quickly up to him, genuinely caring, speedily helpful.

"We'll stop now," he said to her relief. "No point in entering Fu-tu Kwan. It's a filthy place."

"The river is only a little way off the trail to the right," she said, in fervent agreement with him. "Can you stay mounted for just a little while longer, until we reach it?"

He gave her a weary grin. "Yes," he said. "Of course I can. Lead on, MacDuff."

Twenty minutes later she had found a camp site with grazing and water for the ponies and mules. The Chinese helped Charles from the saddle and he sagged against them weakly.

"There's only tomorrow to go," she said encouragingly.

The Chinese lowered him to the ground, sitting him down with his back supported against the trunk of a tree.

"Thank God," he said with heartfelt relief. "You know,

Gianetta, I have the crazy feeling that Zac expected me to continue with the expedition, fractured arm or no fractured arm."

"I don't think so," she lied soothingly. "You would only have been a handicap to him, wouldn't you? Is there anything I can do to make you more comfortable?"

He shook his head, looking pale and drawn. "No, nothing. The Chinese are being very good. They handle me with unbelievable gentleness."

The Chinese were busy making a fire and unpacking provisions for the evening meal.

"Will Zachary have difficulty in finding men to replace them?" she asked with a worried frown.

"No." Charles' voice was confident. "Zac never does have those kind of difficulties. Men are always eager to work for him. I don't know how he does it, but they always turn out to be not only hard workers, but blindingly honest into the bargain."

"Perhaps it's because he doesn't expect them to be anything else," said Gianetta. She had been squatting down on her heels beside him; now she stood up. "Dinner looks as though it will be another twenty minutes or so. Do you mind if I go for a walk and try and find the potentilla? I know we're in nearly the same place as I camped the other night."

"No, I don't mind," Charles said, closing his eyes. "Take my note-book and penknife with you. If you do find it, Zac will be delighted, and at least *something* will have been salvaged from this debacle."

He opened his eyes again. "You know what to put in the notes, don't you? What the soil is like, where you found the plant, its position, whether it is facing north or south, whether the plant is solitary or in a group, how tall the scape is . . ."

"The scape?" she asked, puzzled.

"The stem," he said. "How many flowers it carries, the width of the corolla . . ."

"The corolla?"

"The whorl of petals contained in the calyx."

She thought it best not to ask what the calyx was, in case he decided it was pointless her even looking for the plant.

"Yes," she said, rising to her feet.

"And take another cutting with my penknife," he said, closing his eyes once again. "Then we can press it."

Gianetta left him and walked away down the river bank. In the distance, the walls of Fu-tu Kwan looked just as they had done two evenings ago, neither nearer or farther. The landscape was very bare, the hills treeless apart for a few banyan trees. Poppies gave an occasional splash of colour, but apart from the poppies she could see no wild flowers and no grey-leafed, yellow-flowered shrub. The sound of the Kialing as it flowed strongly southwards was restful and she was glad that they were once more camping beside it. It would help her to sleep and not to lay awake, thinking of the dreams she had left behind her.

She had gone as far as she dared and was just about to turn back when, in the deepening dusk, she saw the beaten earth where she had camped, and nearby, the inconsequential-looking shrub, its small yellow flowers closed but unmistakable.

With an uprush of pleasure she knelt down beside it, taking a cutting, then she rested the note-book on her knee and regarded the shrub thoughtfully. She wouldn't be able to tell how many petals there were until morning, when the flower opened, but she could make notes about its situation and the soil it was growing in.

She looked at the soil and rubbed it with her fingers. It was very gritty. She somehow didn't think that would be quite the kind of description that Zachary would deem as being sufficient. She took a handkerchief from the pocket of her jacket and scooped up as much soil as she could into it.

Charles would be a far better judge of her find than she was. There were no similar plants around it, or any plants at all, so she wrote down the word

81

"solitary". Then she paused. She couldn't measure the stem accurately without a ruler, so that task would also be best left until she returned with Charles, and she couldn't make another drawing because it was too dark.

Gianetta rose to her feet, her hands grubby. She would come back in the morning to sketch it, and Charles would be able to come and look at it and make any notes that were needed.

"I found it," she called out to him as she walked back into the small camp. The fire was crackling merrily and the smell of beans and dried pork rose enticingly into the air.

"Good girl." Charles was still propped against his banyan tree and she saw that one of the Chinese had poured him a restorative brandy.

"It wasn't very far away," she said, sitting down on the ground beside him. "You'll be able to see it for yourself in the morning. However, I did my humble best for the field-notes. I've brought some of the surrounding soil back because I didn't know how to describe it. It just looked gritty to me."

Charles grinned and she wondered whether it was the brandy or her news that had revived him. "Let's have a look," he said, his grin deepening as he read the extent of her notes.

"'Solitary' and 'found near water' aren't really enough, Gianetta. We'll eat first and then I'll show you what you should really have put."

They ate around the fire, and the same spirit of camaraderie that she had experienced the previous night enfolded her. She liked this life of the open air. She liked the satisfaction of doing something worthwhile, and surely finding a plant that in Europe was little known, or perhaps unknown entirely, was worthwhile?

When one of the Chinese had taken their tin plates down to the river to wash, and the other had poured them hot mugs of tea, Charles said, "Now I'll show you how to make proper field-notes. You have to remember that a gardener in England has to be able to grow the plant, so it is very important that he knows the conditions under which it grows here. This scraping of top soil isn't of any use whatsoever. We have to know what the soil is like much deeper down. The Chinese will take care of that for us in the morning."

She listened to him with keen attention, and when he had finished he said to her gently, "You really are serious about wanting to be a plant-hunter, aren't you, Gianetta?"

She nodded, hugging her knees with her arms. "Yes, it seems so wonderful. To perhaps be the first European to see a certain flower growing in the wild, and to bring the seeds of that flower back to England so that English gardeners can grow it. It seems such a marvellous, magical thing to do."

The flames from the fire had cast a rosy nimbus of light around Gianetta. Her face, with its fine-boned, delicate features, enormous dark eyes and gently curving mouth, looked so unbelievably beautiful that a lump rose in his throat.

When he had taken advantage of her the previous night, kissing her so passionately, it had been nothing more than natural reaction at being faced with a girl he had already been attracted to, in inviting, unchaperoned circumstances. Now he knew that it could be far more. That if things were different . . .

"Why are you looking so sombre?" she asked him. "Is it your arm? Do you need to try and sleep?"

"No, it isn't that," he said, though his arm was hurting like the devil. "I was just bitterly regretting that I can't make you an offer of marriage, Gianetta. I'm engaged already, you see."

"Oh!" She didn't know what to say. The sudden turn in the conversation had taken her completely by surprise. They had been sitting, talking, in such easy friendliness that she had momentarily forgotten his disturbing kiss of the previous evening. She didn't know whether to be

83

shocked that he should have kissed her in such a manner when he was betrothed to another woman; flattered that he cared for her enough to wish he were free; or relieved that their relationship could only, after this admission, be one of friendship.

At the troubled expression on her face he said sincerely, "I'm sorry if my behaviour yesterday evening led you to expect anything more honourable from me, Gianetta."

She shook her head, her hair tumbling in wild disarray around her shoulders. "No, I don't think that it did. I was just surprised . . . and bewildered."

He remembered that she had no parents, and that her return to Chung King meant that, in a few weeks time, she would be returning to England and a lonely existence in a house occupied only by servants.

"I can't bear you to look so unhappy," he said, reaching out with his uninjured arm and taking her hand. "It will be devilishly difficult, but I'll free myself, I'll . . ."

Her eyes flew wide. "No!" she said with such obvious sincerity that his first instinct was to be offended. "I'm not in love with you, Charles. I thought at the Residency that perhaps I could be, just a little. But I know now that though I like you enormously, I'm not in love with you. So there's no need for you to feel obliged towards me and for you to break off your engagement."

Charles didn't know whether he felt relieved or shatteringly disappointed. "Then what is it?" he persisted. "Why are you looking so sad?"

She gave him a little smile. "Do I? I don't meant to, but oh, Charles! I did *so* want to go to Kansu and search for blue Moonflowers!"

He was silent for a minute and then he said, "Then why don't you? You know what it's like to ride on your own. Another two days of such riding and you could catch up with Zac. He won't inconvenience himself by returning you to Chung King this time. He will have had enough of inconveniences."

His blue eyes were fierce as they held hers. "Follow

84

your dream, Gianetta. Go to Kansu with Zac. Leave your uncle and the explanations to me."

"But your arm," she protested. "How will you manage? I can't ride off and leave you."

"I'm in very good hands," he said, indicating the Chinese. "There's only another day of riding ahead of us. I enjoy your company, Gianetta, but I don't *need* it. I can survive without it. Take your opportunity, it may never come again. Go to Kansu!"

Her eyes held his, excitement spiralling through her. She *could* still go. All she needed was the courage.

"Set off in the morning," Charles said. "Zac won't have travelled any further than the next town on the road north. He has to pick up the two replacement Chinese there and it will take him at least a day to find suitable men, probably two. You'll have no difficulty in catching up with him."

"Oh, Charles! Do you think I can? Do you think I should?"

Despite his tiredness and his pain, he grinned. "Why the sudden doubts? You had none before, had you?"

"No," she said, her eyes glowing, her face radiant. "And I've none now! I'm going to Kansu and this time nothing, nothing at all, is going to stop me!"

CHAPTER FIVE

Gianetta slept soundly, comforted by Charles' nearness and the deep friendliness that had been forged between them. In the morning he insisted that she take one of his pistols, patiently showing her how to load and fire it.

She set off shortly after dawn, her heart beating fast and light, Charles standing by a grove of trees, waving goodbye to her with his uninjured arm until she was out of sight.

It was the third time she had travelled the same stretch of countryside, and it was becoming reassuringly familiar. Ben cantered uncomplainingly and when the sun indicated that it was lunch-time she stopped, picnicking on the last of her bread and cheese and the melon-seeds, peanuts and candied orange-peel that the Chinese had generously insisted she take with her.

After Ben had had time to rest she mounted him again, the road taking her through hills thick with pine and juniper, the Kialing never far from her left-hand side. She reached the spot where they had camped the previous night, a patch of still warm, blackened earth showing where their fire had been.

From here on, the route she was to take was unknown to her. She knew only that Zachary had said he would be pausing at the next town to engage men to replace those returning to Chung King with Charles, and that he had said the town was some thirty li away, which was equivalent to ten English miles.

"If we stay close to the river we can't go far wrong," she said to Ben, with more confidence than she truly felt.

The midday heat was uncomfortable, the increasingly undulating countryside eerily silent. A blue-jay darted low across the Kialing, disappearing into a narrow gully thick with poppies. The track she had been following and which had, in its earlier stages, been the road leading from Fu-tu Kwan, now disappeared altogether. She remembered her uncle once saying that roads, as Europeans understood them, did not exist in China. "Only narrow footpaths connect one town and village with another," he had said disparagingly, "and except by the waterways, nothing can be transported from place to place but on men's backs."

"Which means the next town *must* be on the banks of the river," Gianetta said to Ben, determined not to be fazed by the increasingly difficult terrain.

Ben's attitude accorded perfectly with her own. As small chasms marred their way he leapt them with nimble alacrity, scrambling bravely down and up shallow gullies, only refusing to do so when she dismounted in order to make it easier for him.

"Come *on*," she panted, after she had slithered to the base of one such gully more on her bottom than on her feet, "What are you waiting for?"

He had stood at the edge of the gully eyeing her disapprovingly, making no effort whatsoever to follow her. In the end, she had had no choice but to scramble back up to him and take hold of his reins. Still he had refused to move. Only when she had reluctantly remounted him did he sedately continue.

Despite all her efforts to keep the Kialing continually in sight, it proved to be impossible. The river entered a deep gorge, cliffs rising sheer from its banks. The only route it was possible to take led to the west, climbing upwards into scrubby pine-forest. Had Zachary, only a day earlier, taken the same route? Vainly she kept her eye out for hoof-prints or the blackened remains of a fire. There was nothing, not even a discarded peanut or melonseed-shell to indicate that she was riding in his wake.

By early afternoon, as they climbed even higher, her

apprehension began to deepen. How many li had they covered? Surely it was more than the thirty or so that Zachary had specified? If their route didn't soon begin to wend downwards, she would have no alternative but to make camp for the night in the pine forest. And in the forest would be wolves, perhaps even leopards.

They rounded the crest of the ravine they had been slowly traversing and there, far below them, was a glinting, shining loop of the Kialing.

It was the most welcome sight she had ever seen. "And there are boats on it, Ben!" she said exultantly. "Punts and sampans and even a junk!"

Their way began to lead down-hill and, though the Kialing soon disappeared from view again, Gianetta was uncaring. She knew now that they were heading towards it, and she also knew that they were heading towards a town. Quite a large town, if the traffic on the river was anything to go by. In the town, they would find Zachary Cartwright.

Light-heartedly she began to sing. Once she met up with Zachary Cartwright she would have nothing further to fear. He would be furious with her, but he had been furious with her before and she had survived the experience.

"And Zachary Cartwright's bad temper is far preferable to Lincolnshire," she said to Ben, leaning forward to give him an encouraging pat on his neck.

Within a very little while the pine trees petered out altogether, to be replaced by minute paddy fields descending in steep terraces. They were now on a recognisable path and the next bend revealed a sizable walled town, a steep, slanting staircase of stone steps leading up to its main gate.

A half-hour later, Ben was scaling the steps gallantly and Gianetta was again bombarded by stench and noise and an almost unbearable sense of claustrophobia. Just as in Fu-tu Kwan, the streets were unpaved, with open drains running down their centre, the houses pressing in higgledy-piggledy on either side.

"We need to find an inn," she said to Ben, wondering how a Chinese inn made itself recognizable.

Ben plodded stoically up first one narrow alley and down another. At last, Gianetta saw a painted wooden screen hanging over an uninvitingly dark doorway. The screen depicted an excessively large lady and she regarded it doubtfully, not sure whether it signified an inn or a house of ill-repute. A couple of mangy mules were tethered outside and Ben came to a halt beside them. Trusting his judgement she dismounted. There was no sign of Zachary Cartwright's sleek and frisky pony. No sign of the pack-mules that had accompanied him.

She adjusted her little round Chinese hat, took a deep breath and stepped towards the foetid, dark doorway. Once inside it took several seconds before her eyes adjusted to the gloom and she was able to discern people and shapes. Small rooms like hutches ran off at either side from the room she was standing in, which evidently served as the inn's lobby. Half a dozen pairs of eyes stared at her with incredulity.

Unable to single out anyone who was obviously the inn-keeper she said to the room at large, "Is there an Englishman staying here?"

There was a murmur of incomprehension. All her audience were male, and all looked to be at least eighty years old.

"An English-man," she said again. "He was hiring men to travel with him to Kansu."

At the word Kansu there were some encouraging nods and one of the wizened figures bravely approached her.

"*Yang-jen?*" he asked, "*Yang-kwei-tse?*"

She wondered what other words, apart from Kansu, would be recognisable to him.

"A round-eye," she said, and was rewarded by half a dozen eager nods of assent.

"*Yang-jen,*" the old man who had taken it upon himself to be spokesman, said again in agreement.

Gianetta physically sagged with relief. "Is he still here?"

she asked, gesturing towards the rows of hutch-like rooms to indicate her meaning.

The Chinaman shook his head vigorously and shuffled towards the door. "*Yang-jen*," he said again, pointing up the alley in a northwards direction. "Many coolie, many mule."

Zachary Cartwright had been at the inn, and he had left the inn. Knowing that it was pointless asking how long ago he had left, Gianetta thanked the Chinaman, who was now beaming toothlessly at her, and stumbled gratefully out into marginally purer air.

Even as she had asked if Zachary Cartwright was still at the inn, she had known the answer to her question. He wouldn't have stayed the night in one of those abominable open-fronted rooms. The minute he had engaged the men he needed, he would have left the town and made camp beside the river. Which was exactly what she was going to do.

With an increasing sense of *déjà-vu*, she rode out of the town at dusk, as she had ridden out of Fu-tu Kwan.

"But this time I have a pistol with me," she said to Ben, determining, for his sake, to camp at the earliest opportunity. "We'll catch Zachary Cartwright up tomorrow and . . ." they rounded a curve in the riverbank and her sentence remained unfinished.

There, not twenty-five yards ahead of her, was a campfire with mules, a pony and a small group of Chinese in attendance. Dominating the scene, his back towards her, was the unmistakable figure of Zachary Cartwright.

Her relief was so intense that she was ashamed of it. She crushed it as quickly as she could, telling herself it would have been no great problem if she hadn't met up with him until the next day. Then she took a deep breath to steady herself for the coming confrontation.

This time, there was no question of her galloping dramatically up into the circle of fire-light. Ben was far too tired to do any more than keep on at a steady plod.

The bells around Ben's neck jingled softly and Zachary Cartwright spun around. As he did so, Gianetta slipped from the saddle, determined to give no hint of the depth of her tiredness. With an apparently carefree smile on her face she walked briskly up to him, saying gaily,

"We're beginning to make a habit of meeting up like this, aren't we? Is there anything good for dinner?"

He uttered an expletive that in ordinary circumstances would have shocked her unutterably.

She pretended she hadn't heard it, walking past him towards the fire. "It has been quite a nice day's ride, hasn't it?" she said conversationally. "The pine forest gave wonderful shade when the sun was at its highest."

"Damn the pine forest! Where the devil is Charles?"

Zachary was standing feet apart, hands on hips, his face thunderous. For the first time it occurred to her that he was more than capable of subjecting her to physical violence.

Defiantly she turned away from the fire and faced him, her head high, her back straight, her eyes meeting his unwaveringly.

"Charles will be in Chung King by now. He told me he had no real need of me."

"Then he's a bloody fool! He should have guessed you would follow me . . ."

"He didn't need to guess," she said spiritedly, interrupting him. "He knew. And he approved."

"Then he's an even bigger fool than I've always privately thought him! Dear God in heaven! Have you any idea of the fix you have put me in?" His face hardened, and without waiting for a reply he continued harshly, "Of course you have, but you have grossly miscalculated, Miss Hollis. I'll be damned to hell before I act as you intend I should."

"And just what is it you imagine I intend?" she asked, genuinely curious.

"You intend that out of a sense of honour I will ask you to marry me. That's what this has been all about,

91

right from the beginning. Originally you set your cap at Charles, thinking that if you could compromise him you would secure a nice advantageous marriage for yourself. Once he opted to return to Chung King you had to reassess things a little. The two of you hadn't been alone together quite long enough for your reputation to be ruined irrevocably and for there to be no other way for him to make amends to you, apart from marrying you. With Charles no longer in the running you're looking to me to save you from spinsterhood and Lincolnshire. Well, I'm going to disappoint you. I don't have a sense of honour, and nor do I have a family who will be scandalized by my behaving without it."

Only the knowledge that he expected her to react in near-hysterical fury enabled her not to do so. When she spoke, her voice was a little unsteady, but it was also ice-cool and withering in its contempt.

"I have heard of men with overpoweringly high opinions of themselves, Mr Cartwright, but I have never before heard of one, much less met one, with such a falsely high opinion that it warrants a strait-jacket and a lunatic asylum."

His hands were no longer on his hips but folded across his chest as he glowered at her, the flames from the fire providing him with a suitably satanic backdrop in the near darkness.

"Marriage to either yourself or Lord Rendlesham has never been my object," Gianetta continued, her words vibrant with truth.

"Then what has?" he snapped back at her. "You will certainly have no hopes of marriage elsewhere when news of your hare-brained escapade is made public. And it will be made public eventually. Such escapades always are."

She reflected on his question and his subsequent remarks with a thoughtfulness that he had clearly not expected.

"I think you are wrong," she said at last, slowly. "My aunt and uncle will certainly not talk publicly of it. If anyone in Chung King should query my absence, they will simply say that I have returned unexpectedly to England."

He snorted derisively and she continued unperturbed, "And if you are right in your assumptions, Mr Cartwright, I truly don't care."

"You'll care very much when you are back in England and socially *persona non grata*."

"I was never destined for high society, Mr Cartwright," she replied, a touch of wry amusement in her voice. "Only if Serena had wanted a season in London would I have been able to have one. And Serena wants no such thing."

One of the Chinese had approached them nervously, a mug of steaming tea in each hand. As Gianetta stepped towards him, gratefully accepting one of the proffered mugs, Zachary Cartwright remained silent.

She sipped the tea and then said quietly, "You say that my action in following yourself and Lord Rendlesham out of Chung King was thoughtless and hare-brained. Perhaps it was. But it is not an action that I regret."

Her lack of response to his anger seemed to have successfully deflated Zachary Cartwright. He took the remaining mug of tea and said tersely, "You seem to be wilfully skirting the only issue that is at stake here. Your reputation."

"I'm not skirting the issue, Mr Cartwright. I've thought about it a good deal. And I have decided that if the choice lies between living a full and interesting life – albeit one that leaves me with a falsely tarnished reputation – and a boring, stultifying life, I will choose the full and interesting one."

"It isn't quite so simple," he said, and this time his still obvious anger was tightly reined. He sounded almost sympathetic. "In eight months time my expedition to Kansu will be at an end. Presuming I was rash enough to agree to your accompanying me, what would become of you then? Your uncle and aunt will most likely disown

93

you. Your cousin's husband will probably refuse to allow her to consort with you. You will have no home, no way of earning a living, you will be totally ruined . . ."

A smile quirked the corners of her mouth. "My future is not quite as bleak you imagine, Mr Cartwright. I have a certain amount of intelligence, and I intend to make the most of it."

His eyebrows rose queryingly and her smile deepened. "I've thought about my future long and hard today, and I intend suggesting to my uncle that I go to Oxford, to Lady Margaret Hall. I don't think he will refuse me. An education will equip me for the kind of life I intend leading. A life that is full of interest and adventure, as yours is. A life that doesn't centre around marriage."

For a second she didn't know if he was going to laugh derisively or explode in renewed rage. He did neither. He simply said curtly. "It's been a long day, Miss Hollis. Both of us are tired. I suggest we eat and get some rest and continue this bizarre conversation in the morning."

She nodded agreeably, careful not to allow her elation to show in her eyes. She had won. She was sure she had won. He certainly wouldn't disrupt his plans by returning with her to Chung King. Neither could he possibly suggest that she return unaccompanied, and even if he did so she wouldn't comply. She was going to go to Kansu to search for blue Moonflowers, and if Zachary Cartwright chose not to take her with him, she would go alone.

Dinner was an unidentifiable stew which she ate with hungry relish. Occasionally she was aware of Zachary Cartwright looking covertly across at her, a deep frown marring his brow. When the dishes had been cleared away he said curiously,

"How did you manage to follow me with such accuracy?"

"You had said you intended stopping at the next town to engage men and another mule. I assumed the town would be on the banks of the Kialing, so I followed the river as closely as possible."

"And when you reached the town?"

He was sitting in his canvas-chair, his plant-hunting box at his feet, his field-book within easy reach.

"I went to the inn. An elderly Chinaman there gave me to understand that you had passed through the town earlier and that you were headed north."

"And just how was this conversation conducted? In Chinese or English?"

A smile tugged at the corners of her mouth. "In a little of both. What does *yang-kwei-tse* mean, by the way?"

This time it was his turn to suppress a smile. "Foreign devil."

Her amusement deepened. It really was most curious how much at ease she felt with him. If the circumstances had been different, if it had been Charles sitting next to her by the fire, she knew that, despite the friendship that had sprung up between them after his accident, she wouldn't have felt half so comfortable.

"Then that is how the local populace regard you," she said, not hiding the amusement she felt.

He gave a grunt that could have been dismissive or equally amused and picked up his field-book.

She glanced across at him as he worked, much in the same way as he had kept glancing at her earlier. He was extraordinarily handsome. His blue-black hair was sheened to a high gloss by the fire-light and as he bent his head over his book, it tumbled thick and low over his brow. His nose was classically straight, his jaw-line strong.

After a little while she said, "I found the *Potentilla Veitchii*. Charles told me how to take a correct cutting and he has taken the cutting and a soil sample with him, to Chung King."

"Good." He didn't look towards her, nor did he pause in the notes he was making.

She stretched her booted feet towards the warmth of the fire. She had already tended Ben, and he was teth-ered nearby alongside Zachary Cartwright's sleek-looking pony. The darkness wasn't oppressive as it had been the night she had camped alone. It was velvety and caressing. Although there was no moon, the sky glistened with stars. She could smell sage and verbena, and the sound of the river surging southwards was as hypnotic as a drug.

His dark, rich voice woke her from her doze. "You must want to bathe and change your clothes. There is very easy access to the river about fifteen yards away, just beyond where the ponies are tethered. If you run into any problems, just give a shout."

She felt a surge of gratitude towards him for the unembarrassing way he was helping her to solve a problem that had been preying increasingly on her mind.

"Thank you," she said, rising from her canvas-chair, her skin itching to be rid of the garments she had worn every day since leaving the Residency.

"There is soap in the right-hand pouch of my saddle-bag," he added, "and don't worry about the Chinese. They won't disturb your privacy."

And neither would he. She knew it with absolute certainty. He had said he was a man without honour, but it wasn't true. She didn't doubt for a moment that he was unconventional and that polite society would often look askance at him, but he knew far more about the true meaning of honour than Charles ever would.

She found the soap and took a towel and clean under-clothes from her carpet-bag. There was no longer any need for her to keep wearing Chinese clothes for safety and she discarded the jacket, rolling it up and stuffing it, with the soft round hat, in the bottom of her bag. The trousers, unfortunately, were a different matter. Without wearing them she couldn't possibly ride Ben. Not unless she was able to obtain a side-saddle from somewhere. Nor could she keep wearing them without washing them. The night was warm, but whether it was warm enough to dry linen trousers she didn't know. It was a risk she would just have to take. She took a blouse and skirt from out of her bag and padded in the direction Zachary had suggested.

Minutes later she was swimming, naked and blissful, in the wickedly cold waters of the Kialing.

It was very heaven. Never again, she vowed, would she be constrained in polite drawing-rooms, embroidering and sketching meaninglessly to fill up the long, boring hours. She was going to become a botanist; an explorer; an adventurer. She was going to become the first European woman ever to see a blue Moonflower growing wild.

When she returned to the bright circle of firelight dressed in her blouse and skirt, her hair hanging wetly and sleekly down her back, Gianetta caught Zachary Cartwright unawares. For a moment there was almost the same look of stunned incredulity in his eyes that she had occasioned in the eyes of the Chinese at the inn. He looked, quite simply, as if he couldn't believe what he was seeing. Then the expression vanished, to be replaced by his usual brooding taciturnity.

"I see Charles had the sense to give you his sleeping-bag," he said abruptly. "I've set it down near the fire. I'll sleep nearer the ponies. Their restlessness will wake me if we should have any four-footed nocturnal visitors."

"I have a pistol," she said helpfully.

His winged brows rose almost into the tumble of his hair. "Have you, indeed?"

Laughter bubbled up in her throat. It was fun surprising and shocking Zachary Cartwright.

"Goodnight," she said, suddenly aware that she hadn't been so carelessly happy for years, not since her parents had been alive and she had lived on the shores of Lake Garda.

"Goodnight," he said gruffly, turning on his heel, his broad shoulders infinitely reassuring.

Next morning she woke to a flushed rose sky. There was no sign of Zachary Cartwright, Gianetta climbed out of her sleeping-bag stiffly, stretching with pleasure. To the far north were pale tawny mountains. Presumably this was a mountain-range they would have to cross before reaching Kansu. By the time they reached it, she would need far warmer clothes than the ones she had brought with her. She wondered if she would be able to buy a quilted Chinese coat in the next town they came to.

She brushed her hair and then walked across to the bush on which she had spread her linen trousers. They were still horrendously damp.

"Problems?" Zachary Cartwright's now familiar voice said from behind her.

She turned quickly. "No," she said swiftly, and then as she saw unconcealed disbelief in his eyes she added reluctantly, "Yes. I washed my trousers last night and they are still damp."

He frowned. "Surely your skirt is perfectly adequate for travelling in?"

"Not for riding in a *miao-tse* saddle, it isn't."

His frown deepened. He looked just as forbidding as he had done the first evening they had met, and she wondered if she had imagined the suspicion of a smile that had touched his mouth the previous evening.

"Then you'll have to wear a pair of mine," he said, as if his solution was the most obvious in the world.

She stared at him. "I beg your pardon? I don't think I heard you correctly."

"You'll have to wear a pair of mine," he said, not bothering to hide his irritation. "I'll ask Tien Tang to get a pair from my saddle-bag and bring them over to you."

It was the first time she had heard any of the Chinese mentioned by name and she made a mental note of it before saying, with stiff politeness, "I don't think that would suit at all, Mr Cartwright."

"It's going to have to suit," he said with disconcerting brusqueness. "Breakfast is ready and waiting, and I intend leaving in just over half an hour."

Zachary was wearing his white linen shirt again. It was open to the waist. With his dove-grey breeches fitting snugly about his narrow hips, and his knee-high, black velvet-cuffed boots, he lacked only gold earrings to make him the perfect storybook pirate.

She opened her mouth to protest again and then decided against it. The last thing she needed to do at the moment was to start causing difficulties. Zachary Cartwright still hadn't actually agreed to allow her to accompany him and, if she began creating inconveniences at the outset, he never would.

With the conversation at an end he swung on his heel, walking back to the crackling camp-fire where breakfast was waiting. She saw him speak to one of the Chinese and minutes later she was being presented with a broad leather belt and a pair of surprisingly fresh-smelling corduroy breeches.

Once again she felt the linen trousers spread on the bush. They were far too damp to wear. Accepting defeat and knowing that she had no other choice, Gianetta walked briskly away down the river-bank until she came to the bend where she had bathed the previous night. There she carried out all her ablutions, slipping reluctantly out of her ankle-length skirt and easing herself into Zachary Cartwright's breeches.

It was the strangest feeling she had ever experienced. The Chinese trousers had been light, and had felt almost feminine. There was nothing feminine about the breeches she was now wearing. They felt rough against her skin, were far too long, and though Zachary Cartwright was pleasingly narrow-waisted, his waist was nowhere near as slender as hers. With an exclamation of irritation, she rolled the legs up until they were at an acceptable height and gathered the waist in with the belt. There wasn't an eye-hole far enough along the length of the belt and with increasing bad-temper she stalked back to camp, holding the belt in place, searching in her carpet-bag for a pair of nail-scissors.

"What the devil do you think you are doing?" an outraged voice demanded as she struggled to pierce an eye-hole in the thick leather.

She didn't pause in her efforts. "It should be obvious, even to you, Mr Cartwright, that I can't wear your clothes without certain adjustments having to be made."

With savage satisfaction she skewered the scissors through the leather.

He stifled a noise that was almost agonized.

"There," she said, smiling up at him with malicious pleasure as she buckled the belt securely around her waist. "That's better."

Zachary Cartwright looked as if he thought it anything but better and she felt a surge of satisfaction. Odds were again even and she was damned if she would ever let them be anything else.

It was almost two hours before Zachary Cartwright could bring himself to even speak to her again. When he did so it was to say tersely, "The moment a situation arises in which you can be escorted back to Chung King, I shall make arrangements for you to return there."

She didn't bother to reply. It was highly unlikely that any such arrangements could be made. They were heading further and further into the remotest depths of Asia, and the chances of their meeting up with other Europeans, let alone Europeans who were heading towards Chung King, was so unlikely as to be not worth troubling about.

A little later, as Ben walked steadily on beside Zachary Cartwright's disdainful-looking pony, she said, "Tell me about the Moonflower. How did it get such a romantic name? What is so special about it?"

The Kialing was entering another narrow gorge, though this time with room enough on the banks for them to continue alongside it. Disturbed by their presence, a hoopoe shot out of a tree, the sun glinting on its camellia-rose plumage and brilliant barred wings.

He said, "It gets its name because it flowers at night, under the light of a full moon. And it does so for only one night in the year. Before the sun rises, the fragile petals wither and it is another year, and another moonlight night, before it flowers again."

Gianetta gave a reverent sigh of pleasure, "And how do you know this? Who first discovered the Moonflower?"

"No-one has discovered it as yet in China. A species has been discovered in the Amazon basin. From reports received at Kew, the Amazon Moonflower is a member of the Cactus family and it flowers in a pale, delicate spray of milk-white petals."

"I thought it was blue?" she said bewilderedly.

"The one I hope to find in Kansu *is* blue. There is a painting of it in an eighteenth century book of Chinese flowers. Its flowering habits are given as being exactly the same as those of the Moonflower found in Brazil. Despite the difference in climatic zones, I'm certain a Chinese version exists. Chinese flower painters don't paint from imagination now and they didn't do so in the eighteenth century. The plant is described as being native to the Min Shan region of Kansu, and that is where I hope to find it."

"There must be lots of other beautiful plants that the western world is ignorant of," Gianetta said dreamily as Ben stepped fetlock-deep through a sea of scarlet-headed poppies. "Plants in the still unexplored regions of the Amazon and in the wilds of Upper Burmah and the desolation of Tibet . . ."

"I intend to mount an expedition to Tibet at the beginning of next year," he said in a moment of such rare candour that Gianetta nearly fell from Ben's back in surprise. "The Royal Horticultural Society believes that many Tibetan plants could be successfully grown in England."

The near impossible had happened again. Despite his bad temper and brooding rudeness, they were on the verge of easy-going camaraderie, just as they had fleetingly been the previous evening.

Zachary reined and looked around. The gorge had widened and was fast diminishing and the meadows now spreading out at their feet were thick with flowers.

"I think a little field-work is called for," he said,

101

swinging himself easily from the saddle. "You know the correct way to take cuttings, don't you?"

Grateful for the crash course that Charles had given her, Gianetta nodded.

Zachary handed her a trowel, a pocket-knife and a small collecting-box japanned green on black, with a snap lid like that of a snuff-box.

"In case you find anything of interest, I have to be able to locate it again. Never be mean with your location notes; they can be invaluable," he said, also handing her a notebook and pencil.

Once out of the saddle she stuffed the notebook, pencil and pocket-knife into the pockets of her breeches, appreciating their usefulness for the first time. Then, as he was now giving instructions to the Chinese and as she was sure he would not want her dogging his footsteps, she set off alone through the deep grass, stopping every few yards to secure flowers that to her inexperienced eye looked rare and priceless.

The heat of the sun was pleasant on her back. Butterflies with azure wings darted amongst purple delphiniums and lilac and cream aquilegia; wax-white orchids grew as thick as daisies in an English field. Occasionally she paused in her task, gazing northwards to the misty tops of the mountains, wondering how she had survived the claustrophobic, circumscribed years in Lincolnshire and the frustrating months cooped up behind the Residency's walls.

When her collecting-box was full to overflowing, and she couldn't possibly carry any more specimens, Gianetta walked leisurely back to where the ponies and mules were loosely tethered. The baggage-mules had been unpacked and the collapsible chairs and table erected. She hoped it was Zachary Cartwright's intention to make camp there. A short day's travelling would be welcome after the last three, long, arduous days.

When at last he joined her, the Chinese at his heels, Zachary said with deep satisfaction, "There's quite a remarkable range of specimens in this area. It's going to be a long evening writing them up and pressing them."

Perspiration beaded his forehead, and there was a streak of dirt on his cheek. She grinned, wondering if she looked equally disreputable.

"I've got a huge collection myself but I've no idea what they are."

"Let's have a look," he said, squatting on his heels by the side of her canvas-chair, wiping the perspiration from his forehead with the back of his hand.

She opened her collecting-box, handing him first one carefully culled specimen and then another.

"A Chinese daisy," he said disparagingly, "and barbery. Both of them practically weeds. And Oxytropis and *Viola Patrinii*. Nothing there to set the world on fire, pretty though they are."

"Haven't I found anything of worth?" she asked, deeply disappointed. "Aren't any of the other plants I've found, rare?"

He looked over her motley collection. "I'm afraid not," he said, and he flashed her exactly the same kind of grin he had flashed at Charles shortly before he had said goodbye to him.

The world seemed to rock on its axis. Her breath hurt in her chest and her heart began to slam in sharp, slamming strokes that she could feel even in her finger-tips.

Unaware of how deeply he had disconcerted her he rose to his feet, walking across to where the Chinese were busy setting up one of the flower presses.

Gianetta remained immobile. What had happened to her? Surely not even Zachary Cartwright was so moody and uncongenial that a grin from him was enough to shock in so disturbing a manner? And yet obviously it was. She wondered if his affability would last and determined that if it did so, her reaction to such pleasantness would be far less dramatic.

When a fire had been lit and a meal was under way,

103

she said to him tentatively, "Would you like me to sketch today's plants for you?"

He nodded. "You can begin now. I'm going to walk back to the mouth of the gorge before it gets too dark to see clearly. I don't think I missed anything when we rode through it, but you can never be sure."

It was bliss sitting in the late afternoon sunlight, sketching not only for enjoyment but for a purpose, Ben companionably close by, the shining waters of the Kialing at her feet, the mountains of Kansu soaring in the distance. She hummed a Schubert melody as she painstakingly drew stem and petal and leaf and calyx.

It was early evening when Zachary returned, his collecting-box full, and it wasn't until after they had eaten that he looked at the sketches in his field-book.

He studied each one for a long time. Her touch was strong, yet delicate. Each line was clean and definite and almost frighteningly effective; she had managed to suggest not only shape, but bulk and texture, by pure drawing with the minimum of fuss.

"They're good," he said briefly, "But then you know that, don't you?"

She nodded, and at her lack of false modesty his mouth tugged into an amused smile.

Once again she felt a dizzying sensation deep within her chest. Once again her heart began to slam in short, sharp strokes.

This time she was left in no doubt as to the nature of her response to him. Horror flooded through her and then hard on its heels came incredulity.

She had fallen in love with Zachary Cartwright. She had fallen in love with a man who had accused her of trying to compromise him into marrying her; a man who had made no secret of the fact that he entertained not the slightest *tendresse* for her; a man with whom it had been her intention to travel hundreds of miles, unchaperoned.

The enormity of her realization appalled her. She

couldn't understand how it had happened, or when it had happened. Nor, now that it *had* happened, what she was to do about it.

It was clearly futile to hope for reciprocation. On the first evening they had met, Zachary had shown quite clearly that it was Serena who attracted him, not herself. Charles had confirmed that it was so, and a man attracted by Serena's delicate blonde beauty and calm nature was highly unlikely to ever be drawn to someone of her own adventurous temperament and dark, Latin looks.

Pain washed through her. She would make a far more compatible companion for him than Serena ever would. She remembered Henry Plaxtol and felt a surge of savage satisfaction. Zachary would never be able to pursue his interest in Serena. By the time he returned to Chung King, Serena would be married and living in England.

"I think we should turn in," he said to her. "I want to make an early start in the morning."

She nodded assent, not allowing her eyes to meet his. If she wanted to save herself pain, the sensible thing would be for her to return to Chung King at the earliest opportunity. But if she did? What would happen to her then?

She rose from her chair and walked across the grass to where her sleeping-bag had been laid at a discreet distance from his. Her uncle and aunt would immediately send her to England in disgrace. With luck they would still assent to her going to Lady Margaret Hall, but she would have no memories of the huge, harsh glory of Kansu to take with her; no memories of finding a blue Moonflower.

She pulled off her boots and looked across to where Zachary Cartwright was making adjustments to the flower presses. His back was towards her and she unbuckled the mutilated belt, slipping quickly first out of the alien breeches and then her blouse.

As she slid into her sleeping-bag Zachary Cartwright moved back towards his chair. She wanted to continue looking at him, but the memory of the response she had elicited when he had caught her looking at him at the Residency was too raw for comfort. She closed her eyes and so did not see him once again pick up his field-book, nor did she see for how long and how broodingly he stared down at the sketches accompanying his notes.

CHAPTER SIX

Despite the fact that he had said he wanted an early night, Zachary Cartwright lay awake for a long time before sleep eventually came. Never before had a woman disturbed his peace of mind, but ever since his brief meeting with Serena Hollis she had been continually in his thoughts. She was as delicate as a piece of exquisite porcelain; as fair in colouring as the most ethereal of flowers; as sweet-faced and as tranquil as a Madonna. To have such a woman waiting for him, on his return from an arduous expedition, would be very heaven.

He wondered what his chances were. He didn't have a title or a private fortune, but he did possess a much-respected name as an explorer and as a botanist. He was on friendly terms with his king. Any woman he married would automatically be accepted amongst Edward VII's exotic inner coterie. He would be made a professor within the next year or so, and a peerage would certainly be his for the asking within the next ten years. All told, he wasn't totally ineligible as a prospective suitor.

But would she have him? He had absolutely no way of telling. He hadn't been in her company long enough to have received any intimation as to what her opinion of him had been. It would be eight months at least before he was back in Chung King. Would she have forgotten him by then? Or would she still be thinking of him, as he knew he would still be thinking of her?

He lay on his back in his sleeping-bag, looking up at the stars. No matter what the future held for him where Serena Hollis was concerned, she was not an immediate and pressing problem. Her cousin, however, was.

Despite the irritation he felt at the problems Gianetta Hollis was posing for him, he was aware also of a feeling of amusement. She was an entertaining little baggage. He wondered if it was true, as Charles had said, that the reason for their continual sparring was their similarity to each other. "As like as brother and sister," had been Charles' description.

He grinned to himself. He doubted that they were so similar, but certainly if he had ever had a sister, he imagined she might have been very similar to Gianetta Hollis. Petite and dark and vibrant and adventurous.

He rolled over, seeking for a more comfortable position on the hard ground. He felt far more sympathy for her than she would ever realise. He knew what it was like to lose both parents and to have to make a home with people who provided it out of a sense of duty. Like her, he had been fortunate enough to have found a friend. Charles was an idiot at times, but not criminally so, and he valued his friendship as Gianetta obviously valued Serena's.

Serena. Once again her blonde beauty filled his thoughts. When he returned to Chung King, he would ensure that his stay at the Residency was a prolonged one. He wondered if she had other suitors in the offing. Gianetta would know. He would have to bring up the subject with the utmost carelessness. He didn't want Gianetta Hollis suspecting his feelings for Serena, for if she did there was no telling in what way she might put the knowledge to use. She was so determined on accompanying him to Kansu that if blackmail would help her to attain her object, he could well imagine her stooping to it.

He felt a pang of regret. Despite her undoubted courage and her admirable determination, Gianetta's dream couldn't possibly be fulfilled. She had said that she was uncaring as to the damage that would be done to her reputation, and she had obviously been speaking

108

the truth. However, if she accompanied him to Kansu it would not be only her reputation that would be ruined. His would also be destroyed. On a personal level he didn't give a damn what the gossips said about him, but things were a little different where his career as a botanist was concerned. He was carrying out the expedition to Kansu at the request of the Director of the Royal Gardens at Kew. If his expedition became the source of salacious gossip, then he would certainly not be requested to make any more expeditions for Kew. His proposed expedition to Tibet would never come to fruition, nor would there be any chance of his one day exploring the Amazon Basin.

And so Miss Gianetta Hollis would have to be returned to Chung King. The next significant town on their route was Peng, and he knew that there was an Anglican Mission there. Although their own journey from Chung King had often been arduous, it had been so through choice and because he had wanted to plant-hunt *en route*. The journey between Peng and Chung King could be undertaken relatively easily by boat and he was sure that when he asked the missionaries if they would escort Gianetta back to Chung King, they would agree to his request readily.

Overhead the stars shone thickly. As he gazed at them it occurred to him that he would miss Gianetta. He would miss her talents as an artist and he would miss her bouncy vitality. His last thought on closing his eyes was that when they descended on the mission he would have to ensure that she was wearing a skirt and that her hair was suitably pinned in a chignon and not in a Chinese queue. He wanted the missionaries to realise she was a lady and to react accordingly. A smile tugged at the corner of his mouth. Her travelling attire at the moment was anything but ladylike. With her Chinese queue and her white blouse tucked into the belted waist of his breeches she looked like a rather exotic stable-boy.

He remembered how she had looked the previous evening when she had stepped into the firelight after her moonlit bathe. With her glossy black hair hanging wetly and sleekly to her waist, and with her skirt moulding itself sensuously to her hips, she had reminded him of a pagan naiad.

He felt his sex harden, and swore with annoyance. The sooner he was able to leave Gianetta Hollis in the safe hands of the missionaries, the better. A pagan naiad was no suitable companion on a long, lonely journey into the heart of Asia, especially for a man who was seriously considering matrimony. As he slid finally into sleep he tried once again to conjure up Serena's image. It wouldn't come. Instead of Serena, with her English milk-and-rose loveliness and sweet demeanour, his last thoughts were of a bright-eyed hoyden desecrating his best leather belt with criminal relish.

Gianetta woke to the sound of the Kialing surging inexorably southwards. She lay for a few moments, peace and tranquillity engulfing her. They would travel northwards again today. They would search for more plants and when they made camp in the evening she would sketch them into Zachary Cartwright's field-book. She would ask Zachary to tell her more about the plants that he found and she would ask him if she could begin to keep a field-book of her own.

With a day of utter satisfaction and contentment ahead of her, Gianetta slipped out of her sleeping-bag. There was no sign of Zachary. Presumably he was already plant-hunting. The Chinese had their backs to her and were busy preparing breakfast.

Dressing quietly and quickly, she first went to say good morning to Ben. Then she took her towel and walked down to the Kialing, washing in the freezing cold, dazzlingly clear water.

There were no sounds from camp to indicate that breakfast was ready and that Zachary had returned, so she began to walk leisurely along the Kialing's bank, wondering how near to its source they would travel. Reeds grew high in the water and the bushes on the bank grew thicker in density. She skirted around them, wondering if the source lay in Kansu or if it lay even further west, in Tibet, or further north, in Mongolia.

She was so deep in thought that she didn't hear the splashing sounds coming from the river-side of the bushes. Idly imagining far distant landscapes, she rounded a giant flowering shrub and came face to face with the sight of Zachary Cartwright striding nakedly knee-deep out of the river.

His hair clung low in his neck in sodden curls, thick as a ram's fleece. Water droplets sheened the olive flesh tones of his broad shoulders and firmly muscled chest. He neither halted in his strides for the bank or made the slightest attempt to shield himself from her sight.

Her horror was total. She had never seen a man naked before, nor had it ever occurred to her that she would do so, outside of marriage.

For a second that seemed to last an infinity, she was too stunned to move. She saw something hot flicker at the back of his eyes, to be immediately suppressed, and then she broke free of the shock that was immobilizing her and span on her heel, running back to the camp, her cheeks scarlet with embarrassment.

It was ten minutes or so before he joined her. When he did so he was dressed in his wine-red shirt, grey breeches and boots. He was also, quite obviously, furiously angry.

"You see now how impossible it is for you to travel with me for months on end?" he demanded, his hair still glistening wet. "The terrain is such that camp-life is a necessity and camp-life conditions, as you have so memorably discovered, are totally unsuitable for a female."

She knew what was coming and her initial horror at surprising him naked was replaced by another kind of horror.

"We should reach Peng in two or three days," he continued brusquely. "There is a Mission there. Hopefully one of the missionaries will escort you by boat back to

111

Chung King. If, for any reason, that is not possible, you will have to remain at the Mission until the time comes when it *is* possible."

Her mouth was dry, her distress so intense that she could hardly breathe. Only a short while ago everything had been golden and glorious. Day after day of travel through wild and beautiful countryside had stretched ahead of her. There had been Kansu to look forward to; a happier relationship with Zachary; strange and exotic plants to find. Now there was nothing. Only the prospect of a journey in tedious company back to Chung King or, even worse, dreary days to be endured in the confines of Peng's Mission.

She said thickly, "It isn't necessary . . ."

"It is absolutely necessary." His voice was curt, clipped and utterly final.

Desperately as she wanted to argue with him, she couldn't find the words to do so. If she was to tell him that it was shock at the unexpectedness, rather than at the nature of their encounter, that had caused her to spin on her heel in confusion and embarrassment, then he would think her shameless. There was no way that she could reassure him that the incident had been unfortunate but not one of any great consequence. Any attempt to do so would automatically label her as a young woman who was far too knowing and worldly-wise.

A faint hint of colour still touched her cheeks. To the best of her knowledge she was neither, but it had to be admitted that her reaction to the sight of Zachary Cartwright naked had not been what might have been expected from a well brought-up young lady. Quite simply, she had thought he had looked magnificent.

Misinterpreting the reason for the flush in her cheeks, Zachary gentled his manner slightly.

"I'll make sure you're not occasioned further embarrassment before we reach Peng. We'd better have breakfast now. The sooner we start off, the sooner there will be an end to this debacle."

He turned on his heel, walking over to the camp-fire where the Chinese were busily at work with a pan and a kettle.

She stood, watching him, feeling completely crushed and with all hope gone. Within two days, three at the most, her adventure would be over and she would have nothing to look forward to but an exceedingly difficult reunion with her uncle and aunt. All because she had walked inattentively along the wrong section of the riverbank, at the wrong time.

A little whinny came from her left-hand side and she turned her head to find that Ben was looking towards her. She walked across to him and hooked her fingers into his shaggy, cream-coloured mane.

"I think we're going to have to go back to Chung King," she said sadly. "There's nothing I can say that will change things now."

"Breakfast is ready!" Zachary called out, his customary impatience back in his voice.

With a heavy heart she walked over to where breakfast had been set out on a crisp white cloth. There were the usual bowls of melon seeds, peanuts and candied peel without which the Chinese seemed to think no meal, even breakfast, complete, and there was a steaming bowl of rice and a bowl of the savoury stew that was the mainstay of their meals.

"It's fortunate that you mastered eating with chopsticks when you were at the Residency," Zachary said in a manner that was, for him, startlingly friendly.

She wasn't won over by it. She knew very well why he had suddenly become civil. It was because he knew he would soon be rid of her, and because he was possibly feeling sorry for her. She felt a spurt of anger. She didn't want anyone feeling sorry for her, least of all Zachary. She wanted Zachary to admire her. She wanted him to look at her in the way he had looked at Serena.

Well aware that he was as likely to do so as fly to the moon, she ate her breakfast in frigid silence. If Serena

113

had followed him from the Residency into the radiant stillness of Upper Szechwan he would, no doubt, have already proposed marriage to her. Perhaps they would have married at the Mission in Peng. Whether they would have done so or not, he certainly would not have described their situation as being a debacle.

She wasn't a small-minded person and she had never before experienced even the slightest twinge of jealousy or resentment, no matter what the situation. She felt something very similar to it now, however. Serena could never have contributed to the success of Zachary's expedition in any way. She would have been unable to travel a yard over rough country unless carried in a sedan-chair. The vastness of the countryside would have overwhelmed her. Her interest in the plants that were Zachary's passion would have been minimal. To Serena, flowers were something to arrange in a vase. Searching for them, drawing and cataloguing them, would have bored her unutterably. And yet, according to Charles, Zachary had been bowled over by Serena and had hopes of furthering their acquaintance when his expedition was completed.

Cross with him for being such a fool, cross with herself for minding so much about his foolishness, she finished her breakfast in silence and maintained her silence as the Chinese re-packed bags and boxes and loaded them on to the patiently waiting mules.

If Zachary Cartwright was disconcerted by her silence, he certainly didn't show it. She might just as well have not existed, for all the notice he took of her. Their route lay once more along the banks of the Kialing and he reined in his pony often, dismounting whenever something of botanical interest caught his eye. He never asked her to join him on his mini-expeditions, and when their journey continued, he never bothered to discuss his finds with her.

As the day progressed and his obliviousness to her presence continued, Gianetta's resentment grew until she

114

could hardly contain it. She wanted to become a botanist. She wanted him to discuss his finds with her. She wanted to learn from him. And she wanted to travel with him to Kansu. That he was not now allowing her to do so was no fault of hers. *She* hadn't been so careless as to bathe nude. The scene by the river bank he was using as an excuse to be rid of her, had been his fault entirely. Nor had she reacted to it in a missish way. She had simply speedily retreated. She had not given way to hysterics. She had not declared herself mortally offended. *He* should have apologised to *her*. And he certainly shouldn't be off-loading her at Peng because of his carelessness and crassness.

It was mid-afternoon when he broke the silence between them. The grass beneath their ponies' feet was thick with pale little starry gentians and along the river bank were drifts of irises, blue and deeper blue and purple.

"Does your cousin like China?" he asked suddenly.

Her eyebrows flew high. So he had been thinking about Serena during their long, unfriendly ride. And from the nature of his question he had obviously been thinking of a possible future with her, in China.

"No," she said crisply, "She loathes it."

It wasn't strictly true. Serena's temperament was too equable for any such passion, but Gianetta saw no reason to encourage the course of Zachary's thoughts. Indeed, she saw no reason why she shouldn't put an end to them altogether.

"Serena is to leave China very shortly," she said, feeling a very unladylike surge of savage pleasure. "She is to marry Henry Plaxtol, the son of Lord Plaxtol."

Whatever his reaction to her news, it didn't show on his handsome, hard-boned face. No eyebrow moved, no muscle twitched. Only his hands revealed his inner emotion. Gianetta saw them tighten on the reins, the knuckles showing almost white.

Strangely enough, her pleasure did not intensify at the sight. She felt only a great wave of desolation.

"Mr Plaxtol is a clergyman," she added inconsequentially.

"I hope they will be very happy together," Zachary said, not turning his head towards her. "There's an unusual-looking iris over there. I'm just going to take a closer look at it."

He slid from his saddle, striding towards the river and a clump of irises so purple as to be almost black.

The depth of Zachary's reaction to news of Serena Hollis's marriage had taken him totally by surprise. He hadn't realised how much he had been assuming where she was concerned. He had never before even considered the possibility of marrying. Marriage was something undertaken by men who led conventional lives. Men who were accustomed to the structure of family life. He was far from conventional and the death of his parents had robbed him of any experience of real family life. He had never been filled with the desire to create a new family life for himself.

Only when he had sat opposite Serena Hollis in the candle-lit dining-room of the Residency had it occurred to him that marriage might, in fact, be a pleasant proposition.

There had been something infinitely restful about Serena. He could well imagine returning to her after a long, arduous expedition and discussing his discoveries with her. He had intended, once his expedition was completed, staying at the Residency for several days in order to become better acquainted with her. Then, if he was not disappointed at what he found on further acquaintance, he would have asked her to marry him.

Gianetta's words had put a swift end to his speculations. A clergyman. Any woman who fell in love with a clergyman would have been very unlikely to have ever fallen in love with himself.

Zachary had been staring unseeingly at the clump of irises. Now, his reflections at an end, he focussed on them clearly. They were nothing special after all. Their

116

glossy aubergine colouring had been a trick of the light. They were purple *Iris tigridia* and he walked away from them, wondering how he could have been so hare-brained as to have imagined that marriage was for him. Apart from Charles' spasmodic companionship, he had grown up alone. As no woman of sense would relish marriage to a man who spent months and sometimes years, hunting for plants in the worlds remotest regions, he would most likely continue through life alone.

"You haven't brought a specimen back," Gianetta said as he returned to his impatiently waiting pony. "Wasn't the iris special after all?"

She was still wearing his corduroy breeches, his broad leather belt cinching her narrow waist. With her hair in a long thick plait and her plain white blouse reminiscent of a man's shirt, she should have looked extremely masculine. She didn't. She looked disturbingly feminine. He remembered his inadvertent physical reaction when he had been thinking about her the previous evening, pondering on the best way of having her escorted back to Chung King. And he remembered his split-second reaction when he had been striding naked from the freezing waters of the Kialing and she had walked around the bushes, facing him from a distance of mere feet.

She was a young lady who could lead even a saint from the path of virtue, and he was far from being a saint. The memory of the way Charles had taken advantage of her vulnerability checked the pleasurable rising he had begun to feel in his crotch. He had no objections whatsoever to amorous adventures with ladies of the town, married ladies, or with any other female well able to take care of herself, but Gianetta had not been in a position to take care of herself. The fact that she had not objected to Charles's amorous overtures was not of any consequence. Charles had taken advantage of her youth and her naivety and the unprotected position she had put herself in and he, Zachary, had felt ashamed of him for doing so.

To Zachary, manipulation of the weak by the strong

was never acceptable, whether it was manipulation of natives by colonial masters, the poor by the rich, or sexual manipulation. And he had no intention of finding himself an offender in the latter category.

"No," he said tersely in answer to her question. "It wasn't special. Can you persuade your mangy animal to get a move on? I want to cover another twenty li before dusk."

The cold, bleak feeling possessing her was instantly transformed into white-hot, bubbling fury.

"Ben is *not* a mangy animal!" she flared, her voice shaking with the intensity of her indignation. "He is brave and gallant and . . . and he is a *friend*!"

Only minutes ago his reaction to the news of Serena Hollis's impending marriage had been so savage that he had had to dismount and stand alone for a little while in order to compose himself. Now, incredibly, he felt a smile tugging at the corner of his mouth. She was quite right to censure him. Her little Chinese pony *had* been brave and gallant, and he knew quite well what she meant about him being her friend. His own strong and sleek pony, named Bucephalus after Alexander the Great's much-loved horse, was very much a friend, and he would have reacted just as she had if he had been insulted.

"My apologies," he said gravely.

For a little while she didn't say anything and then she said at last, reluctantly, "Accepted."

He looked towards her, about to say more. Her face was in hostile profile and there was the glitter of unshed tears on the dark sweep of her eyelashes.

He was seized by a rush of both compassion and affection.

"I wish it could be different," he said sincerely. "But it can't. There is no other alternative but for you to return to Chung King."

The unexpected gentleness in his voice nearly undid her. She tightened her hold on Ben's reins, saying stiffly,

118

"It *could* be different. Women are not so very different from men as men suppose."

At this unexpected sally, the amusement she had aroused in him a few short seconds ago intensified.

"In exactly what sense, Miss Hollis?" he asked, keeping his amusement out of his voice with difficulty. "Biologically, mentally or spiritually?"

At the "Miss Hollis," Gianetta's wilful jawline tightened. Earlier she had been, for a short time, Gianetta. Now it seemed that he was regretting his marginal step towards friendship and camaraderie.

"Some women enjoy adventure and travel just as much as any men," she continued, keeping her eyes fixed firmly on the grassy track ahead of them. "My uncle knows of a Miss Gertrude Bell who has made several first ascents in the Bernese Oberland and has had one of the newly conquered peaks named after her, and there was an obituary in *The Times* only recently of Miss Isabella Bird who travelled adventurously all through the American Wild West *and* to Korea and Japan and Persia."

"And was your uncle admiring of these ladies?" Zachary asked, unable to resist teasing her further.

Gianetta sought for words that would not be untruthful. Her uncle had made no comments on Miss Bird but he had certainly not been admiring of Miss Bell, saying of her that she was a tiresome overbearing female with a far too high opinion of herself and that her only originality lay in her linguistic ability.

"He thinks Miss Bell very . . . original," she said at last and then, remembering her uncle's grudging comments about Miss Bell's translations of Persian poems into English, added triumphantly, glad of the opportunity to make clear that her idol was also a woman of letters as well as a woman of adventuring spirit, "And he thinks her translation of poems by the Persian poet Hafiz very fine."

"And so they are," said Zachary deflatingly.

119

For the first time since they had begun the conversation she looked across at him.

"Have you read them?" she asked, the tone of her voice indicating that she thought it highly unlikely.

His eyes met hers, his eyebrows quirking demonically. "But of course. Both Miss Bell's translation and the original."

She swiftly looked once more ahead of her, unsure as to whether or not he was making fun of her.

"I believe Miss Bell is at the moment exploring the Syrian desert," he said, reluctant to end a conversation he was finding increasingly entertaining.

Gianetta would very much like to have maintained a dignified silence, but curiosity got the better of her.

"To climb?" she asked, doubtful whether or not there were mountains in Syria.

"To seek out and study early Byzantine churches."

She knew that if she expressed ignorance about early Byzantine churches and asked him for information about them he would enlighten her, as he would if she were to ask about early Persian poetry, or Chinese history, or any aspect of botany. Unbidden came the realisation that, even if she were to spend a lifetime in his company, she would never be bored. He was a man who would always be full of surprises; a man whose conversation would always be diverting.

"I can see a town ahead of us," he said suddenly, breaking in on her thoughts, "If there's an inn we'll make use of it tonight, and not camp."

She was just about to protest that the inn would be filthy and that she would much rather sleep out of doors, when she realised the reason for his decision. It was because of what had happened early that morning. He was seeking to protect her from any further embarrassments of camp life.

Miserably, Gianetta remained silent. For an obviously worldly, go-to-the-devil adventurer, he was behaving with deplorable primness. She wondered if he was, perhaps,

120

a misogynist and then she remembered his reaction to Serena and dismissed the idea. Whatever Zachary Cartwright's underlying reasons for wishing to be so speedily rid of her, they were not because of a general dislike of her sex. Not only had he been very obviously physically attracted to Serena, but he had also spoken of Miss Bell in tones of admiration no misogynist would have used.

As the late afternoon sunlight smoked into dusk, she wondered about Miss Bell. She could not possibly be travelling through Syria unaccompanied, and her servants and guides would presumably be male. From the way Zachary Cartwright had spoken of Miss Bell's expedition it was obvious that he found no fault with it. And if he found it acceptable for Miss Bell to camp among members of the opposite sex in the deserts of Syria, why should he find it unacceptable for her to do exactly the same thing in remotest China?

She was still pondering on the best way of presenting this argument to him when they entered the town. It was small and unprepossessing; she had no hopes at all of its having an inn that would be even remotely adequate.

Even Ben appeared to be dispirited, as he plodded up one evil-smelling street and then down another. Gianetta was just about to make a vehement protest to Zachary when he reined in his pony, saying with satisfaction,

"Here we are, and we might be in luck! There's glass in the windows as well as paper. That indicates a relatively high standard of comfort."

The building he was referring to was painted a dark, dismal green and had two storeys. Gianetta looked at it unenthusiastically.

"Does that mean that the rooms might be moderately clean?" she asked with more tartness than she had intended.

He flashed her one of his rare, down-slanting smiles. "Any true traveller eventually has to come to terms with fleas, Gianetta. No doubt even Miss Bell is doing so in Syria."

121

The effect of Zachary's sudden smile, and his once more calling her by her Christian name, filled her with such intense elation that she forgot completely to take advantage of his mention of Miss Bell. By the time she remembered the argument she wanted to confront him with, he was striding away from her towards the inn's open door and the cavernous darkness beyond.

She dismounted but made no attempt to follow him. If only there had been no mention of Peng and of her being returned to Chung King, she would not have cared how many Chinese inns they stayed in. As it was, she cared terribly. He had said that Peng was only two or three days travelling time distant, and that meant only two more nights before her adventure was over. She wanted to spend those two precious nights under the magic of the moon and stars, not in a smelly, claustrophobic inn.

He emerged from the unwelcoming interior and halted in the doorway, beckoning her to join him. Her heart sank down to her boots. He had found it habitable. There was going to be no camp that night. No soothing sounds of slow-moving river-water to lull her to sleep; no sweet-smelling fragrance of juniper and lavender; no gazing up at a sky thick with diamond-bright stars.

Unwillingly she walked towards him.

"I told you we were in luck," he said with annoying satisfaction. "Szechwan's Viceroy was born here, hence the unexpected standard of the inn. It would be shaming to him if his home-town didn't possess a 'semi-foreign' hostelry."

"What does 'semi-foreign' mean?" Gianetta asked, unimpressed.

"Glass as well as oiled paper in the windows, three rooms of honour on the ground floor and three above, kangs and washing facilities."

Despite herself, Gianetta's interest was caught. She had never slept on a kang and had always wondered whether they would be comfortable or not.

"I am to have the ground floor suite of rooms, you are to have the upstairs rooms."

Commonsense told her that it was the only arrangement he could possibly have made, but it didn't sound a very friendly one. She would miss the knowledge that he was only yards away from her, that she had only to say his name to attract his attention. And she would miss Ben's nearness and the occasional, comforting noises he made during the night.

She followed him into the musty interior and up a flight of rickety stairs. The room she was to sleep in was well-swept, the kang huge.

"I'll see you later," he said peremptorily, "when it's time for dinner. Meanwhile, have a rest. I'll have hot water sent up to you so that you can wash."

The prospect of being suddenly left alone in the cheerless, arid room appalled her.

"Ben," she said quickly. "I must see that Ben is properly stabled."

"I'll see to Ben. Have a rest."

It was said pleasantly enough, but she couldn't help feeling that his main concern was not for her tiredness but of his own need to escape her company.

He turned and walked out of the room and she sat down slowly on the uncomfortably hard kang. It was over. All the fun, all the exhilaration, all the adventure. There was nothing to look forward to now. Nothing else interesting or unexpected was going to happen to her.

CHAPTER SEVEN

"How do you feel about being my wife for an evening?"

It was barely thirty minutes later, and Zachary's abrupt entrance woke her with a start.

Gianetta stared at him, blinking rapidly, trying to clear her head. She had obviously been dreaming, and she had an uncomfortable suspicion that she had been dreaming about him.

"I'm sorry," she said, pushing herself up into a sitting position on the kang. "I must have fallen asleep. What did you say?"

He stood with his feet apart, his hands pushed deep into his breeches pockets, a lock of night-black hair tumbling low over his forehead.

"I asked if you would care to be my wife for an evening?"

Her heart began to race erratically. Was he suggesting that he share her room with her? He couldn't be. Not in such an offhand, indifferent manner. And yet what else could he mean? Heat suffused her. There could be no question of her acquiescing to such an insulting suggestion. It had been made without the slightest overture of tenderness. An offer to a woman of the streets would have surely been made with more finesse. And yet . . . and yet . . .

"The Viceroy is at his family home, and word of my arrival having reached him, he would like to meet with me," he said, a gleam of amusement in his gold-flecked eyes. "It isn't customary for Viceroys to give audiences to women, but no doubt an exception would be made if I were to present you as my wife."

She could feel the heat stinging her cheeks. Was he amused because he had guessed the assumption she had so presumptuously and erroneously come to? Even worse, had he guessed her unspoken response? Fury and humiliation fought for supremacy. Holding his eyes with difficulty, Gianetta said stiffly,

"If I cannot be presented to the Viceroy as Miss Gianetta Hollis, then I prefer not to be presented at all."

He gave a slight shrug of his broad shoulders. "Just as you please, although I think it is a decision you may well come to regret. Viceroys may be pretty thick on the ground in China, but audiences with them are not so easily come by, especially for women. You may not get such a chance again."

It was true. And if she didn't go with him, she would have to remain in the inn alone. As the desire to accompany him struggled with her indignation at the terms he was stipulating, there came a small scuffling noise from behind one of the interior walls.

"A rat," Zachary said off-handedly as she looked towards where the noise was coming from. "They're not vicious unless you try and corner them."

She breathed in deeply. She had no intention of trying to corner one, nor had she now any intention of remaining alone in her room while he visited the Viceroy.

"I hadn't thought of the visit from an educational point of view," she said with admirable dignity. "Perhaps I ought to accompany you. It would be really rather negligent of me not to."

"I thought you might see it like that," Zachary said gravely as the scuffling noises continued with increased vigour. "Could you be ready in fifteen minutes or so, looking suitably . . . ladylike?"

It took Gianetta all her self-control not to reach for the nearest object and throw it at his head.

When Zachary had gone, she moved quickly. First she kicked the wall soundly in an attempt to scare off the rats, then she pulled her ankle-length skirt and a high-necked, lace-trimmed blouse from her carpet-bag. Spreading them out on the kang she smoothed the wrinkles from them and began to undo her queue. Fifteen minutes. How on earth did he expect her to make the transformation from dusty, male-attired traveller into elegant femininity in fifteen minutes? There was a bowl and a jug of cold water by the kang and she undressed, sluicing herself down as best she could. The water was freezing cold and she dried herself quickly, reaching into her carpet-bag for clean underclothes. When she had dressed she brushed her hair, sweeping it off her neck with practised ease and piercing the neat twist she created with long black coral pins.

There was no mirror in the room or in her bag but she did not need one to know that her transformation was complete. When she heard Zachary impatiently calling her name she picked up her Eton-styled bolero jacket and walked out of the room to join him.

If he was impressed by the transformation she had effected, he didn't allow it to show.

"You've been nearly half an hour," he said brusquely, leading the way into the inn's courtyard where sedan-chairs and bearers were waiting for them.

His own transformation was almost as complete as her own. He was wearing a snowy-white evening shirt with a high, starched collar and exquisitely cut dark jacket and trousers. His dove-grey waistcoat would have done credit to a London dandy and there was even the gleam of a gold watch-chain across his breast.

His finery must, until now, have been rolled in one of the saddle-bags. Gianetta wondered how many minions had been called into service in order to press it into its present pristine condition.

If he was expecting an apology from her, for her lateness, he didn't receive one. There had been no-one on hand to press *her* skirt or blouse, and it was a wonder she hadn't taken twice as long to complete her toilette.

She was also intensely annoyed at not receiving any acknowledgement concerning her own appearance. She had expected a compliment, even if only a small one. Instead, he had spoken to her as if she were a troublesome young sister.

In icy silence, Gianetta allowed him to hand her into the sedan-chair. It was a form of transport she had never liked, being claustrophobic and joltingly uncomfortable. Seconds later the bearers lifted the chair and she gritted her teeth. The town was small. The Viceroy's family home could not possibly be far. The sedan-chair's curtain swung against her cheek, heavy with the odour of stale perfume. She wrinkled her nose in distaste. To the best of her knowledge, her aunt had never accompanied her uncle when he had visited Chung King's Viceroy. Women, in China, were not usually accorded such privileges. Stringent rules of etiquette were being broken for her benefit. But only because Zachary had requested that they should be

As the sedan-chair rocked and swayed she wondered what his motive had been? Perhaps he had sincerely thought that it would be an educational experience for her and one that she should not miss. It was certainly a possibility, but it was a doubtful one. She suspected Zachary Cartwright of many qualities but altruism was not one of them. It was far more likely that he had made the request merely because it amused him to do so.

The sedan-chair came to a halt and the door was opened. As she stepped gratefully into fresh air she was struck by a third possibility. Perhaps he had requested she be allowed to accompany him for no other reason than that he found pleasure in her company?

He was standing before her, looking down at her with a slight frown.

"You have a smudge on your cheek," he said critically, putting a swift end to any such speculation.

She raised a hand to where she had felt the curtain swing against her cheek, but before she could locate the spot he had brushed the mark away with a kid-gloved forefinger.

"Now you at least look respectable," he said, taking her arm and slipping it through his own.

She was just about to make a suitably stinging retort when the massive gates before which they were standing were flung open and one of the Viceroy's retainers proclaimed loudly:

"Make way! Make way for the Honou'able Mr Zacha'y Ca't'ight and the Honou'able Mrs Zacha'y Ca't'ight."

Even though she had known the identity she was to assume for the evening, the shock of hearing herself announced as his wife was so great that she stumbled.

Zachary's hand tightened its hold of her arm.

"Steady, Mrs Cartwright," he whispered in obvious amusement. "Don't disgrace yourself in front of the Viceroy."

With relief she saw that, despite their having been announced, there was no imposing Viceroy yet in sight. They were in a lamp-lit inner courtyard filled with orange, camellia and azalea trees in large pots on carved stone pedestals. The attendants who had greeted them escorted them across to another set of imposing gates on the far wall of the courtyard. When they reached the gates, they were again flung open, a flight of stone steps was ascended and the pair were again loudly announced.

This time the courtyard was marginally smaller, but again there was no sign of their host.

"How long does this go on for?" she whispered to Zachary as they were led from the second courtyard and up another flight of steps into a third courtyard.

"I suspect the Viceroy will meet us in the fourth court and escort us himself into his inner sanctum. By meeting us in the fourth court, he will not be showing us too much honour, or too little."

"And if we had been European royalty?"

"Then he would have met us himself in the second courtyard."

128

"Not the first courtyard?"

He flashed her one of his sudden, down-slanting smiles. "No, that honour is reserved only for Chinese nobility."

Her stomach muscles tightened as they always did when he looked so directly at her. "And does leave-taking have the same rules?"

He nodded. "The host escorts the guest, and at each gate the guest must protest that he be escorted no further. The host will do so, however, until the gates appropriate to his guest's honour are reached."

She was intrigued and beginning to enjoy herself. "And will both host and guest be in agreement on which set of gates those are?"

His grin deepened. "Not always. The possibilities of insult are infinite, and news as to which gate a guest is welcomed at, and at which gate his host has taken leave of him, travels fast."

"And so if the Viceroy isn't waiting to welcome us at the next gate the entire district will know of it and will judge our status accordingly?"

"Absolutely."

Her hand tightened on his arm as they reached the gates. Brocade-robed servants flung the gates wide.

"The Honou'able Mr Zacha'y Ca't'ight and the Honou'able Mrs Zacha'y Ca't'ight," the attendant who had been escorting them announced loudly.

An enormous, Buddha-like, black satin-clad figure, very obviously the Viceroy, bore down on them. Zachary greeted him in Mandarin and a pleased and surprised smile creased the Viceroy's heavily jowled face.

With further attendants following in their wake every minute, they made a stately progression through the remaining courts and into the Viceroy's innermost sanctum. A banquet had been prepared, and lay spread out on a low round table covered in brilliant scarlet oilcloth. Chinese lanterns bobbed and danced. The Viceroy very formally presented both of them with gifts, a roll of silk for Zachary, an ornament of jade for herself. And then the banquet began.

There were scores of tiny little dishes, all containing a different delicacy, nearly all unidentifiable.

"You've just taken a helping of shark's fin omelette," Zachary said as she followed his example and helped herself from the nearest dish.

"Really?" she said, determined not to gratify his expectations by grimacing. "It looks delicious."

It didn't taste delicious, but no-one could have discerned this from her expression.

"And that is a souse of pigeon eggs," he added as she dipped her chopsticks into another dish.

Her hand didn't waver. She was in the heart of China, and she didn't expect to be served with steak and kidney pudding and apple tart.

A pudding made of dried jujube fruit followed the main dishes and small glasses of hot, fiery liqueur followed the pudding.

Both the Viceroy and Zachary drained their glasses in a single swallow and she lifted the glass to her mouth, determined to do likewise.

"I don't think you should . . ." Zachary began to say to her, but it was too late.

For a second, as the liqueur burned her mouth and throat, she thought she was going to die. She couldn't breathe and her chest felt as if it was about to explode.

"Would you like some water?" Zachary asked, keeping a straight face with difficulty.

She shook her head, unable to speak, furious at the knowledge that she was once again affording him amusement.

When she could finally speak, Gianetta lied in a croak, "How very . . . pleasant."

The attendant behind her chair immediately stepped forward and refilled her glass.

"Good manners don't require that you kill yourself," Zachary said, his amusement turning to concern. "The

130

Viceroy isn't going to take offence if you don't drink any more."

She didn't care about the Viceroy. She cared only about removing the last vestige of amusement from Zachary's gold-flecked eyes.

"I'm not being motivated by good manners," she said with utter truthfulness as she raised the glass again to her lips. "It is an exceedingly . . . warming drink."

Despite all her efforts to the contrary, the liqueur brought tears to her eyes. She blinked them away rapidly, flashing him a brilliant smile.

"It is also an exceedingly intoxicating one," Zachary said dryly, "and two glasses are one too many for anyone unaccustomed to alcohol."

A glow was spreading through her entire body. Instead of being offended at his talking to her as if she were a child, she felt amazingly well disposed towards him. For her benefit, their host had reverted from Mandarin to pidgin-English and, as he discussed his collection of *objets d'art*, she found herself thinking how entertaining he was and how cultured. The evening was becoming even more enjoyable than it had first promised to be. It was exceedingly pleasant to be treated as a married lady and to be acknowledged as her husband's helpmeet, especially when the husband in question was as handsome as Zachary.

The Chinese lanterns hanging low above their heads swayed gently like exotic, giant flowers. The Viceroy's black silk and brocaded robes shone like polished jet. As the conversation turned from the Viceroy's art collection to a discussion of the war taking place in distant Manchuria between the Russians and the Japanese, Gianetta began to feel as disembodied as if she, too, were a lantern floating gently in mid-air.

When the Viceroy rose to his feet, signalling that the evening was at an end, she felt intensely disappointed. As she rose to her own feet she also felt intensely dizzy. Zachary's strong arm instantly steadied her and she was suffused with warmth towards him. He really was proving himself to be a most splendid husband. Previously her body had only ever brushed against his but now, as they were escorted out into the lamp-lit courtyard, she leaned against him, aware of a sensation of pleasure so deep it almost robbed her of breath.

"Are you all right?" he was asking her, looking down at her in concern. "Are you going to be able to make it to the outer courtyard?"

She squeezed his arm reassuringly. "Of course I can make it to the outer courtyard," she said, headily aware of his hip and thigh pressed close against her own. She giggled and then hiccupped, adding in happy certainty, "And I'm not going to make it only to the outer courtyard. I'm going to make it all the way to Kansu as well."

He made what sounded to be an exasperated exclamation under his breath, but she was too happy to pay any heed to it. For the last hour everything had suddenly seemed possible. Of course she would go to Kansu, of course she would remain with Zachary. Any alternative was simply unthinkable.

The Viceroy remained with them as their escort as they made their way down through the courtyards. At each gate Zachary protested against the Viceroy accompanying them any farther; at each gate the Viceroy smilingly insisted on doing so.

At last, when they reached the outermost gate, amid many salutations of friendship and good-will, the Viceroy took his leave of them.

Gianetta looked towards the waiting sedan-chairs. Despite the grandeur of their glass windows and silvered top-knots and pole-knobs, they looked more claustrophobic than ever.

"I think," she said, swaying slightly, "that I would prefer to walk."

Zachary looked down at her, an eyebrow quirking. She tried to make up her mind as to whether the expression in his eyes was one of amusement or concern, and couldn't do so.

"It's probably a good idea," he said as she rested her head contentedly on his shoulder, "But promise me that if you begin to feel ill you'll give me instant warning."

"Silly," she said, hiccupping again. "I feel wonderful. Absolutely, unbelievably wonderful."

She felt, more than heard, his suppressed chuckle. So he was, for some unfathomable reason, amused. Earlier, his amusement at her expense had annoyed her. It did so no longer. She was glad that she amused him; glad that he enjoyed her company; glad that his arm had slipped to a far more supportive position around her waist.

"I think," she said dreamily as Zachary dismissed the sedan-chair carriers, "that I have never been happier. I feel so warm inside, so content . . ."

"Home brewed Chinese liqueur does have that effect," he agreed, his voice sounding even darker and richer than usual.

They had begun walking in the direction of the inn and she halted abruptly, turning to face him.

"I hope you're not inferring that I am intoxicated," she said, trying to sound suitably offended.

His arm was still around her waist, for which she was very grateful. Without such support her legs would have undoubtedly given way.

"Only a little," he said and his voice, so often clipped and curt, was unexpectedly gentle.

As they faced each other in such close proximity, it seemed only natural that her hands should slide in a very pleasant manner up against his chest.

"If I am intoxicated, I am enjoying it exceedingly," she confided, aware of the feel of his heart beating beneath the palm of her hand; of the faint tang of his cologne; of his tantalizing, delicious nearness.

"You may not enjoy the headache you are bound to wake up to quite so much," he said, exercising every inch

133

of self-control in order to turn away from her and continue walking.

As she was obliged to once more fall into step beside him, disappointment flooded through her. It had been inexpressibly pleasant standing so close to him, his arm around her waist, his mouth so very near to her own.

"I should not wake with a headache if we were to sleep out beneath the stars," she said with heartfelt longing and unwitting provocativeness.

His arm was still around her waist and she felt his muscles tense and tighten. After a few moments he said, his voice oddly abrupt,

"You're tempting me like the very devil, Gianetta Hollis, and the sooner we get to the inn and you go to your room, the better."

Laughter rose in her throat, husky and unchained. She felt suddenly extraordinarily powerful.

"In what way am I tempting you?" she asked, knowing the answer with a knowledge as old as Eve.

He stopped walking, turning towards her once again, his hard-boned face looking more Slavic than ever in the star-lit darkness.

"Despite your undoubted innocence you know very well," he said, the grimness in his voice sending shivers down her spine. "But I'm not in the habit of taking advantage of unprotected females, no matter how beautiful they may be."

She stood very still, hardly daring to breathe.

"Do you really think I'm beautiful?" she asked when she could trust herself to speak. "Do you think I'm as beautiful as Serena?"

Slowly he hooked a forefinger beneath her chin, tilting her face to his. Their eyes held. Somewhere nearby, in the velvety-soft darkness, a small creature could be heard scampering about its business.

"I think you are very, very beautiful," he said thickly, and at the expression in his eyes desire spiralled through her.

She leaned against him, sliding her arms up and around his neck.

"And I think you are very, very handsome," she said truthfully.

He lowered his head to hers and she sighed rapturously, closing her eyes and slithering down against him in a state of alcoholic insensibility.

He swung her up in his arms before she ignominiously reached the ground, relief sweeping hard on the heels of intense thwarted desire. He had not only been on the verge of kissing her, but of making love to her. God only knew what would have been the consequences. He certainly wouldn't have been able to ship her back to Chung King under the auspices of one of Peng's missionaries. Gianetta's violated honour would have demanded marriage, and he had not the least intention of being so tritely entrapped.

As he walked through the deserted, unmade streets towards the inn his relief gave way once more to amusement. So she thought him handsome, did she? He wondered if she would remember her declaration in the morning. If she did, he would take good care that she was not embarrassed by it. Inconveniencing as she was, she was a highly likeable baggage and he had no desire to cause her any embarrassment.

He shifted her weight a little in his arms. In fact she was more than likeable, she was lovable. But not for him. When he married he had no intention of choosing as his bride a girl as adventurous and as uncaring of conventions as himself. He intended to marry a girl like Serena. A girl whose peaceful serenity would soothe him when he returned home after months of arduous travelling; a girl who would bring calm and order into his life.

As he approached the inn, the burden he was so lightly carrying moved slightly in his arms, opening her eyes.

"Would you please put me down," she said unsteadily, "for I think I am going to be ill."

He set her on her feet with ungentlemanly alacrity.

Uncaring of his presence, she parted company with a prodigious amount of half-digested shark's fin omelette and soused pigeon's eggs.

When she had finally finished retching, he said sympathetically, "You'll feel much better now."

She didn't feel better. She felt utterly mortified. With as much dignity as she could muster she said stiffly, "It was the pigeon eggs. I shouldn't have eaten them. They were probably ages old."

Despite all efforts to prevent it the corner of his mouth tugged into a grin. "And the liqueur," he said as gravely as he could manage. "That was probably a little old too."

She drew in a deep, steadying breath. "The liqueur was perfectly innocuous. It was the pigeon eggs that were at fault," and, not trusting herself to say another word for fear of disgracing herself again, she walked unsteadily away from him and into the musty confines of the inn.

He didn't follow her. He knew that if he offered assistance it would be refused and though she was certainly far from well he judged that she was capable of mounting the stairs to her room and of putting herself to bed.

He himself didn't feel in the least like sleeping. It had been an odd evening. Enjoyable. Entertaining. And something more. Though what the something more was, he couldn't quite decide.

The narrow unmade street in which the inn was situated was deserted except for a dog scavenging for food. He ducked beneath the inn's inadequate doorway, emerging a minute or so later with a battered chair and a pipe. Sitting on the chair, he tilted it back on two legs against the wall, lit his pipe, and proceeded to ponder what the something more had been.

Women were no mystery to him. He had enjoyed several satisfying love affairs, though always with ladies as worldly and experienced as himself. Yet, satisfying as his previous amorous encounters had been, he had never before experienced such intensity of desire as that which had swept over him in those seconds when Gianetta had been so willingly in his arms, her face upturned to his, her mouth infinitely inviting.

Even now, grateful as he was for the turn of events which had stopped him from making love to her and consequently being under an obligation he couldn't possibly honour, he couldn't help wondering what it would have been like to have kissed that soft-looking mouth. And he couldn't help feeling regret at having been cheated of the knowledge.

He blew a smoke-ring into the still night air. He had certainly never felt such a complexity of emotions for any woman before. His lovers had always been exactly that and nothing more; they had never also been companions or friends, which was what Gianetta Hollis was fast becoming. If it hadn't been for her sex he would have had no doubts at all about taking her with him to Kansu. Her artistic ability was exceptional and would have been a great asset to him. Her intelligence was undeniable, as was her courage. All in all, if she had been a man she would have been an ideal companion. But she was very far from being a man. She was the most engaging, most desirable woman he had ever met.

The chair came down abruptly onto four legs. Where on earth had that last thought come from? She was desirable certainly, but not the most desirable woman he had ever met. That honour was undoubtedly her cousin's. He thought again of Serena Hollis and the overwhelming effect her ethereal blonde beauty had had on him. She had been as delicate in colouring as the palest English rose. He tried to conjure up her soothing image but, to his annoyance, couldn't satisfyingly do so. No matter how hard he tried, her face remained indistinct. He was unsure as to whether her eyes had been green or grey, whether her face had been heart-shaped or oval.

Frustratedly he knocked out his pipe, rose to his feet and made his way to his room and his kang. He didn't sleep well. Serena's image may have been elusive but Gianetta's image was ever-present. His dreams were plagued by visions of her riding Ben, her silk-black Chinese queue bobbing on her back, her white shirt open at the throat, her violet-blue eyes full of laughter, her smiling mouth petal-soft, tormentingly inviting.

When Gianetta woke it was with a groan of pain. Her head was throbbing as if she had a fever. She pressed her hand against her forehead, but it was reassuringly cool. And then she remembered.

With another groan she sat up, doing so very gingerly. Why, why, why had she drunk a second glass of the Viceroy's liqueur? It had been obvious that it was lethal. Even Zachary had treated it with caution and had not accepted a second glass. Zachary. She had a hazy memory of his steadying her as the Viceroy had escorted them down through the courtyards to the outer gateway. And then what? Had they travelled home by sedan-chair? If they had, she had no memory of the journey.

She rose to her feet and crossed the room, pouring water from a jug into a porcelain bowl. They hadn't journeyed back to the inn by sedan-chair. She had a cloudy memory of protesting against the claustrophobia of the chairs and of Zachary equably agreeing that they walk back to the inn. She had the uncomfortable feeling that something else had happened, something that she ought to be able to remember.

She began to splash the icy water on her face and neck and it was when she was patting her face dry that memory of the previous evening returned in full. She had said that she thought him handsome. And then she had collapsed in his arms and afterwards, on regaining consciousness, she had been excessively sick.

With a groan she pressed her small hand-towel against her burning cheeks. What would he think of her? How could she possibly face him? And then she remembered that she had not been the only one to make a confession. He had told her that she was beautiful. And he had been going to kiss her. Surely at one point he had been on the point of kissing her?

Slowly she lowered the towel from her face. If she had cause for embarrassment, so had he. It had been he, after all, who had audaciously suggested that she play the part of his wife for the evening. And as a gentleman he should have warned her well in advance not to touch a drop of Chinese liqueur. And though he hadn't told her that she was more beautiful than Serena, he *had* told her that she was beautiful. He had told her that she was very beautiful. Her mortification faded and a hint of a smile touched the corners of her mouth. Whatever the indignities of the evening, there had also been compensations. And if Zachary Cartwright couldn't take her temporary bout of sickness in his stride, he wasn't half the man she judged him to be.

By the time she made her way to the stables to say good-morning to Ben, her headache had faded into a minor inconvenience. She was quite sure that Zachary would expect her to be awkwardly embarrassed by the events of the previous evening, and she had no intention of satisfying his expectations.

He was in the stables, supervising the loading up of the mules and she saw that both Bucephalus and Ben were already saddled and ready for the road. He was adjusting a saddle-bag and at her approach he turned, a winged eyebrow rising quizzically.

With annoyance she saw that he was wearing a cream linen shirt she had never seen before and that he was looking far more elegant than he had any right to after so many days travelling. It was open nearly to his waist, and she was acutely aware of an intriguing amount of crisply curling dark hair on his firmly muscled chest.

"Are we going to have breakfast on the road?" she asked, determined to give the impression that the events of the previous evening were of no consequence and certainly not worth referring to.

"Yes. I thought you would find it preferable to eating here."

139

He was still regarding her expectantly, as if waiting for an embarrassed apology.

She gave Ben a good-morning pat, pleased to see that he looked rested and well-fed.

"I would," she said, beginning to attach her carpet-bag to the pommel on her saddle, "Are we leaving now?"

An expression flashed through his eyes that she wasn't quite sure of. It could have been mild frustration at her not having reacted as he had expected her to react, or it could have been reluctant admiration. She wasn't sure and she didn't trust herself to hold his eyes for long enough to make sure.

They breakfasted by the banks of the Kialing and then continued on their journey through breathtakingly spectacular scenery. The river ran broad and deep on their right hand side, the water the colour of Imperial jade. On their left were gentle slopes covered in woods of freshest green. The fields through which their ponies were gently walking was thick with wild rosebushes and sun-yellow barberry. The air was heavy with the scent. The peace and beauty were almost more than Gianetta could bear.

"I do *love* China," she said suddenly with deep passion.

He looked across at her with the flashing grin that so dramatically transformed his hard-boned features. "This is a side of China very few Europeans see. They crowd the bund at Shanghai and the Legations in Peking, but they very rarely venture out into the true China."

"They're too frightened of bandits," Gianetta said, remembering the conversations she had heard between her aunt and uncle and their European guests.

"And you're not?" Again an eyebrow was quirked.

She eased Ben around a low-lying rosebush drowning in pale pink petals. "Not enough to forgo seeing all this."

In the far distance, mountains rose silver-grey, silver-green, silver-tawny. A kite wheeled high in the sky above their heads. From an unseen and isolated pagoda, there came the faint tinkle of bells.

As he continued to look at her, Zachary's grin faded. Although dark, vibrant, exotic good looks had never previously been to his taste, he had to admit that the words he had so inadvertently uttered the previous evening were true. Gianetta was very, very beautiful. And devastatingly likeable.

He dragged his eyes away from her, trying to continue with his task of observing the flowers around them. With a slight frown, he found himself remembering the incident that had taken place between Gianetta and Charles. Charles had most certainly been kissing her and she had just as certainly been making no effort at resistance, or at least she hadn't done so until she had heard his own approach.

He had been filled with cold anger at the time, and a quite surprising degree of disappointment. Anger because of the disruption her arrival and behaviour were causing to his expedition and disappointment both at Charles' irresponsibility and at her shamelessness.

He had known, of course, what had prompted her to behave in such an unlikely manner. She was a single young lady with no immediate family and her prospects were grim. She was facing return to England and the choice of living with Serena and her husband or alone, apart from servants, in the Hollis family mansion. It wasn't much of a choice and he could quite well see how attractive Charles, as a potential husband, must have seemed to her. And in order to snare him as a husband she had acted with quite breathtaking audacity.

His frown deepened. The devil of it was, taking her own unquestionable attractions into account and Charles' easy-going and susceptible nature, it could quite easily have worked. Once she had amorously compromised him or, more to the point, allowed him to compromise herself, there would have been every chance of her uncle succeeding in coercing him to marry her.

141

It was disturbingly easy to visualise her as Lady Rendlesham. And surprisingly unpleasant. Charles was, for all his admirable qualities, quite simply not worthy of her. For the first time the question edged into his mind whether he, himself, would not be a far more suitable candidate.

Zachary's first reaction was to be amused by the ridiculousness of such a thought. His second reaction was stunned surprise at the realization that it wasn't ridiculous at all. Gianetta had effected a state of almost permanent sexual arousal in him ever since she had walked into camp after her bathe in the Kialing looking like a water-naiad. As he remembered, desire pulsed through him. There were worse fates in life than marriage to a woman who aroused such reactions, and who was both intelligent and entertaining into the bargain.

And Serena? Serena was probably by now Mrs Henry Plaxtol and, even if she were not, Serena was an unknown quantity. All he knew of her was the feelings the sight of her had aroused. Even if she had not been affianced he had no way of knowing whether, on further acquaintance, her personality and character would have proved to be as he had imagined they would be.

As Zachary continued to brood on the surprising direction of his thoughts, Gianetta rode in silence at his side, equally preoccupied.

She had been premature in assuming there was no alternative for her but to agree to his decision that she return to Chung King accompanied by one of the Peng missionaries. He didn't truly want her to return to Chung King. In the days and nights that they had been together he had become used to her. Despite his often curt and abrupt manner she was sure that he liked her almost as much as she liked him. And so she would take matters into her own hands. When they reached Peng she would seek out and engage a Chinese woman to act as a chaperone. She would be able to help with cooking tasks, and with a little instruction would probably be a great help in changing the botanical drying papers. Her presence in the camp would make it impossible for Zachary to claim that it was her own sexual vulnerability, as a lone woman, that made their continuing any further together impossible.

She leaned forward in her saddle, patting Ben's neck. "It's going to be all right," she whispered confidently. "We're not going back to Chung King. I know we're not."

At lunchtime they picnicked companionably amongst wild roses and yellow barberry. Afterwards, when they resumed their journey, they did so at a slightly brisker pace. As the first hints of dusk began to smoke the air, Zachary said, with surprise, "Good Lord! There's Peng ahead of us. I must have been alarmingly out in my calculations."

Gianetta looked in the direction towards which he was pointing. Through the late afternoon heat-haze, a red-roofed tower and high stone walls were clearly visible. A flare of excitement spiralled through her. She hadn't the faintest idea of how to go about engaging a chaperone, and she knew that she would have very little time in which to do it. For the last few miles, she had been wondering whether she should announce her intention to Zachary or wait until the arrangements were made. After much indecision, she had decided that it would be wiser to wait.

"All I have to do is to be firm," she had said beneath her breath to Ben. "I must simply refuse absolutely to return to Chung King, and persuade Zachary that a chaperone makes my return totally unnecessary."

"The mission is on the south side of the town, outside the walls. We should be there within half an hour or so," Zachary said, breaking in on her thoughts.

His voice sounded rather odd, as if he were annoyed by their unexpectedly swift arrival. She didn't answer him. She was too busy making plans. If the mission was on the south side of Peng, it meant she would have to make some excuse for riding alone into the town itself. Where would be the best place to locate and engage a suitably middle-aged, respectable Chinese matron? The missionaries would know, but she wasn't sure whether, under the circumstances, they would be helpful or not.

"There it is," Zachary said suddenly. "A little piece of England, a world away from home."

They had rounded a tree-shaded corner. In front of them, fifty yards or so from the shingled bank of the river, lay a low, white, clapboard house with a surrounding verandah. A large area around it had been cultivated as if it were an English garden, and Gianetta could see the pinks and purples of carefully tended foxgloves, and the blue of canterbury bells.

A gentleman in European dress was seated on the verandah, enjoying an early evening drink. He was presumably one of the missionaries, and as they cantered nearer Gianetta saw with amusement that his white suit was as formal as if he were a consul or an ambassador.

Zachary frowned, barely noticing the figure now rising to greet them. He had never before felt so undecided. Was he making a mistake in insisting that Gianetta be escorted back to Chung King? Was there an alternative?

The white-suited figure began to descend the verandah steps, stepping out of the shade into the still clear light. As he did so, Gianetta's eyes widened in incredulity.

"Oh no!" she whispered, her hands tightening on Ben's reins, sick apprehension flooding through her. "It can't be! It isn't possible!"

Almost in the same instant Zachary also recognised the figure approaching them. With a disbelieving blasphemy he reined in, his face tightening, a pulse beginning to throb at the corner of his jaw.

Sir Arthur Hollis strode towards them, fury and hostility in every line of his body.

Hardly able to believe that he was real, Gianetta slid from Ben's back.

"Uncle Arthur! What are you doing here? I'd no idea . . . If it's because of me there was no need . . ."

"Of course there was need," her uncle snapped viciously, "You've destroyed your reputation! You've brought

144

shame onto every member of your family! How we are to hold our heads high again, God only knows!"

A few feet away from them, Zachary dismounted.

Sir Arthur spun towards him. "As for you, Cartwright! I hold you ultimately responsible! You should have escorted my niece back to Chung King the instant she caught up with you! You've behaved monstrously and restitution will have to be made!"

"Just what kind of restitution did you have in mind, Sir Arthur?" Zachary asked him, his voice dangerously quiet.

Sir Arthur breathed in deeply, his nostrils flaring. "There is only one kind that is possible in this situation. An Anglican priest is in residence at the mission. I have arranged that a marriage should take place between the two of you at the soonest possible moment."

CHAPTER EIGHT

Gianetta swayed dizzily. It seemed impossible to her that the scene now taking place was real and not a hideous nightmare. How could her uncle have known that Zachary would call at the mission house at Peng? How could he have been so sure that he would be able to waylay them? To have reached the mission before them, he must have travelled by boat up the Kialing, yet during the many hours that she and Zachary had ridden along or near to the Kialing's banks they had seen no boat flying a Union Jack.

She wound her fingers tightly into Ben's mane. It was bad enough that her uncle was here at all, without the further humiliation of his demanding that Zachary should immediately marry her. Almost before he had finished speaking, she attempted to protest, but her mouth was so dry that no words would come.

Zachary was not similarly hampered. To her incredulity he was neither furiously angry nor coldly contemptuous. Instead he said laconically,

"Then you have been wasting the gentleman's time. I have not the slightest intention of marrying your niece."

"You have no option!" Sir Arthur expostulated, frothing at the mouth. "You have lured my niece into a liaison that has robbed her of the last vestige of honour! You have compromised her utterly and absolutely! You have . . ."

"I have done nothing of the kind," Zachary replied indifferently, taking hold of Bucephalus's reins and beginning to walk with him towards the mission.

146

At this affront to his dignity Sir Arthur gasped word-lessly for air and then, rallying himself, spun on his heel, striding after him.

"How dare you turn your back on me, Cartwright! Twenty years ago I would have called you out for such an insult!"

"Pistols at twenty paces?" Zachary asked in mild amusement, looking across at him but not halting in his easy stride. "It could be arranged, if it would give you satisfaction."

"Damn you for your impudence, Cartwright! What will give me satisfaction is a marriage! Only a blackguard would refuse to act honourably in such a situation!"

They had reached the foot of the verandah steps. An elderly, gaunt gentleman in clerical dress had walked out onto the verandah to meet them; a Chinese stable-boy had hurried round from the rear of the mission and was waiting to relieve them of their mounts.

Zachary handed Bucephalus over to him and turned towards his raging adversary. "Then in that case I am quite obviously a blackguard," he said indifferently.

"Of the deepest dye!" Sir Arthur riposted, his face white, his knuckles clenched. "I will see that you are ruined, Cartwright! I will see that the doors of polite society are closed against you! I will see to it that you are never again given a commission by Kew or the Royal Horticultural Society or the Royal Geographical Society or any other Society!"

The white-headed figure in clerical garb at the head of the steps cleared his throat uncomfortably, but neither Zachary or Sir Arthur took the slightest notice of him.

With one foot on the bottom tread of the verandah-steps and his hand and his weight resting on the hand-rail, Zachary continued to face Sir Arthur.

"Such a course of action would be most unwise," he said, and despite the nonchalance of his stance his eyes had narrowed and a hint of menace had entered his voice.

"Don't try and threaten me!" Sir Arthur spat at him,

147

freshly affronted. "Whatever high ideas your friendship with young Rendlesham may have given you, you're a nobody! You can't harm me, Cartwright, but I can damn well ruin you!"

"Sir Arthur . . ." the cleric at the head of the steps intervened, deeply shocked. "I think perhaps it would be wisest if . . ."

"I would take great exception at having my career ruined for no reason other than a refusal to be entrapped into marriage," Zachary said tightly, ignoring the attempted interruption.

"Entrapped! Entrapped! No-one has entrapped you, Cartwright! You've entrapped yourself by behaving like the worst kind of scoundrel!"

"I disagree. Very far from behaving like a scoundrel I have behaved, much to my surprise, as a gentleman. Your niece, possibly with your connivance, attempted first to compromise Lord Rendlesham and then, Lord Rendlesham's arm injury rendering it necessary for him to return to Chung King before enough time had elapsed for her to succeed in her efforts, she turned her attentions to me."

For the first time since Sir Arthur had accosted him, Zachary looked across at Gianetta.

She was still standing where she had dismounted, too far away to hear the conversation now taking place. As their eyes met his face tightened, a pulse beginning to beat at the corner of his jaw.

"Whether or not she knew that you would be here to bring her scheme to fruition, I have no way of knowing," he continued, keeping his voice indifferent only with the greatest difficulty, "but I am beginning to strongly suspect that this meeting was most carefully pre-arranged."

As Zachary's eyes met hers, Gianetta's anger and mortification deepened. How *dare* her uncle have assumed that Zachary had robbed her of her honour? How could he have been so shameless and vulgar as to hurl such an accusation at him without waiting for an explanation of

148

what had, and had not, passed between Zachary and herself? Trying hard not to think of the very definite way in which Zachary had repudiated the demand that he marry her, she began to lead Ben towards the verandah-steps.

Sir Arthur was staring at Zachary as if Zachary had taken leave of his senses.

"*Connived* at? *Pre-arranged*? I haven't the least idea what you're talking about! You lure my niece into the wilds of China! You seduce and disgrace her . . ."

There was an agonized, inarticulate protest from the figure standing impotently at the head of the steps.

". . . you scandalously cast her aside . . ."

"For God's sake, I've done no such thing!" Zachary snapped, his apparent indifference vanishing and his very real anger flaring to the surface. "Your niece's situation is such that she is in desperate need of a husband and a home of her own. She saw what she thought was an ideal way of securing both when Charles and myself visited the Residency. If she travelled after us and was several days alone in our company, she thought she could charm and compromise one of us into an offer of marriage."

"*No!*"

This time the outraged protest was not from Sir Arthur's deeply shocked host, but from Gianetta.

Her eyes burned in her white, disbelieving face. "You can't possibly believe such a thing! I travelled after you because I wanted to see China! Because I wanted to find blue Moonflowers . . ."

"And if Charles hadn't so fortuitously injured his arm and been obliged to return to Chung King, her plan might very well have succeeded," Zachary continued implacably, keeping his attention very firmly on Sir Arthur.

"It isn't true! I had no such designs . . ."

"As for your claim that I have seduced her, your niece is as *virgo intacta* as she presumably was the day she left the Residency."

Sir Arthur sucked in his breath, his eyes bulging. His

149

host galvanised himself into movement, hurrying down the steps and inserting himself between Sir Arthur and Zachary as if fearing that the altercation was about to become physical.

"That is enough, gentlemen!" he said authoritatively. "That is quite enough! This conversation must come to an end before irreparable harm is done."

"There has already been irreparable harm done," Sir Arthur said savagely.

Zachary merely shrugged, once again in control of his temper, one again affecting indifference.

"If there has been, it has not been of my making," he said, and turning his back on Sir Arthur he began to mount the steps two at a time.

"Zachary," Gianetta's voice was steady, drained of anger and disbelief, thick with a grief she couldn't yet give vent to.

Reluctantly he turned, looking down at her from the head of the steps, a pulse still throbbing at the corner of his jaw, his face shuttered and inexpressive.

"Your assumptions are wrong," she said fiercely, her eyes holding his. "I never intended compromising either yourself or Charles. I never had any other motive other than the one I have just expressed."

For a moment she thought he was going to walk back down the steps towards her; he didn't do so. Without a word he simply turned on his heel and entered the mission.

"Unbelievable!" Sir Arthur fumed. "Insufferable!"

The clergyman ignored him. Gianetta's face was so drained of blood that he thought it quite likely she was going to faint.

"Would you like some tea?" he asked her in concern.

She nodded her head gratefully. The Chinese boy who had led Zachary's pony around to the stables had returned, and she gave Ben a comforting pat and handed his reins over to him.

"There can be no question now, of course, of your

sharing a home with Serena and her husband," her uncle was saying in clipped, curt tones. "Nor of your living alone at Sutton Hall. You have shown yourself to be totally untrustworthy. I can only assume that your Italian blood is to be held responsible for your scandalous behaviour . . ."

Gianetta was too heartsick to care what he assumed. Not only had her heady taste of freedom and adventure come to an abrupt end, so had the camaraderie between herself and Zachary.

As she allowed herself to be escorted up the shallow flight of steps, she found it hard to believe that, all the time they had been together, he had believed her to be both scheming and devious. Had he believed her when, a moment ago, she had told him that he had been grossly wrong in his assumptions? And if he hadn't, would she have any further opportunity of persuading him of the truth?

"My father was always vehemently opposed to your parents' marriage, and all his worst fears have come to fruition," her uncle was saying as their host led them into a large, plainly furnished sitting-room. "No good could ever have come out of such an alliance. The Italian nation has always been recklessly hot-headed and regrettably hot-blooded . . ."

"I think it would be wisest if no more was said on the subject, Sir Arthur," his host said with surprising asperity. "Your niece is obviously in need of rest and refreshment . . ."

"She's in need of a good whipping," Sir Arthur responded, "And where she is going she may very well receive one."

Gianetta looked around the room. There was no sign of Zachary.

"And where do you intend me to go?" she asked, finally giving her uncle the benefit of her attention.

"An Anglican convent," Sir Arthur said with crisp satisfaction. "You will remain there until you are twenty-one."

151

Gianetta stared at him, horrified. "But I can't bear feeling closed in, you know I can't. Let me go to Lady Margaret Hall. I'll work hard there and . . ."

"Oxford?" Sir Arthur snorted derisively as a Chinese maid brought a tea tray into the room and set it down on a low cane table. "After the way you have behaved in China, I certainly have no intention of allowing you to run loose in Oxford. You're going to go where an eye can be kept on you, young lady."

"But I don't *need* an eye keeping on me," Gianetta protested vehemently, "I need an education in order that I can earn my own living. I need to go to Lady Margaret Hall. I need . . ."

"You need to do as you are told," her uncle interrupted bluntly. "We shall leave first thing in the morning for Chung King. Until then you will have no further communication with Mr Cartwright." He turned his attention to their host. "I trust that you will give me your full support in this matter, Reverend Daly?"

"I shall certainly try and ensure that your niece isn't further distressed," Lionel Daly replied a trifle obliquely.

Sir Arthur frowned, unhappy at not receiving a more reassuring response. "Then oblige me by making it known to Cartwright that his presence here is offensive. It is unthinkable that he and my niece should spend tonight beneath the same roof."

"It is certainly regrettable and I will, of course, suggest to Mr Cartwright that he find lodging for the night in Peng. If, however, he chooses to remain at the mission then it is an arrangement that will have to be accepted. No-one is ever turned away from here, no matter who they are or what their alleged crimes."

"Then you will one day find yourself murdered in your bed," Sir Arthur snapped caustically. "I take it you will have no objection to my niece being locked in her room tonight?"

"As long as the key is on the inside of the door, none at all."

152

"I have arrangements to make," Sir Arthur said, realising that he was not receiving the whole-hearted support that was his due. "I trust I can leave my niece in your care for half an hour or so?"

Lionel Daly nodded and without so much as a glance in Gianetta's direction, Sir Arthur strode from the room.

When the sound of his footsteps had died away, Lionel Daly said gently,

"Would you like a cup of tea, Miss Hollis?"

"Yes, please."

He poured her a cup, handed it to her, then sat down in a chair twin to her own.

The tea was hot and sweet and wonderfully reviving and she looked across at him gratefully.

"My father always used to turn to tea in a crisis," she said with a small smile of reminiscence, "Now I understand why."

Lionel Daly smiled, his elderly eyes creasing at the corners. "Yes, it's a wonderful restorative. The Chinese use it for anything and everything."

For several minutes they sat in a silence that was strangely companionable. After a little while she said:

"Could you persuade my uncle to allow me to speak with Mr Cartwright before we leave tomorrow morning?"

Lionel Daly's smile faded. "I think that would be most unwise, my dear. Whatever the true circumstances of your relationship with this man . . ."

"We were friends. Nothing more." Her voice was bleak. "All his assumptions are false. I didn't ride after him with the intention of compromising him into marrying me." Her eyes burned with the need to be believed. "I rode after him because I wanted to be a member of his expedition; because I wanted to go to Kansu to find blue Moonflowers."

There was the unmistakable ring of truth in her voice and he said quietly, "I believe you, but regretfully, I doubt if the world at large will believe you. Your uncle was acting in your best interests when he suggested to Mr Cartwright that he marry you."

"He didn't suggest. He demanded." Gianetta's voice was tight. It would be a long time before she forgot the humiliation of that moment, or the way in which Zachary had so emphatically refused to comply with the demand.

Lionel Daly regarded her with wise eyes. "Whatever your reason for riding after Mr Cartwright and for remaining with him, your best course of action now is to acquiesce to your uncle's wishes. An Anglican convent can be an extremely educational place. It could serve as very good preparation for life at Lady Margaret Hall."

At the mention of the convent Gianetta shuddered. No doubt the convent would be in Lincolnshire. Her room would be spartan and the convent grounds would be bounded by high walls. Anything less like the freedom she had recently enjoyed was impossible to imagine. She thought of the nights spent sleeping beneath the stars by the banks of the gently murmuring Kialing; of the mountains that had dominated the far horizon; of the heady scent of wild roses and jasmine and honeysuckle.

"I think I would like to go to my room now," she said, her throat painfully tight.

Lionel Daly nodded, rising to his feet. "Jung-shou will show you to it," he said, lifting a small bell from the tea-table and giving it a sharp ring.

The young girl who had earlier brought in the tea-tray re-entered the room.

"Please show Miss Hollis to her room", Lionel Daly said to her, his gaunt figure looking stooped and rather tired.

Gianetta felt a stab of guilt. He was older than her uncle, possibly in his seventies, and the unpleasant scene between her uncle and Zachary must have distressed him considerably. Feeling suddenly exceedingly tired herself, she followed the Chinese girl from the room, seeing immediately why it was that Zachary had so easily and swiftly disappeared from view.

The inner doors led onto a covered but open-sided

walkway and running diagonally from it at each end were a series of simply built bungalows.

"Are the bungalows for guests?" Gianetta asked, wondering what she would do if Zachary suddenly stepped into view. Her uncle had said that she was to have no further communication with him but she hadn't agreed to the demand. She had made no promises whatsoever.

"They a'e sick 'ooms and school 'ooms and guest 'ooms," Jung-shou said with shy pride.

In one of the bungalows Gianetta could see small children sitting cross-legged on the floor and she could hear, but not see, an English woman instructing them. She wondered if the unseen teacher was perhaps Mrs Daly. There was no sign of a tall, masculine figure in an open-necked shirt, riding breeches and boots. She didn't know whether to be relieved or disappointed.

She continued following Jung-shou along the covered walkway, aware that, where Zachary Cartwright was concerned, her emotions were in such turmoil that it was impossible for her to know which was uppermost. When he had walked away from her into the mission, she had been seized with a feeling of such acute desolation that she had wondered how she was going to survive it. And she had been angry as well. Indignantly, furiously angry. How *dare* he have assumed that she was husband-hunting? The more she thought about it, the angrier she grew. If that was his arrogant assumption, the least he could have done was to have confronted her with it. Then she could have swiftly disabused him.

Jung-shou crossed the open-ended square towards one of the bungalows, and Gianetta followed her. Had Zachary walked straight out to these bungalows and spoken to the English woman teaching the children? Or perhaps he had met another resident of the mission and been escorted to a guest room, just as she was now being escorted. Would he seek her out in order to say goodbye to her? And did she want him to do so?

The guest bungalow Jung-shou led her into was small

and plainly furnished. On one of the white-washed walls was a framed print of Holman Hunt's, "Light of the World," and on a small cane table beside the narrow bed was an oil lamp, a box of matches and a Book of Common Prayer.

If she was not going to be able to see him again in order to disabuse him of his notion that she had been trying to trap him into marriage, then she didn't want to see him again at all. It would be too humiliating.

"You will be comfo'table?" Jung-shou was asking anxiously. "Is the'e anything that you 'equi'e?"

Gianetta shook her head. "No. Nothing. Thank you, Jung-shou."

When Jung-shou had closed the door behind her, Gianetta sat down slowly on the bed. Her adventure was finally and utterly over. She had nothing to look forward to now but three years of stultifying boredom. Unless she took matters very dramatically into her own hands . . .

It was twilight now, and the room was quickly growing dark. Gianetta didn't rise to her feet to light the lamp. Instead, she continued to sit on the edge of the bed, thinking hard. There had to be a way out of her present dilemma. She couldn't simply passively accept the future that her uncle had so insensitively mapped out for her. There had to be some course of action she could take which would allow her to have some say, however small, is her immediate future.

Bouncy optimism was part of her nature, and slowly but surely it began to reassert itself. There *was* a way. There had to be.

The darkness was now total, and she lit the oil-lamp. Shadows flickered on the plain white-washed walls. Gianetta was suddenly reminded of her childhood bedroom in the Villa Simione. Vines had grown thickly outside her window and on hot, sunny afternoons, when she had been taking her siesta, she had watched the dancing shadows of the leaves on the pristine white walls of her room.

Italy. She wondered if it would ever be her home again. She closed her eyes, remembering the scent of lemon groves; the glitter of the sun on Lake Garda; the sound of church bells signalling early morning Mass.

Her eyes flew open. Mass. Despite being married to an Anglican, her mother had always attended early morning Mass. One of the main reasons for her grandparents refusing to come to terms with her mother's marriage had been because of her father's Anglicanism. The breach had deepened after her own birth when her parents had agreed she be baptised and brought up as an Anglican.

The breach had continued until the present moment, but Gianetta was quite sure that contact would be re-established if she were to ask her mother's family to save her from three years in an Anglican convent.

If it had not been for the gulf that now existed between herself and Zachary, Gianetta would have been dizzily happy. She had always wanted to be reconciled with her Italian grandparents, and now she was sure that she would be able to. It was a reconciliation between herself and Zachary that was now the immediate problem.

There was a soft tap on her door and she flew to open it. As she found herself facing a middle-aged, primly dressed Englishwoman, disappointment engulfed her. For a brief, exhilarating moment she had been certain that the caller was Zachary; that he had come to say goodbye to her and that she was going to be able to persuade him that his assumptions about her were wrong.

Her visitor had a homely face but a stunningly sweet smile.

"Hello. I am Elizabeth Daly. I'm sorry I wasn't able to introduce myself earlier, but I was taking a class when you arrived and then afterwards there was a problem in the dispensary. Supper will be served in about fifteen minutes. I'm sure you must be very hungry . . ."

Gianetta wasn't at all hungry, nor did she relish the prospect of sitting at table next to, or opposite, her uncle.

"Would you mind very much if I didn't join you?" she

157

asked, a little apologetically. "I'm not at all hungry, but I am very tired, and I thought I would go to bed early."

"If that is what you would prefer to do, then of course we don't mind. Would you like me to bring you some biscuits and a glass of hot milk?"

"That would be lovely. Thank you."

Elizabeth Daly hesitated for a moment and then said awkwardly, "Mr Cartwright has ridden to Peng and will be spending the night there. If you would like to have your biscuits and milk in the mission sitting-room . . ."

"No," Gianetta said firmly, hoping that her reaction to Elizabeth Daly's news wasn't showing on her face. "I really am very tired."

Elizabeth Daly nodded understandingly. "I'll be back with the milk and biscuits in five minutes."

She took her leave, Gianetta closed the door, leaning heavily against it. He had gone. And he had gone without troubling to say goodbye to her. Her sense of loss was shocking in its intensity. She didn't know at what point she had begun to think of him as a friend and not as an adversary, but that she had done so at some time in their spiky relationship was beyond question. And she had done so mistakenly. Friendship required reciprocated feeling and the feelings she had begun to entertain for Zachary Cartwright were quite obviously very far from being reciprocated.

The pain of this knowledge was so acute that she could deal with it only by succumbing once again to anger. His accusation that she had followed him from Chung King to trap him into marrying was unforgiveble, as was his suggestion that she had pre-arranged the meeting with her uncle. If he thought of her as being so scheming and devious, Gianetta wanted nothing further to do with him. She would leave in the morning with her uncle for Chung King, and she would write immediately to her maternal grandparents, telling them of her uncle's plans for her immediate future. Her Italian grandparents would be appalled at the mere mention of an Anglican

158

convent. They would seize on the chance to further the war between themselves and her father's family and they would, she hoped, be delighted at the prospect of a reunion. She would suggest to them that she attend Lady Margaret Hall. She would study botany and one day she would return to China. One day she would find blue Moonflowers for herself.

Her decisions made, she was able to greet Elizabeth Daly with equanimity when she returned with hot milk and biscuits. Elizabeth told her that a boat had been engaged for the journey back to Chung King, and that it was lying at anchor in the centre of the river.

"You are fortunate that the river is quite deep at the moment. That means a punt will have to be used to take you out to it. The last time we had a visitor travelling down to Chung King, the river was low and he had to endure the indignity of being carried out across the mud-flats pick-a-back."

Despite her still simmering anger where Zachary Cartwright was concerned, Gianetta smiled. The thought of her uncle being carried in so undignified a fashion was highly amusing. Then she thought of Ben, and a slight frown furrowed her brow.

"Will Ben have to travel out to the boat by punt as well?"

"Ben?" It was Elizabeth Daly's turn to frown in perplexity. "I didn't know there was another visitor . . ."

"My pony. Or, to be more exact, my uncle's pony." At the thought of her eventual parting with Ben, Gianetta felt her throat tighten. He had been such a loyal friend. She didn't know how she was going to be able to bear saying goodbye to him.

"Ponies usually swim the short distance to the boat," Elizabeth Daly said reassuringly. "He'll have to be well behaved once he's aboard, though. There's very little room for livestock and he's quite likely to find himself tethered on the open deck amongst the oarsmen."

"Ben is always well-behaved," Gianetta said, trying not to think how disappointed Ben was going to be at finding himself back in his stall at the Residency.

Detecting the faint catch in Gianetta's voice and misinterpreting the reason for it, Elizabeth Daly rose from the chair in which she had been sitting and said gently,

"I'll go now, and let you get to bed. Goodnight and God bless."

Gianetta saw Elizabeth to the door and closed it behind her, grateful for her sensitivity. Thinking about the inevitable parting with Ben had distressed her deeply. As she began to free her hair from its queue she wondered how old he was, if he would still be alive when she eventually returned to China as a botanist, and then she began to wonder if it would be possible to take him with her to England or whether the long sea journey would be distressing to him.

She undressed and slipped her nightdress over her head. The only person who would know such a thing was Zachary and, much as she wanted an answer to her question, she had no intention of asking Zachary Cartwright anything, ever again.

She slid between cool cotton sheets and turned the lamp down low, overcome by an almost suffocating wave of desolation. Even if she had felt differently, she would have been unable to question Zachary, because he was no longer there. He was in Peng and, no doubt, from Peng he would continue travelling north to Kansu.

The emotion that flooded through her was so distressing and so disturbing that for a few seconds she didn't know how to cope with it. Then anger came once again to her aid. Zachary Cartwright was egotistical to the point of mania, and she had been quite right to resolve never to speak to him again. To do so, knowing his assumption about her character and motives, would be to utterly demean herself. If ever they did meet again, whatever the circumstances, she would remain frigidly silent. Nothing and no-one would induce her to speak to him again.

CHAPTER NINE

She was woken in the morning by a hesitant tap on her door. Brilliant sunlight was streaming through the shutters into the room, and Gianetta wondered for a moment whether she had overslept. She opened the door, half expecting to find her uncle on her doorstep, all ready for departure. Instead, she found an anxious-looking Elizabeth Daly.

"I'm sorry to disturb you so early, Miss Hollis, but after the way you spoke about your pony yesterday I thought I had better warn you . . ."

She looked as if she had dressed in great haste. The buttons on the long sleeves of her mauve cotton-dress were undone and her grey-streaked hair looked as if it had been wound into a bun without the benefit of a hairbrush.

As the older woman entered the room, Gianetta stared at her bewilderedly. "Warn me? About what?"

Elizabeth Daly's normally serene face was perturbed. "Ben. Your pony. I gained the impression yesterday that you were exceedingly fond of him and . . ."

Fear gripped Gianetta's heart. "I am. Is he ill? Has he broken a leg?"

"Oh dear. This is very difficult. I'm sure your uncle is going to be very annoyed . . ."

Gianetta was uncaring as to her uncle's emotions. "*What has happened to Ben?*" she demanded in a fever of anxiety.

Elizabeth Daly twisted her hands together unhappily. "Nothing, yet, and he isn't ill, nor has he hurt himself."

"Then what on earth . . ."

"Your uncle has given instructions that Ben is not to accompany you back to Chung King."

At the news that Ben was neither hurt nor injured, Gianetta's fear ebbed and her bewilderment increased. "I don't understand. Is he to stay here instead?"

Elizabeth Daly shook her head. "No. We have all the livestock we need and the Missionary Society monitors our budget very carefully. It isn't possible for us to feed animals that are not needed."

"But if Ben isn't to stay here and he isn't to return to Chung King, what is to happen to him?"

Elizabeth Daly looked as if she wished herself a million miles away. "There may of course be a mistake. Jung-shou may have heard incorrectly . . ."

Gianetta's fear began to return. Whatever Jung-shou had overheard, it had obviously distressed Elizabeth. "What did Jung-shou say?" she demanded urgently. "For goodness sake, Elizabeth, *tell me*."

"She said that Sir Arthur . . . that your uncle . . . has given orders that . . . that your pony be shot."

For a dizzying, disorientating moment Gianetta thought she couldn't possibly have heard correctly. Then with a sob she turned away from Elizabeth and began to scoop up her clothes.

"How could he do such a thing?" Feverishly she began to dress, scrambling into her underthings under cover of her nightdress. "Where is he now? Who did he give the instructions to?"

"I don't know where Sir Arthur is now," Elizabeth Daly said as Gianetta pulled her nightdress over her head, letting it fall unheeded to the floor." He gave his orders to the stable-boy."

"Where are the stables?" Gianetta reached for her skirt, stepping into it and tugging it up over her hips, fastening the button at her waist with trembling fingers.

"At the far end of the other row of bungalows."

She struggled into her blouse. "Please find your husband for me," she said feverishly, leaving the vast majority of

163

her blouse buttons undone and beginning to tug her boots on. "Tell him what my uncle intends."

She yanked open the bungalow door.

"Tell him to come quickly! Tell him there is no time to lose!"

With her hair tumbling around her shoulders, Gianetta ran across the open-ended square.

"Oh dear God, let me be in time!" she panted as she reached the bungalows, racing past a schoolroom and a dispensary. "Let Ben be alive! Let Jung-shou not have heard correctly! Let it all be a ghastly mistake!'

The stables abutted the last of the bungalows. The doors were open, and Gianetta hurled herself into the strong-smelling interior.

In the dim light, Ben's milky-pale coat was immediately visible. Gianetta's relief was so over-powering that for a moment she thought she was going to faint. Weakly she stumbled across the straw-littered ground towards him, pressing her face against the comforting heat of his neck and hooking her fingers into his thick mane.

'It's going to be all right, Ben," she promised, her heart pounding painfully. "No-one is going to harm you. Not now. Not ever."

As she finished speaking a young Chinese boy entered the stables. It was the same boy who had led Ben away the previous evening. This time he had a rifle in his hand.

On seeing her he stopped abruptly.

"Go away," she said succinctly, beginning to put Ben's leading rein on him.

"Pony to be shot," the boy said, standing his ground. "Big Sir say pony old and no use."

"My pony is not old," Her voice shook with the passion of her feelings. "Nor is he going to be shot."

She began to lead Ben from his stall. The boy watched her hostilely.

"Not your pony," he said as she walked past him and out into the sunlight. "Pony belongs to Big Sir."

It was a truth she couldn't refute. In rising panic

she wondered how she could possibly ensure Ben's safety when she had no legal rights to him, when she couldn't even give him away because he was not hers to give.

"*Gianetta!*" Her uncle's outraged voice assailed her. "*What the devil do you think you are doing?*"

He was standing on the covered walkway, dressed as immaculately as ever in a white suit with a matching waistcoat. He was also dressed for travel. There was a pith-hat on his head and a walking-cane in his hand.

"*Stay there if you please!*" he shouted. "*I want a word with you, young lady!*"

As her uncle strode along the walkway towards the intersection with the bungalows, Gianetta's heart began to bang. The next few minutes would be crucial. Somehow she had to persuade him to rescind his instructions; somehow she had to make him see what a crime he would be committing if he did not.

Sir Arthur didn't step from the walkway to cut across the square. Instead, he kept rigidly to the allotted route, turning abruptly at the corner and striding down the pathway fronting the schoolroom and dispensary.

"What in God's name are you doing in the stables so improperly dressed?" he demanded furiously as he approached her. "Have you lost all sense of decency and decorum?"

Gianetta was uncaring of her partially unbuttoned blouse and her tumbled, unbrushed hair.

"I wanted to check on Ben," she said, deeming it wisest not to involve Elizabeth Daly. "I wanted to make sure he was ready to leave for the boat."

"Such arrangements are none of your affair. Please oblige me and return to your room immediately."

Gianetta remained motionless. "Seconds after I arrived at the stables, so did a stable-boy. He said you had given him instructions to shoot Ben. I told him he had obviously misunderstood your instructions and . . ."

She had hoped that she was offering her uncle a

way to rescind his instructions without losing face. He didn't do so.

"Then you told him wrongly. The animal long ago outlived his usefulness, the mission is not in need of him and I have no intention of going to the trouble of transporting him by boat back to Chung King. I would appreciate it if you would now return to your room and dress yourself suitably for the journey ahead of us. We shall be sailing in half an hour."

Gianetta's eyes held his. He was lying about Ben having outlived his usefulness. Ben wasn't old. He was sturdy and strong. With a terrible flash of insight she realised her uncle's true motives. He wanted to hurt her. He wanted to make her pay for the inconvenience and humiliation she had caused him. It seemed incredible that her compassionate and loving father could have been older brother to a man so vindictive and small-minded or that Serena, so sweet-natured and kind, could be his daughter.

She said steadily, "Ben isn't old. He won't be any trouble on the boat trip to Chung King. If you no longer want him then I will find someone who does. Someone who will appreciate him and care for him."

She didn't put into words her hope that he might be able to travel with her to England. She still had to find out whether or not such a trip would be in Ben's best interests.

"You will do no such thing!" Sir Arthur's nostrils were pinched, his lips almost bloodless. "I have taken all the impudence from you that I intend to take. From now on you will do exactly as I say, and you will keep your regrettable opinions to yourself."

All through their altercation the stable-boy had been only yards away, the rifle still in his hands.

Her uncle turned abruptly towards him. "Shoot the beast," he snapped. "Shoot him here and now."

"No!" Gianetta's hand tightened on Ben's rein. "I won't let you!"

166

The boy took up a stance facing Ben and raised the rifle.

"Stand aside, Gianetta," her uncle commanded curtly. "I can assure you I'm not going to be thwarted by any mock heroics on your part. If you want the animal's blood all over your blouse and skirt, then you shall have it."

Gianetta flung her arms around Ben's neck, tears streaming her face. "You can't have him shot! I'll do anything you ask of me, if only you will change your mind! I'll go to the convent! I'll never be rebellious again! I'll . . ."

"It's far too late to make such promises. You're going to be boarded at the convent whether you like it or not, and you will have no opportunities for further rebelliousness. Now stand aside this instant, or take the consequences."

"No!" She pushed Ben behind her, so that she was standing between him and the rifle. "I won't let you shoot him! I won't!"

The stable-boy looked towards Sir Arthur for guidance.

"Prepare to fire!" Sir Arthur commanded him implacably.

Gianetta swayed, certain that her uncle was mad, and that her last moments had come.

"*For the Lord's sake!*" Lionel Daly was running towards them, a terrified looking Elizabeth in his wake. "Put down that weapon, Li Po! Have you lost all reason, Sir Arthur? Can't you see that your niece is terrified?"

The stable-boy looked from Sir Arthur to Lionel Daly and then, realising that the fun was over, regretfully lowered the rifle.

Sir Arthur blasphemed and took two quick strides in the stable-boy's direction. Seizing the rifle from him, he raised the sight to his eye, aiming it directly at Gianetta.

"Stand aside!" he barked, uncaring of his growing audience. "Stand aside immediately!"

"This is an outrage, Sir Arthur!" Lionel Daly panted

as he came to a halt a few feet away from him. "This is a mission, not a slaughterhouse!"

Sir Arthur ignored him, his finger closing around the trigger. "Stand aside," he rasped again to Gianetta.

Gianetta remained immobile, Ben patiently standing behind her. "No." Her voice was cracked and ragged. "If I did, and if you pulled the trigger, you would never forgive yourself."

"Don't tell me what I would or would not do!"

Frustrated in his attempts to get a clear view of Ben's head, Sir Arthur threw the rifle to the ground. For a dizzying moment Gianetta thought that the danger was over, and then he began to walk towards her, taking a small pistol from his pocket as he did so.

"This may not be powerful enough to put paid to him, but he will most certainly have to be finished off afterwards," he said grimly, and raising the barrel of the pistol he pressed it to the side of Ben's head.

There was uproar. Gianetta was aware of hoof-beats fast approaching, of Elizabeth Daly screaming and of Lionel Daly shouting. She sprang towards her uncle, trying to wrench the pistol from his grasp. A shot sliced the air and she fell against him, wondering for a reeling moment if Ben had been shot; if she had been shot.

"*Just what the hell is going on here?*" a familiar voice demanded tersely as Ben whinnied, alarmed but unhurt.

Gianetta pushed herself away from her uncle, turning to face the horseman, never more glad to see anyone in her life.

"He was going to kill Ben," she said, her voice breaking, forgetting all about her vow never to speak to him again. "He was going to do it in order to punish me."

Zachary slid from his saddle, ramming the pistol he had just fired back into his saddle-bag. Then he turned towards Sir Arthur.

"Is that so, Sir Arthur?" he asked, regarding him with undisguised contempt.

"What I may, or may not have intended, is none of your

168

affair. The animal is mine and if I choose to make an end of him I will do so."

His voice was icily unrepentant and though he had lowered his pistol his fore-finger was still curled around the trigger.

"You will not do so here," Lionel Daly said unsteadily, still breathing harshly after his arthritic sprint towards the stables. "Your behaviour this morning has been inexcusable, Sir Arthur. Quite unforgivable. I can only imagine that you are ill. Yesterday's heat perhaps . . . or reaction to distress occasioned on your niece's behalf."

"Any distress Sir Arthur has felt or is feeling is purely on his own behalf, not anyone else's," Zachary said darkly. "May I ask what your intentions are now, Sir Arthur?"

Ben was nuzzling Gianetta's hair; Elizabeth Daly was crying softly; Lionel Daly was listening as intently as Gianetta for Sir Arthur's reply.

"I am returning to Chung King with my niece."

"And Ben?" Zachary asked, a winged eyebrow rising queryingly. "What future do you intend for him?"

"His future is none of your affair, Cartwright, nor do I intend to submit to the impudence of this cross-examination any longer."

He put the pistol back into his jacket pocket and adjusted his jade cuff-links. "The boat I have engaged will now be ready to sail," he said, as if nothing exceptional had taken place. "Good-day, Mrs Daly, good-day, Reverend Daly. Your hospitality has been much appreciated."

He began to walk away and Zachary said in raised tones, "Just one moment, Sir Arthur. Before you leave I would like to pursue the question of Ben's future."

Sir Arthur swung around, his face livid with hatred. "Such concern ill becomes you, Cartwright! If my niece hadn't stolen him in order to follow you into the wilds of China, his fate would not now be in question. If anyone is to be held responsible for the decision I have taken, it is you."

"Then in that case I must obviously make amends."

Sir Arthur's eyes narrowed. "Exactly what kind of amends did you have in mind?"

"I'll buy Ben from you."

Sir Arthur snorted. "Buy a mangy pony from me? You call that making amends? The insult you have occasioned my family requires amends of a far higher order, Cartwright. Have you considered what my position will be when Rendlesham returns to London? News of my niece's scandalous liaison with you will be all over town. My family name will be irretrievably besmirched. The only way you can possibly make amends is to marry my niece forthwith."

Gianetta sucked her breath in between her teeth but before she could make a protest Zachary raised his hand slightly, motioning her to keep silent.

"And if I don't?" he asked, "what other punishment do you intend for her, over and above shooting Ben before her eyes?"

To Sir Arthur's stupefied fury and to her husband's amazement, Elizabeth Daly answered for him.

"When she returns to England she is to be boarded in an Anglican convent," she said, sensing that nothing but good could come out of the disclosure.

Zachary looked from Sir Arthur to where Gianetta was standing, one hand curled in Ben's shaggy mane, her hair tumbling wildly around her shoulders, her blouse indecorously open at the throat. A less likely candidate for convent life was hard to imagine.

He sighed heavily, aware that there was only one course of action he could take if her life were not to be made a misery. Fatalistically, he returned his attention to Sir Arthur.

"If I were to make amends to your niece, there would be a stipulation."

"Name it."

"You will give Ben to her as a wedding present."

"Agreed."

The last verbal exchange had taken place so quickly

that Gianetta was unsure as to whether she had heard aright.

"I still want to sail to Chung King today," her uncle was saying to Lionel Daly. "Could the wedding take place this morning? Before luncheon?"

"*No, it could not!*" she erupted explosively, under no doubt at all now as to what was being discussed.

All eyes swivelled towards her.

Her eyes were focussed solely on Zachary. "How *dare* you assume I am willing to marry you? What gives you the temerity? The utter gall . . ."

Behind her Ben nuzzled her neck.

"He does," Zachary said dryly. "If you don't marry me, the instant you reach Chung King your uncle will have him shot."

She stared into his suntanned, hard-boned face. It was true. And not only would Ben be shot, she would be packed aboard the first available boat for England *en route* to a dismal, claustrophobic existence in Lincolnshire.

The silence was so complete that a pin could have been heard to drop. It was Lionel Daly who broke it.

"This is a quite insupportable situation. I have not the slightest intention of performing a marriage ceremony under these circumstances. Miss Hollis is being most shamefully coerced . . ."

"She is being nothing of the kind," Sir Arthur interrupted briskly, determined not be thwarted now that a satisfactory conclusion was so tantalisingly within reach. "She has behaved in a manner which ensures she can only feel deep gratitude to Mr Cartwright for his offer . . ."

Despite the enormity of the subject under discussion, Gianetta felt a flash of amusement at the speed of her uncle's new-found politeness where Zachary was concerned.

". . . and by marrying her to Mr Cartwright, you will be rendering her a very great service."

"By marrying her to a man she has no desire to marry

I shall be rendering her a very great *dis*service," Lionel Daly retorted crisply.

Gianetta was still looking towards Zachary. He was wearing the wine-red linen shirt that so enhanced his gypsyish good looks. In the brilliant sunlight his glossy hair was night-black and flecks of gold were clearly discernible in his brandy-dark eyes. She remembered the morning when she had surprised him bathing in the Kialing; the evening at the Viceroy's when she had been sure that he was going to kiss her; the camaraderie of their day-long rides; the excitement she felt just being in his company.

"Miss Hollis needs to be assured that the pony will not be shot," Lionel Daly was saying firmly. "It would also be helpful if arrangements concerning her future were made in a spirit of love, nor vindictiveness. Convents do not exist to be used as places of punishment, Sir Arthur . . ."

As her eyes continued to hold Zachary's, Gianetta was acutely aware of the quality she found so attractive in him. It was his fearlessness and daring, his unequivocal determination to live life on his own terms. As she wanted to do. Time seemed to waver and halt. As she wanted to do with him.

". . . and so I advise that fresh arrangements are made for Gianetta's future."

Gianetta looked away from Zachary and towards Lionel Daly. "No," she said, surprised by the steadiness of her voice. "I would like to marry Mr Cartwright."

"But my dear child! A moment ago you made your objections to such a marriage quite obvious . . ."

"I have changed my mind."

It was impossible for her to explain why she had changed her mind. Zachary would no doubt think his assumptions had been correct all along, and that she had followed him from Chung King with no other intention than marriage. Elizabeth Daly would assume she was agreeing to the marriage in order to save Ben's life, and her uncle and Lionel Daly would think she was agreeing to it in order to save her reputation.

"That's it then," her uncle said, highly satisfied. "I suggest we all meet in the mission church in half an hour."

Elizabeth Daly stared at him aghast. "Half an hour? But Miss Hollis has no suitable clothing with her!"

"She can be be married in what she is wearing," her uncle retorted, uncaring of trivialities.

"I think not," Zachary said laconically.

All eyes turned towards the groom-to-be.

For a heart-stopping moment Gianetta thought he was going to announce he had been having a joke and that not even for Ben's sake was he prepared to marry her.

"I would prefer my bride to be married in something a little more suitable than a travel-creased blouse and skirt," he said, walking over to Bucephalus. "I'll be back in about an hour with a wedding-gown."

He mounted with supple ease and for the first time since she had said that she would marry him, his eyes sought hers.

"And flowers," he said to her. "I think flowers are essential for a plant-hunter's bride, don't you?"

There was amusement in his eyes and something else as well. Something that sent desire coursing through her.

Her cheeks flushed hotly. "Yes," she said a trifle unsteadily. "Wild white roses and yellow jasmine and honeysuckle."

He nodded and at that moment, as their eyes held, Gianetta was certain there were no longer any misunderstandings between them. Whatever he had once believed as to her reasons for following him from Chung King, he believed no longer. And he wasn't marrying her solely in order to save Ben's life. He was marrying her for the same reason she was marrying him. Because he was irresistibly drawn towards her, because he couldn't envisage life without her.

As he wheeled his pony around and began to gallop away from the mission in the direction of Peng, exhilaration coursed through her. He would teach her all she longed to know about botany, and together they would travel to the most exotic and remote regions of the world, seeking out plants unknown to British gardeners, collecting seeds and cuttings. And he would be more than a husband and a teacher to her, he would also be her lover and her friend.

She would have staked her life on it.

"If you have any doubts, my dear," Lionel Daly was saying in deep concern, "If you would like to speak to me alone . . ."

She turned towards him. "No," she said, her radiant face reassuring him more than any words could have done. "Is there a stable-boy other than Li Po who could groom Ben for me? I want him to look absolutely splendid for the wedding."

"Of course," he said gently, not querying her stipulation that the task of grooming Ben should not be given to someone who had so recently been on the point of killing him.

"For goodness sake, let's move away from the stink of these stables," her uncle said irritably. "There are things to do and not much time to do them in."

He began to march down the pathway fronting the bungalows, wielding his walking-cane vigorously. "I must inform the boatman that I will be departing for Chung King later than I had anticipated, hymns must be chosen for the wedding service, notice that the wedding has taken place must be despatched to *The Times*."

Gianetta walked quickly, keeping up with him with ease, the Dalys following more slowly behind them.

"Lord Rendlesham must be informed, of course," he continued, "A pity he isn't here to act as best man."

When they reached the covered walkway, Sir Arthur waited for the Dalys to catch up with them and then said peremptorily,

"The wedding will take place the instant Mr Cartwright returns. I shall be in my room until then, and would appreciate being informed of his arrival."

"It would be much more seemly if there were less haste,

Sir Arthur," Lionel Daly said stubbornly, disliking his guest's high-handed manner. "In the ordinary way of things, banns would be called on the three Sundays prior to the wedding. I would prefer it if this were done. Mr Cartwright can reside in Peng for the next three weeks and Miss Hollis can remain here."

Sir Arthur regarded him with animosity. "It is my understanding that the purpose of banns is to proclaim an intended marriage," he said witheringly, "and to allow any persons who have reason to object to the marriage an opportunity of stating their objection. No-one in this remote corner of China is going to be even vaguely interested in my niece's marriage to Mr Cartwright, and there is certainly no-one in the vicinity who can have an objection to it. Banns, therefore, are unnecessary. A speedy marriage, on the other hand, is highly necessary."

Lionel Daly did not look at all convinced, and Gianetta said quickly, "Mr Cartwright is *en route* to Kansu, in search of blue Moonflowers. A delay of three weeks could mean his not reaching Kansu until the flowering season is over, and then his journey would have been in vain."

"And if Mr Cartwright decides he cannot wait for the banns to be read and continues his journey without marrying Miss Hollis, it will cause untold distress," Elizabeth Daly ventured, envisaging Ben's corpse floating down the Kialing.

Her husband misunderstood her. Thinking she was intimating to him that the marriage had perhaps been anticipated and that Gianetta was possibly pregnant, he said reluctantly, "Then in that case I shall perform the ceremony as requested. Twelve o'clock would be a suitable time, I think, providing that Mr Cartwright has returned from Peng by then."

"That's it then. Settled." Sir Arthur was highly pleased with himself. He had always found his guardianship of Gianetta an inconvenience, and now he would be free of it.

"I shall give you away, of course," he said magnanimously to her, adding as an afterthought, "What your father would have said about today's arrangements I can't imagine, though as his own wedding was equally unconventional I think we can assume he wouldn't have been overly critical."

Lionel Daly's mouth tightened. It seemed to him that Sir Arthur was incapable of saying anything that wasn't either insensitive or rudely dictatorial.

"I think perhaps Gianetta should get ready for her wedding in our room," he said to his wife, determined to give Sir Arthur no opportunity of pursuing the subject of Gianetta's parents' marriage. "It has facilities, such as a hip-bath and mirror, that the bungalows lack."

Elizabeth didn't hesitate. Sir Arthur's behaviour had been deplorable. The sooner she turned her back on him, the better she would like it.

"Come along, my dear," she said to Gianetta. "I'm sure Jung-shou will be able to rustle up some hot water."

As they walked away towards the double doors leading into the mission's drawing-room, she added zestfully, "And we must find you something blue to wear, and something old and something new and something borrowed."

Gianetta could have hugged her for her kindness. With Elizabeth's help, her wedding was going to be delightfully traditional, instead of being prosaically make-shift.

"I believe some brides wear blue garters, but I doubt if we'll find any of those in the mission," Elizabeth continued, amusing Gianetta vastly. "I do have a blue ribbon though. We could pin it on your underskirt, or tie your bridal bouquet with it."

"And will you be my matron-of-honour?" Gianetta asked as Elizabeth began to lead the way up a wide flight of shallow steps.

Elizabeth was so surprised that she almost lost her footing. "But I'm nearly fifty, my dear! Isn't that a little old to be a matron-of-honour?"

"Matrons-of-honour can be any age."

Elizabeth flushed with almost girlish pleasure. "Then I would love to be your matron-of-honour. Now, we must choose at least two hymns. Jung-shou's sister plays the piano for church services. She doesn't have a very wide repertoire but I'm sure she could manage the Twenty-third Psalm or 'The Voice that Breathed O'er Eden'."

"Then 'The Voice that Breathed O'er Eden' it shall be," Gianetta said, enjoying herself enormously. "And what about the children, Elizabeth? I saw a host of small children yesterday in one of the school-rooms. Could they be guests at my wedding?"

"Of course they can. It's a wonderful idea. We've never had a European wedding here before."

They entered a large sunny bedroom and she said in sudden consternation, "Oh my goodness! Chinese wedding-dresses are red! You don't think Mr Cartwright will return with a red wedding dress, do you?"

Their eyes held in temporary dismay and then Gianetta began to giggle. "It won't matter if he does. As the wife of a plant-hunter I'm going to have to accommodate myself to all kinds of strange experiences. Being married in red will be a symbolic reminder of what I'm letting myself in for."

The next couple of hours were a flurry of activity. Jungshou filled the hip-bath with steamingly hot water. Elizabeth donated a packet of fragrant bath-crystals she had been keeping for a special occasion. Lionel Daly informed the missionary teaching the children that she and her charges were invited to a wedding that was taking place at midday. Then he asked the mission's cook to prepare a simple wedding breakfast.

By the time Zachary returned laden with a wedding dress and wild flowers, the atmosphere at the mission was of joyous celebration with no-one, other than himself, remembering the circumstances that had necessitated it.

With a frown, he handed the flowers and a wrapped package to Elizabeth Daly. For a decisive moment, when he had looked across at Gianetta after being told of her uncle's plans for her future, he had been suddenly sure he had been wrong and that she hadn't followed him from Chung King with the intention of ensnaring a husband; that instead she had followed him for reasons he totally sympathised with. She had wanted to explore the wonderful world around her and she had wanted to find blue Moonflowers. And so, rather than allow her to be barbarically boarded in a claustrophobic convent, he had said he would marry her. Now he couldn't help wondering if he hadn't been a mite impulsive.

"The wedding-dress is red," he said to Elizabeth, unable to quell the growing suspicion that his proposal had been anticipated all along and that he had been manipulated into making it with Machiavellian artistry. "Perhaps you will explain to Miss Hollis that red is the customary colour for brides in China."

"She already knows, and she is more than happy to be married in red," Elizabeth said, intending to be reassuring.

Zachary was anything but reassured. He had made his offer to marry Gianetta in order that she would be free of Sir Arthur and his petty tyranny. She had agreed to the marriage primarily in order that Ben should not be shot. In such circumstances, stoic resignation on her part would have been understandable, perhaps even gratitude. The apparent happy enthusiasm indicated by Elizabeth seemed, however, decidedly out of place.

His frown deepened. He wasn't a man who people took liberties with. He certainly wasn't a man who was easily fooled. Was he being fooled now? More to the point, if he was, did he mind?

Deep in thought, he turned on his heel and strode out of the room and on to the verandah, leaving a slightly disconcerted Elizabeth Daly behind him.

A hundred yards or so away the Kialing surged inexorably southwards. The junk in which Sir Arthur intended sailing to Chung King lay at anchor, a boat-man and a large black dog asleep together near the prow. On a hill on the far bank a small pagoda emerged from a cluster of pine trees. The heat was intense. The silence profound.

Common sense told him that with the doubts he now had, his only sensible course of action was to call the wedding off. With his hands pushed deep in his breeches pockets, he continued to stare out over Elizabeth Daly's carefully tended garden to where a cluster of small boys were playing on the bank of the river.

He didn't want to call it off. He wanted to marry her, God help him. He wanted a future where he no longer travelled alone, but where she travelled at his side. He wanted to sleep with her by the banks of the Kialing and by the banks of a hundred other yet-to-be-visited rivers in a score of other, yet-to-be-visited countries.

From somewhere a little distance away, a piano began to play. After a few bars the pianist stopped, going back to the beginning again, repeating and practising assiduously. The tune was Handel's "Wedding March".

With a slight, wondering shake of his head, still unable to believe what he was about to do, Zachary turned and re-entered the mission, intent on finding a room in which he could change into clothes more suitable for a bridegroom.

CHAPTER TEN

At twelve-o-clock Gianetta walked across the verandah and down the steps, one hand lightly resting in the crook of her uncle's arm, the other holding a posy of white roses, jasmine and honeysuckle. Her glossy dark hair was swept into a chignon decorated with white rosebuds. Her dress was of crimson silk, the high mandarin-neck emphasising the long, lovely line of her throat, the ankle-length skirt seductively narrow, exquisite gold embroidery edging the short side-splits and hem.

Elizabeth Daly was a step or two behind her, dressed in a becoming gown of dove-grey silk, and carrying a posy of roses and larkspur and gardenias.

At the foot of the steps, Jung-shou and a flower-garlanded Ben were waiting for them. As Sir Arthur led Gianetta the short distance to the mission chapel, girl and pony fell into step behind Elizabeth.

Sir Arthur contained his distaste at leading a procession which had, at its rear, a pony of indiscriminate breed, deeply thankful that no-one of note was there to witness the indignity.

Elizabeth wondered why more European brides, marrying in China, didn't follow Chinese custom and marry in red. Gianetta looked absolutely wonderful; petite, vibrant and exotic. She was glad that when Zachary Cartwright had asked Sir Arthur what his plans were for Gianetta, she had not waited for Sir Arthur to answer but had answered for him. Lionel had afterwards chided her for behaving so improperly, but she wasn't even slightly repentant. If she hadn't spoken out, Sir Arthur would have given a prevaricating answer and Zachary Cartwright would never have known of the future Gianetta was facing. If that had been the case, he might very well not have insisted on marrying her.

Gianetta was aware that she was living through moments she would never ever forget. Beneath the brassy blue bowl of the sky, the small stone-built chapel was as pristine as a child's toy; the only sound in the still, heat-filled air the evocative chords of Handel's "Wedding March". For the hundredth time, she marvelled at the speed with which she had become a bride. Only days ago she had thought Zachary Cartwright the most aggravating and objectionable man she had ever met. Even now she wasn't sure of the exact moment when she had fallen in love with him.

She wondered when he had fallen in love with her. That he had done so she hadn't a shadow of a doubt. His suggesting they marry in order that Ben should not be shot had been a pretext, nothing more. If he had really wanted to, he could have somehow secured Ben's safety without going to such extravagant lengths. He had suggested marrying her, not because of Ben, but because he *wanted* to marry her. Just as she wanted to marry him.

As she neared the open chapel door she could see the children in the pews and edging the aisle, large terra-cotta vases full of roses and irises and camellias. Zachary was standing alone, facing the altar and a grave-faced Lionel Daly. Just for one moment she was aware of a pang; she wished that Charles was acting as Zachary's best-man and that Serena, as well as Elizabeth, were her matron-of-honour.

With butterflies fluttering in her stomach she stepped into the chapel's cool shade. Zachary's head didn't turn, though a score of smaller ones did so, button-black eyes wide with wonder. Jung-shou and Ben remained in the tiny entrance porch and Gianetta walked down the aisle to Handel's timeless music.

Even when she reached his side, Zachary did not turn his head towards her. Her eyes rested for a moment on his strong-boned profile and then she, too, gave Lionel Daly her full attention.

He looked at her questioningly for a moment and then, seeing the happiness shining in her eyes, he said solemnly:

"Dearly beloved, we are gathered here today in the sight of God and in the face of this congregation, to join together this Man and this Woman in Holy Matrimony . . ."

Zachary wondered if he would be able to have the marriage annulled later, on the grounds that he was certifiably insane at the time it took place.

". . . which is an honourable estate, instituted of God in the time of man's innocence, signifying unto us the mystical union that is betwixt Christ and his Church . . ."

Always, all his life, he had been strong-willed and impulsive, living life exactly as he wanted, never conforming to society's many unwritten and boring rules. He had never before, however, acted quite as rashly as he was now doing.

". . . which holy estate Christ adorned and beautified with his presence, and first miracle that he wrought in Cana of Galilee . . ."

The first time marriage had even fleetingly crossed his mind had been when he had sat opposite Serena Hollis in the Residency dining-room. Then he had envisaged a marriage in which he continued his lone travelling and his wife waited tranquilly for his return; a marriage in which the adventurous life-style he so enjoyed would continue unchanged, the only difference the domestic comfort awaiting him whenever he returned to England in order to make plans for yet another trek, to yet another country.

". . . and is commended of Saint Paul to be honourable among all men; and therefore is not by any to be enterprised, nor taken in hand, unadvisedly, lightly or wantonly . . ."

Lionel Daly's eyes were fixed firmly on Zachary.

". . . to satisfy men's carnal lusts and appetites, like brute beasts that have no understanding; but reverently, discreetly, advisedly, soberly, and in the fear of God; duly considering the causes for which Matrimony was ordained . . ."

Zachary's eyes held Lionel Daly's with difficulty. It was a long time since he had listened to the words of the Marriage Service. There was certainly no mention of marriage being ordained in order to save a Chinese pony from death or a young girl from being boarded in a convent.

"I require and charge you both, as ye will answer at the dreadful day of judgement when the secrets of all hearts shall be disclosed, that if either of you know any impediment why ye may not be lawfully joined together in Matrimony, ye do now confess it . . ."

It seemed to the bride and groom and to the bride's uncle, that Lionel Daly waited far longer for a reply than was politely necessary.

Sir Arthur coughed impatiently. The matron-of-honour gave her husband a steely stare.

Bowing to the inevitable, Lionel Daly proceeded with the service. Giving Zachary his full attention he said gravely,

"Wilt thou have this Woman to thy wedded wife, to live together after God's ordinance in the holy estate of Matrimony? Wilt thou love her, comfort her, honour, and keep her in sickness and in health; and, forsaking all others, keep thee only unto her, so long as ye both shall live?"

This time it was the groom's silence which caused Sir Arthur's heart to palpitate unpleasantly.

Zachary's eyes held Lionel Daly's. He was aware of Gianetta at his side and of the faint perfume emanating from her hair and skin. He could still bring a halt to the proceedings; he could still walk from the mission a bachelor. He took a deep breath. Out of the corner of his eye he was aware that the hands holding the posy of roses and jasmine and honeysuckle were trembling ever so slightly.

"I will," he said in dark, rich tones, his voice as steady as the Rock of Gibralter.

From the first pew on the left-hand side of the chapel there came an unmannerly sigh of relief.

"And wilt thou have this Man to thy wedded husband?" Lionel Daly said gently to Gianetta. "To live together after God's ordinance in the holy estate of Matrimony? Wilt thou obey him and serve him, love, honour, and keep him in sickness and in health; and, forsaking all other, keep thee only unto him, so long as ye both shall live?"

"I will," Gianetta said, her voice low, husky and absolutely unhesitating.

"Will you now take the bride by the right hand, with your right hand," Lionel Daly said to Zachary.

For the first time since Gianetta had entered the chapel, Zachary turned and looked directly at her.

Shock-waves sliced through her. He was so devastatingly handsome that she couldn't imagine how she had ever thought him tedious. As he took her hand in his she gave him a smile so dazzling that Lionel Daly almost forgot where he had got to in the service. Previous brides whose marriages he had conducted had kept their eyes demurely lowered throughout the service, and had certainly not bestowed such frank and sunny smiles upon their husbands-to-be.

The husband-to-be now in front of him was not remotely disconcerted by his bride's blatant and vibrant happiness. His white teeth flashed as he shot her a sudden, answering smile.

"Will you please repeat after me," Lionel Daly said to him, wondering how he could ever have believed that Zachary and Gianetta were not hopelessly in love, "I, Zachary Cartwright, take thee, Gianetta Hollis, to my wedded wife,"

Zachary's voice sent little tingles down Elizabeth Daly's

184

spine as he made the responses. The children sat quiet as mice, enraptured by the sight of a European lady in a Chinese wedding-dress. Ben shifted restlessly, anxious to be out on the open road instead of standing at the doorway of a strange building, flowers garlanded annoyingly around his neck.

"To have and to hold from this day forward," Zachary repeated after Lionel Daly, "for better, for worse, for richer, for poorer."

His eyes held Gianetta's. Neither of them was smiling any longer. Neither of them was aware of the presence of the children, or of Elizabeth, or of Jung-shou and Ben.

"In sickness and in health, to love and to cherish, till death do us part, according to God's holy ordinance; and thereto I plight thee my troth."

He meant every word. Whatever her reason for marrying him, whatever his reason for marrying her, he wanted nothing more than to take care of her for the rest of his life.

"Now loosen hands," Lionel Daly said quietly, "and Gianetta, please now take hold of Zachary's right hand, with your right hand and repeat after me, I, Gianetta Hollis, take thee, Zachary Cartwright, to be my wedded husband . . ."

She marvelled at how inwardly calm she felt; how sure she felt that what she was doing was utterly right.

". . . to have and to hold from this day forward," she repeated after Lionel Daly, "for better for worse, for richer for poorer . . ."

Sir Arthur took his gold pocket-watch from his waistcoat pocket and looked at it impatiently, anxious to be off to Chung King.

". . . in sickness and in health, to love, cherish, and to obey, till death do us part, according to God's holy ordinance; and thereto I give thee my troth."

Sir Arthur replaced his watch in his pocket with satisfaction. It was all over now, save for the groom putting the ring on the bride's wedding finger.

185

"The ring," Lionel Daly was saying to Zachary. "Please place it on the fourth finger of the bride's left hand and say after me . . ."

Zachary frowned slightly. "There isn't a ring. It wasn't mentioned, and I doubt if I could have bought one in Peng even if it had been."

Four pairs of eyes stared at him, appalled.

"I can't continue the service without a ring, or without something symbolic of a ring," Lionel Daly said with quiet firmness.

Sir Arthur sprang to his feet. "Of course you can!" he contradicted furiously. "The vows have been exchanged, all that remains is for you to pronounce them man and wife."

"Not without a wedding-ring."

"What about a curtain-ring?" Elizabeth was asking. "Will a curtain-ring do?"

Zachary looked away from Lionel Daly and towards Gianetta. In the cool shade of the chapel, her eyes were the colour of smoked quartz. "There's no need to search for a curtain-ring," he said, pulling his signet ring off his left-hand little finger.

Elizabeth Daly and Sir Arthur visibly relaxed. Gianetta's generous mouth curved into a deep smile. She had known that Zachary would not allow their wedding to be spoilt by an unseemly search for a curtain-ring.

"Place the ring on the fourth finger of the bride's left hand," Lionel Daly again instructed, "and say after me. 'With this ring I thee wed'."

Zachary's fingers were warm and dry as he slid the ring on to her finger, holding it there as he said steadily, "With this ring I thee wed, with my body I thee worship, and with all my worldly goods I thee endow: In the name of the Father, and of the Son, and of the Holy Ghost. Amen."

Elizabeth Daly gave a deep, tremulous sigh. In the porch, Jung-shou wiped tears from her eyes. Lionel Daly smiled benevolently at them both and then said to his small congregation,

186

"Forasmuch as Gianetta and Zachary have consented together in holy wedlock, and have witnessed the same before God and this company, and thereto have given and pledged their troth to each other, and have declared the same by giving and receiving of a ring and by joining of hands; I pronounce that they be man and wife together. In the Name of the Father, and of the Son, and of the Holy Ghost. Amen."

Sir Arthur stepped out of his pew, anxious to make a speedy get-away, but was foiled by the pianist launching into the opening notes of "The Voice that Breathed O'er Eden." He ground his teeth together, obliged to remain respectfully immobile as the bride and groom and small congregation began to sing. The children's voices were discordant but enthusiastic, the bride's voice a lovely, lilting contralto, the groom's voice a surprisingly pleasing baritone.

Jung-shou's sister had no intention of cutting her performance short. Sir Arthur had to endure all eight verses before, to the stirring strains of "Jerusalem", the newly married couple walked arm in arm out of the church.

"Congratulations, and now I must be on my way," he said the instant they were over the porch threshold. "I shall tell your aunt that she has absolutely nothing to worry about where you are concerned, Gianetta. As for you, Mr Cartwright. I'm obliged to you for acting honourably towards my niece. I would appreciate it if, on your eventual return to London, no mention was made of the regrettable circumstances necessitating your marriage. No doubt you will again be my guest at the Residency when you pass through Chung King on your eventual homeward journey. Until then, good-bye."

He shook Zachary's hand briskly, gave Gianetta a perfunctory kiss on the cheek, and made his goodbyes to the Dalys.

No-one made the slightest effort to delay him. His bags had already been carried out to the waiting junk. Without further ado, Sir Arthur marched off in the direction of the river, the set of his shoulders proclaiming the personal satisfaction he felt at having so adroitly brought a difficult situation to an acceptable conclusion.

"Congratulations!" Elizabeth Daly said to them, beaming radiantly. "It was a wonderful wedding service, quite beautiful despite the hitch over the ring. Cook has prepared a wedding breakfast and I've asked her to serve it on the verandah. We don't have any champagne for the toasts, unfortunately, but we do have fresh orange juice."

Zachary was accepting Lionel Daly's congratulations, and Gianetta was overcome by a sudden flash of shyness. The tall, broad-shouldered figure shaking Lionel Daly's hand was her husband. They were married. It seemed too incredible to be true. She wondered what Serena would say when she heard of their marriage; she wondered what Charles would say.

As it was obviously inappropriate to toss her bouquet in Elizabeth's direction, she threw it over the heads of the children clustering around her. There were squeals of delight as a sea of hands vied for possession of it. The victor was a little girl of about six years old. Gianetta blew her a kiss, and Lionel Daly and Zachary finished their short conversation.

"We mustn't linger too long over our wedding breakfast," Zachary said to her as the Daly's began to lead the way back to the mission. "Not if we want to camp tonight out of sight and sound of Peng."

Despite all her determination not to be coy and missish, her cheeks flushed rosily. She had wanted a wedding night by the banks of the Kialing, and now she was to have one. With sudden fervour she wished that her mother were still alive in order that she could talk to her, woman to woman. Elizabeth Daly was kindness itself but they hadn't known each other long enough to be able to hold such a conversation without embarrassment.

"I think we should hold hands," Zachary said to her,

undisguised amusement in his voice. "I think our wedding guests expect it."

Her hand felt very small and fragile in his. More than anything else in the world she wanted to be able to smile at him and meet his eyes as directly and joyfully as she had done in church, but she couldn't. She was too acutely conscious of the night that lay ahead.

A circular table had been set out on the verandah and covered with a white lace tablecloth. There were plates of prettily arranged, very European sandwiches. A Victoria spongecake held pride of place as a wedding-cake, and there were glass jugs of orange-juice and chilled China tea.

With her hand still securely in Zachary's, Gianetta mounted the short flight of steps. As she sat down, Zachary on her right hand side and Lionel Daly on her left, she could see the distant figure of her uncle as he stepped into a punt. In the middle of the river, on board the waiting junk, a dog was barking, wagging its tail vigorously.

A smile quirked the corners of Gianetta's mouth. Her uncle would certainly not relish the dog's company on the long sail to Chung King. She thought of how easily she might have been in the punt with him, and shuddered with relief that she was not.

Zachary flashed her an enquiring look and for the first time since he had mentioned the night to come, her eyes met his without constraint.

"I was just thinking how glad I am that I am not aboard the punt," she said with disarming frankness.

Zachary grinned. She was so entertainingly honest about her feelings that he was finding it increasingly difficult to believe that she was a deceiver of Machiavellian proportions. And if she was not, if every word she had ever told him had been the truth, then there was no reason at all why their bizarrely contracted marriage should not be a happy and glorious one.

"A toast," Lionel Daly said, rising to his feet, a glass

189

of orange-juice in his hand. "To Gianetta and Zachary. May they have a lifetime of happiness ahead of them."

Elizabeth and Jung-shou rose to their feet, raising their glasses, echoing his sentiments.

When Elizabeth sat down she said to Zachary, a deep blush flushing her cheeks, "If you would like to stay here for the night or even for several nights, arrangements can easily be made. There is a double bungalow and . . ."

"No," Zachary said gently, aware of her embarrassment. "That is a very kind offer, but Gianetta and I are in agreement that we will spend tonight by the banks of the Kialing."

Instead of being relieved of her embarrassment, Elizabeth turned even pinker. She thought it the most romantic notion she had ever heard of, worthy of a Byron or a Shelley.

"And we must depart very soon," Zachary added, reaching for another mouth-sized sandwich.

Out on the river the punt had returned to shore and the junk's large, square, umber-brown sail had been hoisted. The dog was in the stern, its tail still wagging vigorously; Sir Arthur's white-suited, pith-hatted figure was seated near the prow, as far removed from the dog as he could get.

As the junk began to glide away down the centre of the river, Sir Arthur made no attempt to wave a last goodbye. His face was turned southwards towards Chung King, and he did not look towards the mission.

The seated figures on the verandah watched the junk's departure, each keeping their thoughts to themselves. Gianetta was thinking of all the wonderful places she would see and of all the beautiful flowers she would find, before she would meet with her uncle again. Zachary was resolving that he would never meet with Sir Arthur again and that he would strategically bypass Chung King when he and Gianetta made their return journey home. Elizabeth was thinking that she had never met a more disagreeable man than the Consul and was fervently hoping that he would never again demand hospitality of her. Her husband was resolving to include the Consul in his future prayers in the hope that the Lord would touch Sir Arthur's heart and make him a more likeable human being.

"We must be going," Zachary said at last, rising to his feet, "but we'll meet again, I hope."

The Dalys and Gianetta rose from the table. "I very much hope so," Lionel Daly said sincerely, clasping him by the hand. "Will you return this way from Kansu?"

"Most definitely."

"Then we can we look forward to you staying with us for a few days," Lionel Daly said with satisfaction.

"I gave orders before the wedding for an extra saddle-bag to be loaded on my horse and for Ben to be saddled in readiness. Could you send someone to tell the stable-boy that we're ready for them to be brought round to us?"

Lionel Daly nodded and Gianetta said a trifle regretfully, "I shall have to change out of my dress and into my riding clothes."

"Your dress is silk," Elizabeth Daly said reassuringly. "It won't spoil if you roll it up and squeeze it into your saddle-bag."

The sun was no longer high overhead but moving quite rapidly westward. On the Kialing the umber-brown sail of the junk could no longer be seen.

"If you will excuse me,' I'll go and change now," Gianetta said to the Dalys, knowing that there was no time to be lost if she and Zachary were to be on the far side of Peng before nightfall.

"I come with you," Jung-shou said shyly. "I help you get 'eady."

"Lay tissue-paper from my hat-box onto Mrs Cartwright's wedding-dress, before you roll it up," Elizabeth instructed her, "and put a sachet of lavender on the dress as well."

It wasn't the first time Gianetta had heard herself referred to as Mrs Cartwright, but it was the first time that anyone had done so correctly.

As she made her way to the Daly's bedroom, Jung-shou at her side, she thought back to the evening at the Viceroy's. It had never occurred to her then, when she had been falsely introduced as Mrs Cartwright, that within days the name and title would be legally hers. Somewhere between her pelvic bones, desire and excitement began to deliciously spiral. It had been on the evening they had visited the Viceroy that Zachary had so nearly kissed her. And tonight he *would* kiss her. Tonight they would make love on the banks of the Kialing.

When she returned to the front of the mission, Ben was placidly waiting for her, still flower-garlanded. On seeing her he tossed his neck, and reading his message she removed the flowers, handing them to Jung-shou.

"Did they tickle, my love?" she said to him fondly.

He gave a whinny, nuzzling her with his head. She thought of how near her uncle had come to shooting him and tears pricked the backs of her eyes.

"Where are your bearers?" Lionel Daly was asking Zachary.

"At Peng. They are going to stay there tonight with the pack-mules and catch up with us sometime tomorrow afternoon."

Gianetta slipped on her bolero jacket, mindful that the day's heat would soon be turning cool, and mounted Ben.

"Goodbye, my dear," Elizabeth said to her, her eyes suspiciously bright. "And God bless you."

Zachary shook hands with Lionel Daly, and swung himself up into his saddle. Twenty-four hours ago he had ridden up to the mission a bachelor, now he was leaving it a married man. Never again would he think life incapable of surprising him.

"Goodbye!" the Dalys and Jung-shou called out as they began to canter away in the direction of Peng. "Have a safe journey! Goodbye! God Bless!"

Their shouts rang out after them until, when Gianetta turned and waved for the last time, they were so far distant as to be mere doll's figures.

She looked across at Zachary. In profile his face was as hard-boned and as sensually aware as ever. A smile touched her lips. At moments like this, when he seemed broodingly lost in his own thoughts, she no longer found him intimidating or taciturn. The long silences that had always existed between them when they were riding together were not uncompanionable and they made the moments when they did communicate and when he shot her one of his sudden, flashing smiles, all the more heady and precious.

They drew nearer and nearer to Peng, and as they did so activity on the river and on its banks increased. Punts and one-man skiffs plied to and from the many landing-stages; junks lay at anchor, some of them upturned for repairs; buffaloes wallowed in the shallows; housewives trudged towards the river with empty buckets and toiled away from it with full ones.

They entered the town by the main gate and Gianetta was surprised to see that it was much cleaner and pleasanter than any of the other towns they had passed through. The gatehouse and main buildings were built of beautiful, russet-coloured sandstone; the inn-yards they glimpsed were spacious and well-swept and the little shops lining the busy, bustling streets were stocked high with rolls of dazzling coloured silks.

Despite the hubbub of activity, they traversed the town at a steady pace, emerging down the wide, stone steps of the north gate with nothing to mar their view but the glittering, glorious curves of the Kialing and the distant, cloud-topped mountains of Kansu.

Gianetta gazed rapturously northwards. "This is the happiest day of my life," she said with utter truth.

Zachary grinned, amused as always by her disarming frankness. His eyes, however, as they rested on her, were still speculative. Even if she had married him for mere convenience, her sentiment would still, no doubt, have been the same. He wondered how, and when, he would ever know the truth of the matter. The memory of walking in

193

on her love-scene with Charles still rankled. It had hardly been the behaviour of a young girl intent on nothing else but finding blue Moonflowers. She had previously spoken barely two words together to Charles and, despite all her subsequent protestations and his own recent doubts, he couldn't quite rid himself of the conviction that if Charles had asked her to marry him she would have acquiesced just as readily as she had acquiesced to his own proposal.

"How long will it take us to reach Kansu?" Gianetta asked, her eyes still fixed on the diamond-hard brightness of the distant mountains.

"Four weeks, maybe five."

His sex stirred pleasurably. He had never wanted to make love to a woman more. He wondered if, when he did so, he would finally know the truth about her motivations for leaving Chung King. However adept she might be at deception, he knew with utter certainty that she would never be able to deceive him in bed. She didn't have the sexual experience for that particular kind of deceit.

As Peng fell farther and farther behind them, the day began to lose its steamy heat. Woodland scattered the gentle slopes flanking the river and the bank itself was a sea of golden Globeflowers, as thick on the ground as buttercups in an English meadow.

"I think we'll camp here," Zachary said suddenly, reining in his horse.

On the hillside behind them, peeping through the trees, was the rose-red roof of a pagoda. To the south, Peng was lost in a fold of the hills; to the north there was only the distant mountains, their summits milky-white and as ephemeral as a Chinese water-colour in the gathering dusk.

As she reined Ben in and slipped from the saddle, Gianetta was again overcome by a wave of shyness and apprehension. What if he had truly only married her in order to save Ben from being shot? What if he had not the slightest intention of consummating their marriage? Even worse, what if he had every intention of consummating their marriage but expected her to be far more worldly-wise than she in fact was?

He unrolled the bedding bundles from his pack, rolling them out on top of the Globeflowers, not assiduously adjoining each other, but intimately near. Far nearer than they had ever been previously.

"Can I leave you to unload Ben and Bucephelus while I get a fire going?" he asked, his eyebrow quirking slightly.

She nodded, wanting to trace the satanic line of his eyebrow with her forefinger; wanting to feel the crisp coarseness of his hair against her palms; wanting to feel his mouth, hot and ardent, against her own.

As he strolled the few yards to the river bank in search of stones to edge the fire, she began to unload Ben. In the nearby trees a bird warbled. Somewhere, far out in the river, she heard a fish jump.

In easy silence he brought back stones, and as she loosely hobbled Ben and began to unload Bucephalus he began to build a fire.

The crackle and the aroma of the wood-smoke was infinitely comforting, reminding her of the many camp-fires they had shared previously.

"Are you hungry?" There wasn't the slightest trace of nervousness in his voice.

She shook her head, knowing that even if she had been she couldn't possibly have eaten. Her mouth was too dry, her throat too constricted.

"Then I think we should go for a walk."

There was a hot flush at the backs of his eyes and she was suddenly sure that it was, in fact, the last thing he wanted to do. He had suggested it in order to give her a breathing-space; in order that when he took her as his wife it would be in the moonlight, and not in partial daylight.

"Yes," she said huskily, agreeing with his suggestion, grateful for the surprising sensitivity he was showing.

He hobbled Bucephalus and then took hold of her hand, beginning to walk in the direction of the woods and the pagoda. Her fingers slid willingly between his, her shyness ebbing with the same rapidity with which it had engulfed her. Everything was going to be all right between them. There was absolutely no need at all for a disabling emotion that could only mar, and not enhance, the precious experience of their first night together.

The pathway was narrow and obviously little used, and she half expected to find the pagoda a deserted shell. Instead, the ground-floor room was meticulously swept, the enormous statue of Buddha in its centre, splendidly ornate.

"Do we light candles?" she asked, a little breathless after the steep climb through the trees.

Zachary shook his head, "No," he said, amused. "We're not in St Peter's."

They stood, hand in hand before the statue, in the gloom and the rapidly deepening dusk.

"What do Buddhists believe?" she asked at last, quietly.

"They believe that existence is unhappiness, that unhappiness is caused by selfish desire, that desire can be destroyed and that it can be destroyed by following the noble eightfold path."

There was respect in his voice and she said curiously, "What is the eightfold path?"

He turned towards her, drawing her very close.

"Right views; right desires; right speech, plain and truthful; right conduct, including abstinence not only from immorality but also from taking life, whether human or animal; right livelihood, harming no-one; right effort, always pressing on; right awareness of the past, present and the future; and lastly, right contemplation or meditation."

She was as close to him as she had been on the evening when they had visited the Viceroy and when he had so nearly kissed her.

With her heart beating fast and light she slid her hands up against his chest. His lips brushed her hairline and then he hooked a finger under her chin, tilting her face to his. For one long, electrically charged moment, their eyes held and then he bent her in towards him, his lips coming down on hers in swift, unfumbled contact.

Unleashed desire sang along her nerve-endings. In happy submission her hands slid up into his hair and her mouth parted, her tongue slipping lovingly and willingly past his

CHAPTER ELEVEN

Shock roared through him. Whatever response he had expected, it had not been one so passionately ardent, so headily unrestrained. For a fleeting second he wondered if she were still virginal, and then common-sense returned. A girl who had lived a shielded life behind the high walls of the British Residency could be nothing else. The sensuality she was now so artlessly displaying was innate, not practised. He remembered her Italian blood, her warm and generous nature, the fearlessness and daring she had displayed in riding alone from Chung King through bandit-ridden and leopard-inhabited country. He knew that where physical love was concerned, such a girl could never be anything else but stunningly hot-blooded.

And she was his wife. As he thought of his great good fortune, he trembled. Never in his life had he expected to feel such a fierceness of emotion for another human being. The knowledge that he was irrecoverably in love with her swept through him with the suddenness and certainty of a forest-fire. How could he ever have imagined that he had volunteered to marry her simply to save her from her uncle's petty tyranny? He had wanted to marry her because she was the most bewitching, most arousing, most intriguing woman he had ever met. Because she was his soul-mate; his other-half; because they were going to spend a lifetime travelling the world together, searching for flowers still unknown in Europe.

As she pressed herself close to him, he raised a hand to her still-chignonned hair. The white rosebuds fell to the ground, her hair tumbling, silky and scented around her shoulders. His mouth continued to move hotly and demandingly over hers. He wanted to take her now, in the pagoda, without any further preliminaries. As his hand moved to her breast he felt her sway slightly.

"It's all right," he whispered hoarsely, drawing his head away from hers, looking down at her in the now near darkness. "I'm not going to hurt you. I will never hurt you."

"I want to make love by the banks of the river." She was so confounded by desire for him that she was amazed she could still speak articulately, and even more amazed that she should be suggesting delaying the consummation of their marriage by so much as a moment.

His breath was raw in his throat, his sexual need of her so great he thought he was going to explode. Gently and with superhuman restraint he took hold of her hands, raising them to his mouth, kissing her fingers one by one.

"Then let's go," he said, his voice so charged with emotion that it was all she could to prevent herself from sinking to the ground there and then.

With fingers tightly entwined, they turned their backs on the inscrutably carved face of the Buddha and ran towards the woods and the path. The darkness made their swift descent hazardous and their headlong run was intermittently halted as Zachary pulled her out of the way of low-lying branches, swinging her round to him every time he did so, kissing her until he lost his breath in the passion of her mouth.

When they finally emerged from the trees, only the glow of their campfire and Ben's rough pale coat were visible in the moonlight. Both of them were panting from the exertion of the run, both of them were sweat-soaked.

"Let's go for a swim," Zachary said, pulling his shirt over his head.

As he did so Bucephalus whinnied and cantered towards him, his hobble trailing loosely.

"The bank is too stony just here to be able to walk

in comfortably," he continued, attempting to catch hold of Bucephalus as he veered in his direction, and failing. "There's a sandy shore a little further up, where the trees dip almost into the water. I'll secure Bucephalus and join you there."

In the moonlight, both man and beast looked magnificent. Bucephalus's coat shone like black satin as he pranced annoyingly out of Zachary's reach, and Zachary's broad shoulders and magnificent arm and chest muscles were sheened with perspiration.

Unhesitatingly she turned, running through the grass and the closed heads of the Globeflowers towards the point he had indicated. The trees spilled down to the water's edge and she had to slow down, picking her way through them with care until she reached the bank.

As she unbuttoned her blouse, letting it fall onto a damp, narrow arc of sand, she remembered the time she had surprised him while he was bathing. Not in a million years would she have believed then that the day would come when she would bathe naked with him. She laughed joyously as she slipped out of her riding breeches and then, in her lace-edged undergarments, she stepped into the delicious iciness of the water, wading out until she was out of her depth and then swimming languorously, her skin tingling, her hair eddying around her.

As Bucephalus charged once again out of Zachary's reach, Zachary made a dive for the trailing hobble-rope and missed. Blaspheming, he picked himself up off the ground. With Bucephalus in such a mischievous mood he couldn't take the risk of letting him run free. He had to be caught and hobbled no matter how much precious time was wasted in the process.

"Bucephalus!" he called exasperatedly into the darkness, "Come here, you damned nuisance."

Taking his time about doing so, Bucephalus eventually came. As Zachary led him towards the firelight and Ben he felt the ground tremble beneath his feet. He halted abruptly, listening hard. Faintly but distinctly there came the sound of galloping hooves. They were approaching fast. Too fast to signal the arrival of a casual traveller who would gallop past their camp-fire without stopping or disturbing them. Too fast to be the hoofbeats of a Chinese mule or pony. Whoever was approaching was European. And he was approaching intentionally.

With frustration and apprehension almost swamping him, he hobbled Bucephalus and then stood waiting, his thumbs hooked into his broad leather belt. Even before horse and rider pounded into view he knew the rider's identity. Knowing that his wedding-night was going to have to be indefinitely postponed, regretting with every fibre of his body his decision not to make love to Gianetta in the pagoda but to return to the banks of the Kialing, he awaited Charles's arrival, a pulse throbbing at the corner of his tightly clenched jaw.

Charles knew enough of Zachary's travelling habits to know that he would be hugging the Kialing's banks and camping beside them for as long as was possible. In the inn at Peng, Zachary's head-bearer had told him that they were under instructions to catch up with Zachary late the next day and that he and the English lady had only departed an hour or so earlier. Assuming that Zachary had asked them to stay behind at the inn in order that they could carry out the changing of drying papers in relative comfort, he had thought nothing odd about the arrangement. In happy ignorance of Zachary and Gianetta's marriage he had cantered out of Peng, optimistic that he would be able to catch up with them by nightfall.

Despite being handicapped by his injured arm, which was tightly bound in a Chinese splint and a sling, he had made good progress. When darkness fell, however, his quarry was still not in sight and he had been on the verge of reining in and making camp alone when he had seen the gleam of their camp fire. Digging his spurs in his horse's flanks he galloped down towards it, almost running Zachary down as he did so.

"Good God, Zac!" he expostulated as he brought his horse around. "Why the devil didn't you call out?"

"What the hell are you doing here?" Zachary rasped, ignoring the question, feeling as if there were bands of steel around his chest.

Charles grinned and slid from his horse's back. "I've come for Gianetta. I decided in Chung King that I'd been an absolute ass to return there without her – and that I'd also been an ass to listen to your words of advice on the subject."

Despite Charles clapping him affectionately on the back with his good hand, Zachary remained immobile, his thumbs still hooked in his belt.

"What advice?" he asked, his voice so tightly charged that Charles laughed.

"Don't lose your rag. What you said was sense and I appreciated it. But when I reached Chung King I had a long conversation with Serena and I knew then, without any doubt whatsoever, that your assumption was wrong."

"What assumption?"

"That Gianetta was mercenarily trying to compromise me into marriage." He walked across to the fire, warming his uninjured hand at it. "I knew of course, right from the evening when you so precipitately walked in on our . . . er . . . conversation," he threw Zachary a sheepish grin, "that she was eager to marry me, but I don't have such a high opinion of myself that I found it perfectly natural that she should do so. As you so succinctly pointed out, she barely knew me; and her following me from Chung King and declaring herself in the way she did, was all rather suspect."

Zachary stared at him, the bands around his chest tightening with every second that passed.

"Just how did she declare herself?" he asked, his voice

taut. "You never did tell me what led up to the little love scene I disturbed."

Charles cleared his throat. He wasn't a liar by nature, but he had been mortified at Zac thinking badly of him and now that Serena had told him the truth of Gianetta's feelings for him he saw no reason why he shouldn't elaborate the scene a little and reinstate himself in Zac's eyes.

"She told me she had fallen in love with me at first sight," he said, trying to sound modest about it. It was, after all, what Serena had told him had happened and he didn't see what harm could come from putting words Gianetta had been too shy to speak, into her mouth.

He thought back to his last conversation with her. He had told her that he was engaged to be married but that, for her sake, he would break his engagement off. She had been horrified at the suggestion and had told him that she didn't love him, that her only reason for following him from Chung King had been to find blue Moonflowers.

Serena had stared at him as if he had been a madman when he had recounted the conversation to her. With her bags all packed and ready to leave for England as Henry Plaxtol's bride, she had said quite categorically that Gianetta had behaved as she had because she believed that he, Charles, had fallen in love with her.

"Why else would she have ridden after you?" she had asked, wide-eyed. "And now, because she doesn't want to cause your fiancé unhappiness and because she doesn't want to face Papa's wrath, she is obliged to remain with Mr Cartwright's expedition. Someone must rescue her from such an impossible situation, and the only person who can do so is yourself."

"That was the real reason she followed us from Chung King," Charles continued, blithely unaware of the effect his words were having. "You were quite right in assuming that she wanted to marry me, but your assumptions about her reasons were wrong. They weren't mercenary. Serena was absolutely adamant that there isn't a less mercenary or calculating girl alive than Gianetta. And I know now that I will never be happy with anyone else. I have written to my fiancé, asking her to free me. And I am going to ask Gianetta to marry me."

"Are you, by God!"

Pain sliced through him. All along, deep down, he had known he had been living in a dream-world. Now he had no more doubts. She had married him because she had wanted a husband; any husband. Her first choice had been Charles, rich and handsome and titled. And when he had warned Charles off, and when Charles had returned injured to Chung King, she had transferred her attentions to him.

Again he wondered about the depth of collusion between herself and Sir Arthur. Whatever it had been, he had most certainly been gulled. And if Charles had not returned at such a crucial moment, he might have lived the rest of his life with her and never have known.

His fists clenched, the knuckles white. God help him, but he wished he had done so. He wouldn't now be suffering this terrible fury and desolation. He wouldn't now be facing a future without her.

"Where is Gianetta?" Charles asked, looking around curiously.

"She's swimming."

As Charles looked in the direction of the silky-black Kialing, he kicked the two bedding rolls into a heap. The less Charles knew about his true intentions where Gianetta was concerned, the better it would be.

"Your horse needs rubbing down," he said tersely. "There are no Chinese so you'll have to see to it yourself. I'll go and tell Gianetta that you're here."

Before Charles could make any protestation he turned on his heel, striding away from the fire and into the darkness. It was an action he found profoundly symbolic. The passion and joy that had so suddenly entered his life had been extinguished in two carelessly spoken sentences. There was no way, now, that his marriage would be consummated. On the grounds that it had not been so, Gianetta would eventually be free to accept Charles's proposal of marriage. Marriage to Charles was, after all, what she had wanted all along. He had only been the consolation prize.

Grimly he entered the outcrop of trees reaching down to the bank. He was going to need superhuman control if he was to live through the next few hours without revealing the tortured depth of his hurt, but he would not do so, he would be damned to hell before he would do so.

Gianetta was unsure how long she had been in the water, swimming a few leisurely strokes and then floating on her back, looking up at the moon and the stars. The Pleiades were heartachingly bright and she was able to locate Aldebaran and Venus. Dimly she became aware of voices and stopped swimming, apprehension flooding through her. Surely the Chinese hadn't misunderstood Zachary's instructions and ridden from Peng to join them? And if they had, why was Zachary not sending them speedily back the way they had come?

As the minutes ticked by and as Zachary failed to make an appearance, her concern grew. Perhaps she hadn't heard more than one voice. Perhaps she had only heard Zachary calling a still wayward Bucephalus.

She swam towards the narrow arc of shingle and when she was within her depth began to wade out, her lace-trimmed undergarments clinging to her like a second skin.

This time it was Zachary who surprised her as she waded for the shore. Though she wasn't naked, she might as well have been. Beneath her saturated cotton camisole her breasts were full and lush, her nipples dark and prominent.

She stopped walking, smiling at him, expecting him to join her.

"What took so long?" she asked lovingly. "Did Bucephalus refuse to be hobbled?"

The husky quality in her voice sent heat coursing along

his veins and nerve-endings. Christ, but he wanted her! If Charles hadn't blundered in on them, if his blithely happy words hadn't faced him with harsh truth, then they could have been happy together. Despite all her past deceits and even her reason for marrying him, he knew in his blood and in his bones that they would have been blissfully happy together.

For a minute he was tempted nearly beyond endurance. He could tell Charles that he was not only married to Gianetta but that he intended to stay married to her. He could pretend that his conversation with Charles had never taken place. The blood pounded in his ears. If he did so, his deceit would be on nearly as grand a scale as hers.

He said tightly, "We have a visitor. Charles."

The welcoming smile vanished from her face. She stared at him horrified, still knee-deep in the silky-black water. "*Charles*?"

There was no mistaking the disbelief in her voice. Whatever else she may have planned, she had not planned this particular reunion.

"He's waiting for us by the camp-fire." His voice was so oddly brittle that he barely recognised it as his own.

She began to walk slowly towards him, ripples eddying around her.

"Then . . . we're not going to be alone?"

"No." He turned abruptly away from her, knowing that if he did not do so he would be lost.

"Zachary! Wait for me!"

Her voice sounded utterly stricken, as if she was as devastated by Charles' arrival as he had been.

He didn't pause in his swift stride through the trees and onto the grass and the closed Globeflowers. He had made up his mind what he was going to do, and nothing was going to deflect him. A scene now, at night, would be too horrific to bear. He knew that when he had said everything that had to be said, he would need to leave immediately.

The morning would be soon enough for revelations, his

as well as Charles'. And the long, barren, intervening night would just have to be endured.

As Zachary walked away from her, Gianetta stared after him in incredulity. She could understand his frustration and anger at Charles's untimely arrival, but she didn't understand why his entire attitude towards her should have changed so drastically. Surely he realised that she was just as disappointed as he was? Surely he realised that she needed loving commiseration from him, not chilly abruptness?

She shook the sand from her breeches and tugged them up over her wet underthings, before pulling on her blouse. She was now excessively uncomfortable and excessively cold. Leaving her boots where they were she began to run after him, her teeth chattering.

By the time she caught up with him they were too near the camp-fire, and Charles, for her to be able to have any private conversation with him.

"Gianetta!" Charles strode quickly towards her, taking hold of her by the hand, kissing her warmly on the cheek. "I don't suppose you expected to see me again till you were back in London?"

Considering the friendship that had sprung up between them before he had left her to travel on to Chung King alone, his warm greeting was not overly excessive, but Gianetta couldn't help but be aware of Zachary's eyes on them and of his stony silence.

"No," she said, disengaging her hand from his.

At her coolness, he looked pathetically bewildered and she felt immediately ashamed of herself. It wasn't his fault that he had unknowingly gate-crashed her wedding night. At any other time, and in any other place, she would have been delighted at seeing him.

She forced a smile. "How on earth did you manage to catch up with us, riding with one arm in a splint?"

A boyish grin split his good-natured face. "I travelled by boat from Chung King to Peng."

"Did you call at the mission?" Zachary asked, standing several yards away from them.

Charles shook his head. "No. I didn't fancy being preached at. I disembarked at the landing-stage in the town and went straight to the nearest inn. Your men told me you had only left a few hours previously and that I would easily be able to catch up with you."

It was obvious that Charles knew nothing of their wedding. Gianetta looked towards the bedding rolls and saw with a spasm of anguish that they been hurriedly kicked together into an insignificant pile.

She waited for Zachary to tell Charles about their marriage. Charles had obviously rejoined them with the intention of once again being part of their expedition to Kansu. How awkward was it going to be for the three of them travelling together, when two of them were man and wife?

As Zachary remained silent, she realised that he wasn't going to embarrass Charles by telling him he had walked in on their wedding night. He was going to wait until the morning before he broke the news of their marriage to him. She understood his reasons; he didn't want Charles insisting on returning to Peng in the dark, especially when he was so handicapped by his injured arm; neither did he want to cause her the embarrassment of having Charles know that they had been on the point of making love.

"Have you eaten?" Charles was saying, looking towards the camp-fire, surprised at seeing no cooking pots.

"No."

Zachary's voice was so tersely abrupt that Gianetta found it unbelievable that Charles was not taking offence at it. She shivered, the night air striking chillily through her damp clothes and saturated under-garments.

"You need to change into dry clothes," Zachary said to her, as tersely as he had spoken to Charles.

Gianetta looked across at him, trying to catch his eye, hoping to exchange an intimate, complicit smile with him. His eyes studiously avoided hers. Unhappily resigning

208

herself to the fact that Zachary wasn't going to betray their relationship by so much as the flicker of an eyelid, she turned away and walked over to the rim of the firelight where her carpet-bag lay.

"I'd like to speak to Gianetta tonight," she heard Charles say to Zachary.

She pulled her skirt and a blouse from her carpet-bag.

"Leave it until the morning," Zachary replied, his voice still tight-edged. "There'll be lots of talking then."

Bleakly she set off once again for the discreet cover of the trees, vividly aware of how joyously she had run towards them only a short half hour ago.

As she stripped off her wet clothing and clambered gratefully into her serviceably thick skirt and modestly highnecked blouse, she began to chide herself for what she was now beginning to see as her excessive reaction to Charles' arrival. Zachary could have behaved in no other way, not if he was to ensure that Charles did not feel agonizingly uncomfortable. It was good manners which were dictating his behaviour, and her own manners, when Charles had greeted her so warmly, had left a lot to be desired.

She fastened her blouse buttons, ashamed of the childish resentment she had felt towards him. She and Zachary were going to spend the rest of their lives together. One lost night was of no importance. Far more important was loving behaviour towards a friend.

Much comforted, she walked back towards the fire. Cooking pots had been unpacked and two pans of water were beginning to boil, one for rice and one for the hot drink she was now very much looking forward to.

"Serena sends you all her love," Charles said, sitting cross-legged, Indian-fashion, by the fire. "It's been arranged that she and Henry Plaxtol are to marry in Shanghai before travelling on to England. That way, Sir Arthur and her mother will be able to be present at the wedding without too much inconvenience."

"When is it to be?" Gianetta asked, wishing that,

without separating from Zachary, she could be at the wedding and be Serena's matron-of-honour.

"Pretty soon. When I left Chung King, Serena and her mother were ready to leave and were only waiting for Sir Arthur to return from a visit to some Viceroy or other, before doing so."

Gianetta found it interesting that no-one had told Charles of the real reason for her uncle's absence from Chung King. Her aunt, of course, would not have told him, but she was certain that Serena would have done so had she known. The corner of her mouth crooked into an amused smile. Presumably her uncle had kept his intentions to himself so as not to look foolish if unsuccessful.

Her smile faded as another thought struck her. "I hope Serena didn't suffer on my account when it was discovered I had gone," she said anxiously. "My uncle and aunt didn't think she had aided and abetted me, did they?"

Charles looked a little nonplussed. "I don't think they did. To tell the truth, Gianetta, I spent very little time with your family. I simply got my arm patched up, and though I talked to Serena, we didn't discuss what your uncle's and aunt's reactions had been to your leaving. She simply told me your reasons for doing so and I immediately left by boat for Peng."

She hugged her skirted knees, staring into the fire, not seeing the loving, meaningful look he gave her. If her uncle and aunt had permitted Serena to meet with Charles and to talk to him alone, then they quite obviously did not believe she had known of the escapade in advance and had failed to tell them of it.

Her bare feet were as near to the heat of the fire as she could bear them to be and she wriggled her toes in delicious comfort, relieved that Serena had not been accused of colluding with her.

Zachary had melted a chocolate bar into the pan of boiling water, and he now poured the contents into three tin mugs.

As he wordlessly handed her one she didn't again try and meet his eyes. She knew, now, the way he wanted her to behave, at least for that evening, and she had no intention of letting him down.

"The news in Chung King is that the Americans are about to intervene in Manchuria and pull the Russians' chestnuts out of the fire for them," Charles said, equally constrained.

Zachary's refusal to allow him to speak privately to Gianetta that evening was a damned nuisance. For an impatient moment he was tempted to do so irrespective of Zachary's wishes. He glanced across at his friend, and as he saw the tension in his powerful arm and shoulder muscles, he quickly changed his mind. For some strange reason, Zac's temper was being held on a very short leash, and he had no intention of provoking it unnecessarily.

"Good," Zachary said, staring into the leaping flames. "The sooner the Japanese and Russians finish fighting on Chinese soil, the better."

No-one made any further comment. Gianetta's thoughts were a million miles away from Manchuria. Charles was not overly interested in the subject and had only mentioned it because, until he had spoken to Gianetta, there was nothing he really wished to talk about.

It was Zachary who brought the uncomfortable silence to an end.

"I think we should be turning in," he said, rising to his feet.

As he walked across to the bedding rolls, disengaging hers from his, Gianetta felt a pang of almost unbearable sadness. Why, oh why, had Charles decided to rejoin them? The last few hours had been so perfect and now, instead of sleeping in each other's arms, she and Zachary would be sleeping a very proper and very prim distance apart.

"Goodnight, Gianetta," Charles said, rising to his feet as she rose to hers. "I'd like to talk to you in the morning. Perhaps we could take a walk by the river before breakfast?"

His voice was oddly thick. Gianetta wondered if he had laced his hot chocolate with a dash of brandy, or if his arm was perhaps paining him.

"Yes," she said with tired politeness. "That would be nice, Charles."

Zachary had already removed his bedding-roll to the far side of the fire, and she knew that he was not going to wish her a loving goodnight.

Seeking comfort from the thought that not doing so was costing him just as much pain as she herself was feeling, she wrapped her skirt around her legs and, not bothering to undress in any way, slid into her bedding-roll.

Neither Zachary or Charles spoke again, save to wish each other goodnight. The fire crackled, sending an occasional flurry of sparks skywards. Gianetta lay looking up at the stars, wondering if perhaps Charles would decide against accompanying them when he learned of their marriage; wondering if, by tomorrow evening, she and Zachary would again be alone together.

CHAPTER TWELVE

When she woke the sun had already risen and the sky was the colour of pale apricots. She lay for a moment, listening to the familiar sounds of the Kialing surging southwards, of the early morning fire crackling and spitting. A deep smile of happiness curved her lips. This was the first day of her life as Mrs Zachary Cartwright. She pushed herself up on one arm, looking towards Zachary's sleeping-bag, hoping that they could perhaps exchange a few whispered words together before Charles awoke.

His sleeping-bag was empty and there was no sign of him. It was Charles who looked across at her.

"Good-morning, sleepy-head," he said with a grin. "I thought you were never going to wake up. Would you like some coffee?"

She nodded, trying not to be too disappointed that it was he, and not Zachary, who was greeting her.

"Zachary's doing some early morning woodland plant-hunting," Charles said as he poured coffee into her mug. "He didn't say so, but I get the feeling he hasn't been bagging quite as many specimens as he would like. He was extraordinarily uncommunicative about his catch last night and said barely two words to me this morning."

Gianetta's disappointment deepened. She had been hoping Zachary had spoken to Charles about their marriage. That he hadn't yet done so was going to make her own conversation with Charles exceedingly difficult.

"I don't think he's disappointed at the way things are going," she said, accepting the mug from him. "We saw some wonderful irises the other day. Zachary said they

213

were completely new to him. They were very small with grey-green leaves and with crowns of soft blue and sulphur yellow and falls of the most splendid deep purple."

"That's interesting," Charles said, sitting down near the fire again, his arms hugging his knees. "I would have thought it a a bit late in the year for them. I saw some marvellous peonies from the deck of the boat and there were cascades of blush-tinted *Stellera* almost everywhere I looked."

He paused a little awkwardly and then said, "When you've finished your coffee, could we go for our walk? I don't know when Zachary plans on returning, but there is something I would like to say to you before he does."

Without being unmannerly, Gianetta didn't see how she could possibly refuse. No doubt he was wanting to know whether she thought Zachary was pleased at his rejoining them or whether his uncommunicativeness was because, bearing in mind Charles' injury and the way it would impede their progress, he wasn't pleased.

"Yes," she said, sipping at her coffee. "Just give me a minute or two to brush my hair and find my boots."

As she walked barefoot to the narrow arc of shingle, she wished fervently that Zachary would return. The longer she and Charles were together, with Charles ignorant of her marriage, the more deceitful she was beginning to feel.

Her boots were easily found and she brushed the shingle from them and pulled them on. Presumably Zachary had refrained from telling Charles earlier because she was still asleep and he wanted her to be with him when he broke the news. Wishing that he hadn't been so thoughtful, wishing that, knowing of their marriage, Charles had made the decision to return to Chung King, she walked back towards him

"Can you feel the difference in the air now that we are further north?" he said to her. "It's wonderful. I can almost smell the cleanness of snow in it."

His good humour was infectious and she said with a

grin, "I shall have to acquire some far warmer clothes if I'm going to be faced with snow."

"And not only snow," he said, as they began to walk away from the camp-fire. "I've read that the autumn winds in Kansu can be horrendous. They blow in straight from Tibet with only the Min-Shan range offering protection from them."

"If you are trying to put me off, you are failing," she said in amusement. "We shall be in Kansu and have left it behind long before autumn approaches."

A slight flush of colour touched his handsome, good-natured face and she realised with a stab of shock that she had guessed his motives exactly. He *was* trying to dissuade her from travelling further north.

They had reached the banks of the Kialing and he stopped walking, saying awkwardly, "I had a long talk with Serena while I was at the Residency, having my arm patched up."

"Yes?" She felt a slight frisson of apprehension. He had told her the previous night that he had talked with Serena but he had given no indication then that it might be best if she gave up her dream of travelling to Kansu. "What's the matter, Charles? Have you something to tell me that couldn't be said in front of Zachary?"

He turned towards her, his wide-set eyes and curly hair reminding her of a picture she had seen of a Medici princeling. Like Zachary, he was a man more given to action than small talk, and he was obviously finding what he was about to say very difficult.

"She told me your true reason for riding after Zachary and myself."

As she stared at him, bewildered, he took hold of her hands, drawing her towards him.

"There's no need to feel embarrassed or shy, Gianetta," he said tenderly. "You were quite right in assuming that I had fallen in love with you. The only problem was, you realised it long before I did. When we parted and when I travelled on to Chung King alone, I knew almost instantly that I had made the biggest mistake of my life . . ."

Her bewilderment deepened into horror. "Charles . . . Please . . . You hadn't made a mistake," she said, desperately trying to interrupt him. "I . . ."

"I should have known I was ruining all my chances with you when I mentioned that I was engaged, but . . ."

"Your engagement had nothing to do with what was said between us before we parted," she said urgently. "Please believe me, Charles, I . . ."

He was smiling down at her lovingly, her hands still clasped in his. "I'm not engaged any longer, Gianetta, and I don't want you feeling any guilt over my breaking off my engagement. Not to have done so would have been grossly dishonourable. It's you I love, Gianetta. It's you I want to marry."

As he looked down at her, sincerity darkening his eyes, her horror was total.

"Will you marry me, Gianetta?" he asked, confident of her reply. "Will you marry me in Chung King?"

There was now no way in which she could leave it to Zachary to break the news of their marriage. Numbly she shook her head and then she withdrew her hands from his, saying unsteadily,

"I'm sorry Serena so misunderstood my motives for joining you and Zachary. I told her what my real reason was. I told her that I wanted to travel to Kansu to find blue Moonflowers."

His happy smile of expectation grew uncertain. "I don't understand," he said, his eyes anxious. "You do love me, don't you? You do want to marry me?"

"I love you as a friend," she said gently, trying to save his pride, "not as a prospective husband." She lifted her left hand and held it out towards him. "I already have a husband," she said, unable to keep the happiness out of her voice. "I married Zachary yesterday."

Charles stared at her as if he had been pole-axed. When

216

at last he could speak, he said hoarsely, "You did *what*? When? Where?"

"I married Zachary yesterday, in the mission church at Peng."

Charles ran his hands through his hair, struggling for understanding. "You mean it was *Zac* you fell in love with when we dined at the Residency? *Zac* was the reason you followed us from Chung King?"

"*No*." Gianetta's voice was sharp with irritation. "Why will no-one believe me when I tell them the truth? I followed you because I wanted to go to Kansu; because I wanted to find blue Moonflowers; because if I hadn't done so I would have been obliged to return to England and live alone in a mausoleum of a house in the middle of the Lincolnshire fens!"

"But I still don't understand," Charles said, staring at her incredulously. "If you didn't follow Zac because you had fallen in love with him, why did you marry him? And why didn't Zac tell me he had married you? Why all the secrecy?"

Gianetta turned and began to walk back towards the camp-fire. As he fell into step beside her she said delicately, avoiding his eyes, "I think the reason he didn't tell you was because he didn't want to embarrass you."

"Embarrass me?" he said, his bewilderment increasing. "Why on earth should it have . . ." He stopped short, his face flushing. "Good God! You mean last night was your wedding night? Is *that* why the bearers were in Peng?"

She nodded, laughter rising in her throat at the unwitting farcicality of it all.

Their eyes met, and as Charles saw the laughter in her eyes, his hurt and incomprehension died. If she was not embarrassed, there was no reason why he should be. He began to grin. Maybe it was for the best after all. They were loving friends and they would remain loving friends. If they had married, the friendship between them might very soon have become a thing of the past, as he had seen happen so often in his friends' marriages.

"You have all my best wishes and congratulations," he said with sincerity, salvaging his pride and gallantly overcoming his disappointment, "but there's one thing I shall be a long time forgiving Zac for."

"And what is that?" she asked, glad that their relationship was once again on its old happy footing.

"Marrying, without having me as his best man."

They were both laughing when they returned to the campfire. As they did so, Zachary rode out of the woods towards them and Gianetta felt her stomach muscles tighten. What was his reaction going to be when he found out that Charles knew of their marriage? Was he going to be annoyed? Was she going to have to tell him why she had made the disclosure and if she did, would Charles mind?

There was no time in which to ask Charles. Bucephalus was galloping down on them and with deepening apprehension she saw that Zachary's face was forbiddingly grim.

Charles, too, was experiencing a flash of deep unease. He now understood his friend's ill humour of the previous evening, but the tension visible in every line of Zac's body was indicative of a far deeper and more sinister emotion. Trying to ignore it, he grinned welcomingly.

"Did you get a good haul?" he called out as Zachary reined in and slid from Bucephalus's back.

"A few."

There was no sign of a collecting-tin bulging in his breeches pocket, and Charles was sure that he was lying.

He walked over to him, clapping him on the back, saying affectionately, "Congratulations. Gianetta's told me of your marriage. I know it's something you wanted to tell me yourself but believe me, the circumstances were such that she had no option."

For the first time since Charles had joined them, Zachary's eyes held Gianetta's steadily. It was then she knew she had been living in a dream-world, and that something was deeply and profoundly wrong.

"Where Gianetta is concerned, circumstances often leave one with no option," he said tightly, his eyes glittering. "When she told you of our marriage, did she also tell you of the circumstances which occasioned it?"

Even Charles could no longer pretend that everything was as it should be. Bewilderedly he turned towards Gianetta, hoping for some clue as to the cause of Zac's barely controlled fury. Shock rocked him on his heels. Seconds ago her eyes had been dancing with laughter and she had been radiant and vibrant. Now she looked like a ghost.

He swung back towards Zac. "What the devil is going on here?" he demanded, anger on Gianetta's behalf surging through him. "Why all the doom and gloom? I'm sorry that I rode in on your wedding night in the way that I did, but there's no reason why it should spoil the rest of your honeymoon. Obviously I'll return to Peng for a few days and if you think it would be better if I didn't travel with you to Kansu, I'll return to Chung King and be on my way back to England."

Zac broke eye contact with Gianetta, striding across to the far side of the camp-fire and picking up his saddle-bag.

"A return to Chung King would be your best option," he said, his voice a whiplash as he slung the saddle-bag over his shoulder and once more faced them. "And Gianetta will accompany you."

From the moment he had dismounted from Bucephalus and met her eyes, Gianetta had known that her happiness and joy was at an end, but she hadn't known why and she still didn't. Now, her eyes dark with pain and incomprehension, she moved swiftly towards Zachary.

"*Why*?" she demanded passionately. "For God's sake, Zachary, *why*?"

He looked down at her, his face a tightly controlled mask. "Hasn't Charles made his intentions clear? I gave him enough privacy this morning for him to be able to do so."

She felt as if she were in quicksand, floundering deeper and deeper.

"Yes," she said, knowing that Charles must have told him the previous evening that he was going to ask her to marry him. "But what has that got to do with anything? What has it got to do with *us*?"

"I would have thought that was obvious," he said smoothly, only the pulse throbbing at his jawline betraying his inner emotions. "Charles was your first choice of a husband. It was because of Charles that you left Chung King. Our marriage was nothing but a marriage of convenience and, as it has not been consummated, I imagine it can quite easily be annulled. When it is, you and Charles can marry and live happily ever after."

Dimly she was aware of how stupid she must look, staring at him wide-eyed, her mouth gaping in disbelief.

"But I don't *want* to marry Charles," she said at last when she was able to speak. "I never *have* wanted to marry Charles!"

Suddenly she felt all her fears receding. The reasons behind his change of attitude towards her were so ludicrous as to be hysterically funny. He thought she didn't love him. That she loved Charles. That she she had only married him in order not to have to return to England under her uncle's guardianship. Lovingly she took hold of his hand, certain that within seconds he would be laughing at his idiocy.

"The only person I have ever wanted to marry is *you*," she said, smiling up at him, willing him to meet her eyes, knowing he would see the truth of her words in them when he did so.

He neither looked at her or spoke to her. Instead he removed his hand from hers and began to walk towards Bucephalus, the saddle-bag still over his shoulder.

"We were married because Britain's consul in Chung King demanded that we be married," he said to Charles as if she had not spoken, as if she were not there. "If I hadn't complied, he was going to shoot Ben and ship Gianetta to England."

He slung the saddle-bag across Bucephalus's broad back. "As he felt that Gianetta needed close supervision, he wanted her to be boarded in a convent until either he and Lady Hollis returned to England or until she came of age. Rather than allow him to exercise such petty tyranny over her, I agreed to marry her."

He began to secure the saddle-bag and Bucephalus whinnied, eager to be off.

"And as Gianetta had no desire to return to England under the conditions her uncle was specifying, she agreed to marry me."

With the saddle-bag secure he turned to face them both. "That, I think, sums up the circumstances surrounding our marriage pretty succinctly. As you can see, Charles, love played no part. When Gianetta returns with you to England she will be able to secure an annulment and she will then be free to marry you."

He turned away again, swinging himself up into the saddle.

"You both have, of course, my very best wishes for your future."

Gianetta was ice-cold. It was as if small, frozen fingers were squeezing her heart. He had never loved her. He had never even come close to loving her. He had married her because he felt sorry for her. Doubtless, if Charles hadn't arrived when he had, he would have consummated their marriage and taken what sexual comfort from it he could, but he had never *wanted* to marry her. And now he was off-loading the responsibility he had felt for her onto Charles.

For several disbelieving seconds Charles had been rendered equally dumb and immobile. Now he sprang forward, seizing hold of Bucephalus's reins, his fury at Gianetta's obvious hurt nearly unhinging him.

"You're a madman! Gianetta wouldn't have married you unless she were in love with you! And you love her!

221

You must do! No man in his right senses could help but love her!"

The corner of Zac's mouth crooked into a mirthless mile. "There was a time when I would have been in full agreement with your sentiments, Charles. Fortunately for me, you disabused me of them last night."

Charles felt the blood drain from his face. Through all the insanity of the last few minutes it had never occurred to him that he was anything but an unwilling voyeur. Certainly it had not occurred to him that he was in any way responsible for what was being said.

Now, as Bucephalus attempted to prance away, he held onto the reins with difficulty.

"You're being bloody stupid, Zac," he said hoarsely. "Not everything I said last night was the literal truth. Gianetta never told me herself that she wanted to marry me, and Serena was wrong when she said that Gianetta was in love with me. She wasn't. She told me she wasn't this morning . . ."

"I rather think Gianetta was trying to avoid complications," Zachary said brutally.

He had determined that he wouldn't torture himself further by looking at her again, but as he wrenched the reins from Charles's grasp he could no more help doing so than he could have stopped from breathing.

Her face was as pale as a carved cameo and as expressionless, her eyes so dark it was impossible to tell iris from pupil.

"Leave Ben with my bearers," he said, wheeling Bucephalus around. "He can serve as an extra pack-mule. I promise I won't over-burden him."

She felt as if she were in a nightmare from which she would never wake. He wasn't leaving camp to go on a short plant-hunting expedition. He was leaving it for good. His sleeping-bag lay tightly rolled behind his saddle. His mug was tied to the strap of his saddle-bag.

She had told him she loved him and it had made not the slightest difference. He didn't love her and now that Charles had arrived he saw no reason for accepting responsibility for her. He was going to do as he wanted, just as he had always done. He was going to travel to Kansu and search for blue Moonflowers and he wasn't going to take either her, or Charles, with him.

The only thing she could save from the ashes of her dreams was her dignity. Tears and further protestations were useless. He was going away from her and she might never see him again.

"Thank you for offering to look after Ben," she said through lips so dry they felt as if they were cracked.

He knew if he made a response his voice would break. Instead he looked towards Charles, saying tersely, "I've put two letters in your saddle-bag. One is to my solicitor, instructing him to begin proceedings for an annulment, the other is to my bank giving instructions that, until such time as you are able to marry, a suitable allowance be made to Gianetta and that she is to have the keys to my London house," and without waiting for Charles to respond, without looking again in her direction, he dug his spurs into Bucephalus's flanks.

"No!" Charles shouted, appalled. "Come back, Zac! Listen to me, for God's sake!"

He began to run after the galloping horse, but Zachary made no attempt to rein in and Charles staggered breathlessly to a stop, almost crying with frustration.

Gianetta remained frozen. The enormity of what had happened was too terrible for her to come to terms with. With a speed she could scarcely comprehend, her life had once more been turned completely upside-down; her sense of loss was total.

A hundred yards or so away from her, Charles shook his head in despair, then turned and began to make his way wearily back towards her.

Beyond him, in the distance, Zachary and Bucephalus grew smaller and smaller.

It was finally over. She knew now that she would never go to Kansu, never find a blue Moonflower. And she knew that neither of those dreams had ever been really important. Only her relationship with Zachary had truly mattered.

"I'm sorry," Charles said bleakly as he approached her, his boyish face haggard. "I shouldn't have spoken to him as I did last night. I had no idea how things stood between you."

She didn't ask what things he had said to Zachary. She didn't need to. He had told her himself that he had thought she was in love with him. No doubt he had told Zachary the same. Whatever he had said, there had been no need for Zachary to have believed him.

"It wasn't your fault, Charles," she said, moved to compassion by his very obvious anguish.

She stood for another moment or so, staring northwards. Zachary and Bucephalus were no longer visible. All that she could see were gently rolling hills and ever denser thickets of woods until, far far away, they merged into the fairytale landscape of Kansu's distant mountains.

The shock which had numbed her nearly beyond all feeling was beginning to ebb. She hugged her arms, wishing that she could remain frozen, wishing there was some way she could escape the pain she knew she would now have to live with.

Wondering how on earth she was going to survive it, she turned and began to walk back towards the dying campfire.

"I shall, of course, look after you," Charles was saying awkwardly. "I know you said you didn't want to marry me, but I still very much want to marry you . . ."

She bent down to her sleeping-bag, beginning to roll it tightly.

". . . the minute we reach London I'll talk to both Zac's solicitors and my own, and find out what the position is regarding an annulment or a divorce. It will probably take some time but . . ."

"No," she said gently, standing upright again. "When

we spoke this morning I was telling you the truth. I love you as a friend, Charles, but I'm not in love with you. And I'm married to Zachary. If he wants an annulment then he will have to put it in hand himself. I am not going to do it for him."

Her eyes held his gravely, and he understood at last. Deep personal regret swamped him. Despite the ease with which he had overcome his disappointment when he had proposed and she had told him she was married to Zachary, he knew beyond any shadow of doubt that marriage to her would give him life-long happiness. For a few bewildering and turbulent seconds he had thought that such happiness was again within his reach. Now he saw that it was not and never would be.

He picked up his bedding-roll. "You'll still allow me to be your friend though, won't you?"

Incredibly, she felt a ghost of a smile touch the corner of her mouth. "I'll always think of you as a friend, Charles," she said truthfully.

He began to kick the remains of the fire and she walked with her bedding-roll and carpet-bag towards Ben.

He hurrumphed in pleasure at her approach, and the frozen feeling which had enabled her to keep her emotions under such super-human control finally deserted her.

As the pony nuzzled her with his head, tears scalded her cheeks. There was no way she could take him with her back to England. He would have to be left with Zachary's bearers in Peng.

"But you will be well looked after, Ben," she said thickly, her fingers curling in his mane. "And you'll travel to Kansu and be far happier than you were in the Residency stables."

It was a long time before she felt able to walk him over to where Charles was attempting one-armedly to saddle his horse.

"Let me help," she said, wondering how he would have managed to camp by himself if he had failed to catch up with them the previous night.

His equable good-temper had already reasserted itself and he grinned ruefully. "Your aunt thought I was a maniac riding north again alone and with an arm in a sling."

"For once, my aunt was right."

There was an echo of her old vitality in her pert rejoinder but he saw with pain that tears were glittering on her eyelashes.

Damning Zachary for being the biggest fool in all Christendom, Charles swung himself with difficulty into his saddle. Perhaps when Zac finally returned to London, he would be able to make him see sense, perhaps there was still a chance that the two people he loved most in all the world could be reunited.

"I can't ride in my skirt," she said to him as he waited for her. "You carry on and I'll change into my riding breeches and catch you up."

Knowing that there was more than modesty in her request, and that she wanted to be on her own for a few moments, he nodded acquiescently and nudged his horse into movement.

For the last time she turned and looked northwards. There was no pinprick of movement that could have been Zachary and Bucephalus. Presumably they were in one of the many valleys and gulleys running between the hills.

It was very peaceful. On her right-hand side the Kialing surged glitteringly southwards. On her left, high on the wooded hill-side, the russet-red roof of the pagoda peeped gleamingly above the trees. She remembered the precious, passion-filled moments when they had stood in the twilight before the carved figure of the giant Buddha. She remembered the heat of his lips as they had crushed hers; the spring of his hair as it had curled beneath her palms; the strength and hardness of his body.

From the north a light breeze blew, tugging gently at her hair. She brushed a stray tendril away from her face. She would never forget. Not ever.

She mounted Ben, knowing with an aching heart that she was doing so for the last time, and then she turned him round and began the long, bleak journey south.

CHAPTER THIRTEEN

They met Zachary's bearers on the shallow stone steps
leading to Peng's north gate.

"Mr Cartwright wants you to take Miss Hollis's pony
with you," Charles said to Tien Tang as they all came to a
halt amidst a crush of pedestrians. "He isn't a pack-mule,
so you're not to load him up too heavily."

"You're not to load him at all," Gianetta said fiercely,
slipping from the saddle, her eyes stinging as she fought
to hold back her tears.

"It might take you a day or two to catch up with Mr Cartwright," Charles said, privately wondering if they would
ever succeed. "He set off at quite a pace this morning."

"Is all 'ight," Tien Tang said to him confidently. "We
follow Kialing. We find him."

For Ben's sake, Charles hoped they did. He dismounted, tucking Gianetta's bedding-roll under his good
arm and picking up her carpet-bag.

"It's time for us to be on our way," he said to her
gently.

She nodded. They were being jostled on all sides. A
pedlar with a yoked pannier of rice-cakes barged between
them; a housewife clasping a bulky sack in her arms
bustled in his wake.

She slide her arms up and around Ben's neck. "Goodbye," she whispered thickly, "Be happy in Kansu."

The bearers had wasted enough time.

"We go now," Tien Tang said impatiently, attaching
Ben's rein to that of the mule he was riding. "Goodbye.
Best wishes to King Edwa'd."

The string of mules began to clatter away down the shallow stone steps, Ben alongside them.

"Zac will look after him," Charles said, offering her the only comfort he could think of.

She nodded. She knew that Ben would be all right. She knew that, when the journey to Kansu was over, Zachary would make sure that he continued to be well cared for. And she knew that she was going to miss him dreadfully.

"The first thing we must do is acquire a boat," Charles said as they walked up the remaining steps to the north gate. "I know where the town landing-stage is, so that isn't going to be a problem. Lord, but I hate the stink of Chinese towns! You'd think a culture thousands of years old would have devised a decent sewage system by now."

From the middle of the town they descended to the landing-stage via a series of long, narrow alleyways. There were several junks at anchor and Charles went expertly from one to another, trying to find one that had plenty of room aboard.

"I'm not gliding down to Chung King amid a pile of rotting cargo," he had said determinedly, before setting out on his quest. "The boat I sailed upriver in was loaded to the gunwales with putrefying fruit."

The boat he eventually engaged was carrying only a few plump and tidy-looking sacks.

When Gianetta was safely aboard and his horse had also been boarded and carefully tethered, he stretched himself out on the most comfortable sack that he could find.

"Ah, bliss," he said, beaming at her with boyish pleasure. "This by far the most sensible way to see China."

"But it's not the easiest way to pick flowers," Gianetta said as the boatman galvanised his three-man crew into action and they began to move slowly and surely into the centre of the river.

"Nonsense," Charles responded equably, closing his eyes and turning his face up to the heat of the mid-day sun. "We can always drop anchor and swim to the shore if we want to pick flowers."

Gianetta smiled faintly at his idiocy, but the smile didn't reach her eyes. As the boat glided downstream and the town receded, the mission could clearly be seen. Small and white, surrounded by the English flowers Elizabeth so carefully tended, it looked exquisite. She could see the bungalows at the rear, the adjacent church in which, a mere twenty-four hours ago, she had been married; the verandah on which her wedding breakfast had been served.

Zachary's ring was still on her finger. She touched it, her heart aching. It was going to remain there. Even though he didn't consider himself truly married to her, she felt herself to be married to him. She would ask Charles not to deliver Zachary's letter to his solicitor. If Zachary wanted an annulment of their marriage or a divorce, he would have to put it in hand himself when he returned to London. She was not going to do so on his behalf.

The boat drew abreast of the mission. Jung-shui was sweeping the verandah. There was no sign of Elizabeth or Lionel Daly. She remained seated in the prow, not calling out, not waving.

Slowly the distance between the boat and the mission widened. Slowly Jung-shui and the flowers and the church grew blurred and indistinct. She remained looking in their direction long after they were no longer distinguishable, her face pale, her eyes bruised dark with misery.

At dusk the boatmen moored to the shore. Within a very short time, rice was being boiled. They all ate together while ducks and herons massed on the river shingle in anticipation of lefttovers.

"What reason will you give your aunt and uncle for returning to England without Zachary?" Charles asked her as the dusk deepened into night.

"I'll tell them that Zachary thought it would be best if I returned to London and waited for him there."

Charles nodded. She would not be telling any lies, and

he doubted if Sir Arthur and Lady Hollis would find it strange that she was not accompanying her husband into such a remote region as Kansu.

"I don't know about you, but I'm ready for bed," he said, as the boatmen gathered in a circle at the stern of the boat and, squatting down, began to roll dice.

"Do we sleep on the boat or on the shore?"

"On the boat." He pushed himself up from the sack on which he was still comfortably sprawled and went in search of their bedding-rolls.

When he returned with them, he spread them out on the cramped deck space.

"Sorry about the close proximity," he said a little awkwardly. "There's nothing else for it, I'm afraid."

"It's all right," she said truthfully. "I shall be glad to know that you're nearby, and I won't cause any embarrassment by undressing. I'm growing quite accustomed to sleeping in my clothes."

His teeth flashed in the darkness as he gave her a broad grin. "Me too. Thank the Lord we'll be able to have a decent bath when we reach the Residency."

The Residency. Her thoughts had been too full of Zachary for her to have thought yet about her impending arrival in Chung King. She squeezed into her bedding-roll and lay looking up at the stars. Her uncle would not yet have arrived there. When he did, she would be so hard on his heels that she would arrive before he had time to depart for Shanghai with her aunt and Serena.

A ray of warmth touched her heart. She and Serena would be reunited. She would be able to travel to Shanghai with her, and she would be able to be her matron-of-honour when she married Henry Plaxtol.

Charles wriggled with difficulty into his bedding-roll, hampered by his injured arm.

"Goodnight, God bless," he said with deep affection when he had eventually made himself comfortable.

A small smile touched the corners of her mouth. Their easy camaraderie had become almost fraternal.

"Goodnight," she said, grateful for his friendship and his nearness. "Sleep well."

Within a very short time, Charles's breathing deepened and he began to give an occasional snore. From the stern there came the sound of dice being rolled across the deck.

Tired as she was, Gianetta remained awake, wondering if she would be able to travel to England with Serena and Henry, or if they would be honeymooning in China before sailing home. If they were, then she would travel with Charles. She knew that her aunt and uncle would be appalled by such an arrangement, and didn't care. She was a married woman now and, as such, she could make her own decisions.

Her heart hurt as she thought of Zachary. She had been so sure that he had fallen as suddenly and as violently in love with her as she had with him, and she had been so very wrong.

She wondered where he was sleeping; if he was again by the banks of the Kialing; if his bearers had managed to catch up with him and if Ben was again tethered near to Bucephalus.

At the stern end of the boat the dice fell silent, Charles's snoring became more deeply rhythmical and finally, more emotionally exhausted than she had ever been in her life, she fell into a troubled sleep.

When she woke, the boat was already under sail.

"Breakfast is served," Charles said to her with a grin, proffering a bowl of dried apricots. "The sooner you rise and shine and we pack the bedding-rolls away, the better. The skipper tells me we'll be reaching the first of the rapids quite soon."

Remembering the surging torrents she and Zachary had seen when riding along the Kialing's banks, Gianetta felt a thrill of excitement. It was obvious from the ease with which her uncle had travelled from Chung King to Peng and the ease with which Charles had engaged their

232

own boat, that boats could negotiate the more dangerous stretches of the river, but when they had been riding on the bank she had never seen one doing so.

An hour later the sail was lowered and the crew manned the oars.

"Here we go," Charles said tensely, fearful for the safety of his horse and wishing to God his arm wasn't uselessly bound in splints and a sling. If the worst happened and they capsized, he would be gravely disadvantaged.

Turbulent eddies caught hold of the boat. Spray rained on their faces. The crew began to shout out a rhythmic "*ai-oh, e-oh, ai-oh, e-oh,*" which increased in volume and intensity as the skipper, handling the giant rudder-pole with practised ease, negotiated the boat through the foaming maelstrom of water.

When they emerged once more into calm, no harm had been done. Charles's horse, his legs carefully packed about with soft, plump sacks, was blithely unconcerned by the experience. Gianetta had loved every moment of it.

"Perhaps we should form an expedition of our own," he said to her with a grin. "We could sail up the Amazon or search for the source of the Mekong."

Despite her heartache, Gianetta laughed, knowing his remark was merely a piece of nonsense. Charles was not a committed explorer and botanist as Zachary was. She doubted if, when he returned to London, he would ever again venture further from it than to Paris or Nice or Florence.

As they sailed southwards the landscape began to change. Bluffs and cliffs and gorges gave way to much gentler countryside. Thickets of bamboo grew denser and more sumptuous; carefully tended orange groves began to appear.

Their days were spent sitting companionably in the prow on the soft sacks of cargo, and at night Charles joined the crew in their games of dice.

233

Zachary was rarely mentioned. Charles was too mystified by his friend's behaviour to be able to throw any light on it. Gianetta hugged all her thoughts of him to herself.

By the time Chung King was in sight, Gianetta appeared to be the same vibrant and vivacious girl who had ridden out from it such a short time ago. Only her eyes betrayed the profound change she had undergone and the depth of the unhappiness she was hiding.

As they moored beneath the great high wall that was Chung King's river frontage, she was relieved by the knowledge that her uncle would, by now, have apprised her aunt and Serena of her wedding; Serena would not be happily expecting that she had returned with Charles as his fiancée.

"Lord, how I hate this ascent," Charles said to her as they disembarked and waited for sedan-chairs. "Why couldn't they have built the town in a more accessible position? Why does every visitor arriving by river have to risk life and limb just to be able to enter it?"

She didn't answer him. When she had left Chung King, Gianetta had been certain that she wouldn't be returning until after she had journeyed nearly to the roof of the world. Until after she had found the blue Moonflowers. Now, here she was again, having journeyed no farther than Peng.

"Cheer up," Charles said to her as their chairs arrived. "Serena is going to be overjoyed to see you."

"My uncle isn't," she said dryly. "He thought he had seen the last of me. Now he's going to have to endure travelling with me all the way to Shanghai."

Charles shuddered. "And to board the steamer for Shanghai we'll have to descend this cliff-face again," he said as they both stepped into their chairs. "It doesn't bear thinking about."

Gianetta was uncaring of the steep ascent to the town and the perilous descent. She had been looking forward to scaling much steeper and far more dangerous heights.

234

Zachary had told her that the Min-Shan range in Kansu was nicknamed "the stone mountains", and she had been determined to emulate Gertrude Bell's exploits in the Alps by climbing where no European woman had ever climbed before.

She hated the confining mustiness of the sedan-chair. It reminded her of the intense claustrophobia she had suffered all the time she had lived in Chung King. Even worse was the sensation she experienced when, after being carried up the long stone flights of steps and traversing the narrow streets, she once again entered the Residency grounds.

Dusk was fast falling and from behind the lightly curtained dining-room windows she could see the flicker of candles.

She stepped from the sedan-chair, more grateful than ever that she was not alone and that Charles was with her. She hoped he had been right when he had said that Serena and her aunt were waiting only for her uncle's return before setting out for Shanghai. A long stay at the Residency would be more than she could endure.

"Mrs Zachary Cartwright and Lord Rendlesham," Charles said to the minion who opened the door for them.

Almost before they had stepped into the chandelier-lit entrance-hall, news of their arrival had spread.

"Gianetta!" Serena shrieked, running towards the head of the grand-staircase along the balcony that overlooked the entrance-hall. "Oh my life! *Gianetta!*"

Aunt Honoria erupted from the downstairs drawing-room in a sea of violet satin, her aristocratic face stunned almost into stupidity. "Gianetta! What on earth are you doing here? And with Lord Rendlesham? Has there been an accident? Is Mr Cartwright injured?"

As Serena hurtled down the stairs and as her aunt waited impatiently for an explanation, her uncle marched into the hall.

"What the devil are you doing here?" he demanded unceremoniously. "Where's Cartwright?"

"He's continuing with his expedition to Kansu," she said coolly before Charles could answer for her and then, her explanation made, she ran towards Serena with open arms. Two hours later, when dinner was over and when Charles had convinced her aunt and uncle that there was nothing odd or suspicious about their returning to Chung King together, Gianetta was still trying to convince Serena that she had married Zachary because she had wanted to and that she had never, at any time, been remotely in love with Charles.

"But I simply don't *understand*," Serena said for the umpteenth time as they sat together on her bed. "Lord Rendlesham told me he was in love with you and that he wanted to marry you."

"But I have never been in love with him," Gianetta said patiently, trying hard not to remember that, if Serena hadn't been so convinced otherwise, Charles might never have rejoined Zachary and herself, that she and Zachary might still be together.

"And you married Mr Cartwright and he *abandoned* you?" Serena asked incredulously. "Why on earth would he do such a thing?"

"He didn't marry me because he loved me," Gianetta said, keeping her voice steady with a great effort. "He married me in order that I would be free of your father's guardianship."

Serena's grey-green eyes widened. "But Papa isn't a tyrant," she protested with daughterly loyalty. "Why would Mr Cartwright think him one?"

Gianetta thought of Ben, her uncle's pistol pressed close against his head.

"I don't know," she lied, not wanting to cause Serena unnecessary hurt. "And now that I have told you every-thing that has happened to me, don't you think it's about time you told me of the arrangements for your wedding?"

The wedding was held in the Anglican Church in Shanghai.

On the day she walked down the aisle behind Serena, Gianetta bitterly regretted her earlier, lovingly given promise to be her matron-of-honour.

The notes of Handel's "Wedding March" filled the church, and the memory of her own wedding was almost more than she could bear. As the vows that she and Zachary had exchanged were echoed by Serena and Henry, Gianetta needed every ounce of her inner strength in order to remain composed.

There was to be no Chinese honeymoon for the bride and groom. Immediately the wedding reception was over, the wedding party left for the port and the ship that was to take them to England. If several of the guests were bemused at the bride's newly married cousin being accompanied by the eminently eligible young Lord Rendlesham, it was a bemusement they kept to themselves. Sir Arthur and Lady Hollis had let it be known that Lord Rendlesham was accompanying Mrs Cartwright on the voyage to England at her husband's request, and that he was an old and trusted family friend.

Once aboard the ship, Gianetta made her way to the highest deck. She looked beyond Shanghai, turbulent and sprawling, to the vast countryside beyond. It was flat and monotonous, bearing no similarity to the glorious landscape in the far west and the north. Her eyes ached as she strained to see into the heat-haze where sky and land shimmered and merged. Somewhere, over a thousand miles away in the crystal-clear brightness of Kansu, Zachary was searching for plants, drawing and documenting them, waiting for them to seed. She wondered if he would find a blue Moonflower and, if he did, if he would think of her.

Tears stung her eyes as the hawsers were released and the massive ship began to move slowly away from the dock-side. She was seeing her last of China. From now on there would be no towns crammed with pedlars and street-barbers and rope-dancers; no distant wooded hills crowned with small temples or red-roofed pagodas; no foaming, rushing rivers.

With intolerable sadness she remained on deck, watching as Shanghai slowly disappeared from view, watching until dusk fell and the flat, dun-coloured land could be seen no longer.

In the high uplands of Kansu's borders, Zachary sat alone before his camp-fire. A little distance away, Ben and Bucephalus were loosely tethered in companionable closeness. Further away, the bearers were gathered around a camp-fire of their own, their pack-mules fed and rested and tethered in the shadows.

Zachary stared grimly into the leaping flames. Gianetta and Charles would be on the high seas now, heading towards the white cliffs of Dover. He didn't have any doubts that, where Gianetta was concerned, he had made the right decision in insisting that she return with Charles to England. Charles would immediately hand the letter he had given him to his lawyer and no doubt by next spring, when he arrived in England to apprise Kew and the Royal Horticultural Society of his findings, the annulment of their marriage would be a *fait accompli*, save for his signature on the relevant documents. Gianetta would then marry Charles and, as Lady Rendlesham, would be instantly taken into the bosom of London's high society and live in luxury for the rest of her life.

The fire hissed and crackled, sending showers of sparks into the velvet-dark air. For his part, he would continue with his life as if their insane marriage had never taken place.

A log rolled from the fire and Zachary rose to his feet, kicking it savagely back into place with a booted foot. He would learn to live without Gianetta by his side, and he would discipline himself to stop thinking about her. He would continue with his journey into Kansu, and next year he would mount an expedition further west, into Tibet. And he would travel as he had always travelled. Apart from bearers, he would travel alone.

*   *   *

A month later, he wondered how it was that he had mounted and completed so many previous expeditions to remote corners of the globe without ever once being lonely. He was crucifyingly lonely now. At his feet, a tributary of the Wei-Hor tumbled white-spumed over its rocky bed. The Kialing and its head-waters had long since been left behind and it had been the mighty cliff-edged Wei-Hor that had led him into Kansu's heartland.

Zachary gazed broodingly down into the gushing water, his hands thrust deep into his breeches pockets. His trek had so far been highly successful. His field-book bulged with notes. His portable presses were full almost to capacity. He had found a large number of first class hardy plants unknown in England, and in the autumn he would take seed from them. Instead of feeling highly satisfied with the results he had achieved, instead of the all-pervading joy he had always previously felt in such a spectacular, stunning landscape, he felt only a deep black depression that nothing pierced.

One thing was certain. If he wanted to remain sane he would have to avoid meeting Gianetta when he returned to London. The mere thought of seeing her, arm in arm with Charles, was enough to make him clench his fists until the knuckles were white. He would not return to his Chelsea home, where she would be living until the annulment was finalised. He would book into a hotel, make his report to Kew and the Royal Horticultural Society, give the public lectures that would be expected of him and then immediately leave town without seeing either her, or Charles. Somehow he would survive his intolerable longing for her. Some day he would, eventually, forget her.

It was three weeks later when he found the Moon-flower. He made camp some distance from it, so that his nightly vigils would not be disturbed by his bearers or their mules.

On the night that the pale spray of delicate blue petals opened, it took him all his time to steady his hand in order to reverently sketch it. Then, his sketches complete, he sat in the moonlit darkness, gazing at it and breathing in its heady fragrance, thinking of Gianetta and wishing that she were with him. It was then he knew that she was in his blood and in his bones and that his hope of one day being able to forget her was futile. He would never be able to forget her. Not as long as he lived. Not ever.

CHAPTER FOURTEEN

In London, Gianetta was beginning to think herself the only one of Charles' friends who was still in town and not basking on the sea-front at Nice or Biarritz. Charles' mother had invited her to holiday at the family home in the Scottish Highlands, but she had politely declined the invitation. The gentleman who was privately tutoring her in the natural sciences had expressed his willingness to continue with her lessons through the summer, as had her botanical drawing tutor, and the thought of being able to concentrate on her lessons for a few weeks, without any social diversions, was a pleasant one.

She strolled through Green Park, her blouse of Alencon lace high at her throat, her lavender *crêpe-de-Chine* skirt skimming the ground. Charles' mother had been exquisitely kind to her, inviting her to every family occasion and outing. She had been grateful for the friendship and the affection. After visiting Plaxtol relations, Serena and Henry had departed for a delayed long honeymoon in Switzerland. If it hadn't been for Charles's family, she would have been virtually friendless.

When Charles had told his mother quite bluntly what the situation was between Gianetta and Zachary, his mother had immediately invited her to stay. Charles had his own, separate establishment, and it was not an arrangement that would cause embarrassment. It had been an offer that Gianetta had unhesitatingly accepted. The thought of living in Zachary's home, when he did not truly want her there, had been abhorrent to her. Charles' mother's kind invitation meant that she had a temporary home while she decided her future.

The first thing she had done was to ask Charles not to deliver Zachary's letter to his solicitor.

"When Zachary returns, he can give his solicitor whatever instructions he pleases," she had said to Charles, her face very pale. "But I would prefer those instructions to be given later rather than sooner."

"Zac won't change his mind," Charles had said to her gently, knowing full well what she was hoping. "He never does."

She hadn't replied. The hope she still clung to was so tenuous that it could only exist in silence. To put it into words would be to realize how foolish she was being, how totally unrealistic.

The second thing she had done on her return to London was to apply for a place at Lady Margaret Hall. The third had been to write to her grandparents in Italy.

Replies to both letters had far exceeded her expectations. She could go up to Lady Margaret Hall next year, and for the first time since her mother had died, her grandparents entered into correspondence with her.

They invited her to visit them in October, when they returned from a long-planned trip to Greece, and they approved of her decision to study at Oxford. Suddenly the world had seemed a brighter, sunnier place. She had a family again, a future to look forward to. All that she needed to make her happiness complete was a reconciliation with Zachary.

She bought herself a giant map of China and every evening she spread it out on her bed, tracing the route of the Kialing from Chung King to Peng and beyond, wondering where he was, wondering if he had found a blue Moonflower.

All through the autumn she followed what she imagined would be his route along the Wei-Hor into Kansu's heart. In the winter she thought of him holed up in a Chinese inn in Lanchow, Kansu's capital, waiting for the weather to break in order that he could begin his return journey. In the spring she waited for him to arrive in London, her nerves stretched almost to breaking point.

When he did arrive, she did not know for several days. It was Charles who told her.

"He must have been here for quite some time," he said awkwardly, a copy of *The Times* in his hand. "He's giving a public lecture at the Royal Geographical Society on Thursday evening."

Their eyes held. His pitying, hers anguished. He hadn't been in touch with either of them, and he quite obviously didn't intend to be.

"I think it's time I delivered his letter to his solicitor," Charles said unhappily. "He'll know by now, of course, that I haven't done so, but it will show him that you accept the situation. That you're not going to fight him."

"Yes," she said thickly. "Of course. If that is what you think is best. Thank you, Charles."

She felt as bereft, as heartsick, as she had done on the long riverboat journey down the Kialing to Chung King. Since then hope had, little by little, returned. She had imagined him returning to his Chelsea house, expecting to find her in residence. She had imagined his consternation when he did not do so and of how he would then seek out Charles and of how Charles would tell him that she was staying with his mother. She had imagined their meeting in the drawing-room of the Rendlesham town house; of how she would tell him the annulment had not been put in hand because she didn't wish their marriage to be ended; that she didn't want to marry Charles; that she wanted to stay married to him. And she had imagined him being almost pole-axed with relief, had imagined him taking her in his arms, kissing her as he had done in the moonlit pagoda.

Now she saw her imaginings for what they were, foolish daydreams without a hint of substance. That she had not been at his Chelsea home had not concerned him in the slightest. He had made no enquiries as to her whereabouts. He hadn't cared.

She knew that the time had now come for her to face reality. And she would do so. But first she would see him for the last time and she would say goodbye to him in her own way, silently and from the rear of the Royal Geographical Society's public lecture hall.

"*What the devil do you think you are playing at?*" Charles demanded of Zachary furiously.

The last time they had faced each other it had been Zachary who had been hardly able to contain his inner hurt and jealous anger. Now it was Charles who was almost beside himself with frustration.

"Why the devil didn't you get in touch when you arrived? How long have you been here? What are you trying to achieve by behaving like this?"

In the bland anonymity of his hotel suite Zachary continued dressing for his lecture.

"I'm behaving in a way I think is best for all of us," he replied tersely, fastening a starched collar onto his collar-button with some difficulty. "If you and Gianetta are impatient to be married, it's an impatience that will just have to be curbed."

His hard-boned face was as devoid of expression as his eyes. "I'd thought things would have been more or less sorted out by now," he continued with apparent indifference. "As they obviously are not, I shall see my solicitor in the morning and I'll ask him to expedite matters as quickly as possible."

Charles tossed an envelope dismissively down onto the nearest flat surface. "It's the letter you gave me to hand to your solicitors," he said abruptly. "At Gianetta's request I didn't do so. Considering your present behaviour I told her I thought holding off any longer was pointless and that it should be delivered. I was going to do it myself, as you asked, but it seems rather needless when you can now do it for yourself."

Zachary finished fastening his shirt-collar and stared at him. With a surge of satisfaction Charles saw that he had managed to shock him.

"You mean nothing has been put in hand with regard to an annulment or a divorce?" he asked, suddenly very still. "You and Gianetta aren't on the verge of getting married?"

"No." He wondered if Zac's trek had been a success. Whether it had been or not, it had obviously been far more exhausting than any of his previous expeditions. There were deep lines carved around his mouth, and his near-black eyes had a haggard look he had never seen before.

As Zac continued to stare at him uncomprehendingly he said impatiently, "For the Lord's sake, Zac. When will you believe that Gianetta doesn't love me, has no desire to marry me and never has had?"

He walked away from Zachary and over to the high windows looking down over Albermarle Street. "I know I told you she had fallen in love with me at first sight, but it was just wishful thinking. Serena had mistakenly thought it to be the truth and when she told me, I so wanted it to be true that I believed her."

"Why did you lie to me?"

His voice was so taut that Charles wondered again if the expedition had been a success or if Zac had been ill.

"I lied to you because of the kiss I forced from Gianetta," he said unwillingly, staring down into the busy street.

All his anger had now deserted him. He felt ashamed of the boastful lie, ashamed of the incident that had given rise to it, and he hated the coolness and barely veiled hostility that now existed between himself and Zac.

"I knew you thought badly of me for kissing her against her will when she was in such a vulnerable situation and when I should, instead, have been offering her my protection. I wanted you to think you had misjudged things and that I had been given encouragement."

"You *stole* the kiss from her? It wasn't freely given?"

There was something so odd in Zachary's voice that Charles turned round to face him.

"Yes, I stole the kiss and no, it wasn't freely given," he said, bewildered. "You knew that at the time. I've never known you be so angry . . ."

"And Gianetta doesn't want to marry you? She isn't impatient for an annulment?"

"No. She's only living with my mother because she felt you didn't truly want her living in your home and . . ."

Zachary grabbed hold of a bow-tie. "You means she isn't at Chelsea?" he demanded, throwing the tie around his neck. "She's never been at Chelsea?"

Charles's bewilderment turned to stupefaction. "For the Lord's sake Zac! Didn't you know? Haven't you been home?"

Zachary shook his head and snatched hold of his jacket. "No, I just assumed . . ."

There was a knock on the door and a young boy's voice called out, "Your Hackney is waiting to take you to the Royal Geographical Society, Mr Cartwright."

"I'll be down presently."

Zachary struggled into his jacket. Everything he had assumed had been wrong. He had caused himself months of unnecessary loneliness and tortured misery. Worse, he had inflicted the same loneliness and tortured misery on Gianetta.

Cursing himself for being the biggest fool of all time, joy roaring through him as he thought of the future that awaited him, he snatched up his lecture notes.

"Come on, Charles!" he exhorted, striding for the door. "The sooner I get this bloody lecture over, the sooner I can be reunited with Gianetta!"

It was a mild evening and the lecture hall was full. Gianetta squeezed onto a row at the very back. On one side of her was an elderly, eminent-looking gentleman with a profusion of white side-whiskers. On the other side of her was a studious-looking young man wearing a pince-nez.

She clasped her hands tightly together on her lap. On the wall behind the empty speakers' platform was pinned a large map of China. She wondered if any of the august audience were as familiar with it as she was.

A whisper of anticipation rippled around the crowded room as a distinguished looking gentleman entered and took his place on the lecture platform. And then Zachary entered.

The sheer force of his personality brought a sense of excitement and danger into the room. He strode onto the lecture platform with almost insolent assurance, his shoulders seeming broader than ever beneath his closely-fitting evening jacket, his blue-black hair curling as indecently low in the nape of his neck as ever.

There was fierce welcoming applause, but Gianetta was unable to join in. Even at such a distance, his masculinity came at her in waves and she felt sick with longing for him.

The gentleman who was chairing the evening was now introducing him. She caught the words "privileged", "distinguished" "Kansu" and "Blue Moonflower", but the blood was pounding in her ears to such an extent that she could not string the words together. She was aware of nothing save that it was the last time she would ever see him; the last time she would hear his voice.

As he stepped forward to begin his lecture and as the applause eventually subsided, his eyes scanned the hall. She looked downwards swiftly, terrified that he would see her and that she would have to endure the added torment of his open indifference.

Only when he began to speak did she again raise her eyes. Any rag of hope that he had missed her as she had missed him, vanished once and for all. His eyes blazed with happiness so deep, his sun-bronzed face was transfigured by it. Obviously he had found the blue Moonflower; obviously, where she was concerned, he had not one regretful thought.

"In discovering the blue Moonflower and bringing the seed back to Great Britain, I have taken upon myself the customary privilege of naming it," he said to his attentively listening audience.

It was then that his brandy-coloured eyes swivelled to hers; then that she knew he had seen her even before he had begun to speak.

"It is to be called *Ipomota Alba Gianettii*, after Gianetta, my wife."

She couldn't breathe. The blood was roaring in her ears. Her heart was slamming so painfully that she thought it was going to explode.

His eyes burned hers. "My wife accompanied me on the first part of my expedition to Kansu but, due to deeply regrettable circumstances, was not able to continue with me into Kansu itself."

Suddenly he was no longer speaking to the room at large, instead he was speaking only to her. "Will you join me on the platform, Gianetta?" he asked, his voice throbbing with emotion. "I need you by my side, now and for always."

It was as if they were the only two people in the room; as if no-one else existed. With eyes shining with joy she rose to her feet. There was a burst of applause as she began to squeeze along the row towards the aisle. Dimly she was aware of Charles looking towards her, smiling broadly, and of Serena and Henry in the row in front of him.

On the platform Zachary was waiting for her and as she walked toward him the audience, sensing that far more was going on than met the eye, applauded louder than ever.

His hands reached out for hers.

"Will you forgive me?" he asked huskily as their fingers entwined and she stepped up onto the platform beside him.

"Yes," she said lovingly as he drew her close, wondering how he could ever have doubted it.

Relief, so palpable that she could feel it, jarred through him.

"I love you," he said fiercely, "I shall always love you,"

248

and then still holding her by the hand, he turned once more to his audience.

"Though my wife was unable to travel to Kansu, she will be travelling with me on all my other expeditions. In June we are to leave for Tibet in search of species of roses and rhododendrons still unknown in Europe."

A chair was placed on the platform for her and, as his lecture had to continue, Zachary had no option but to lead her towards it. He didn't release hold of her hand until she was seated and then he did so only with the deepest reluctance.

She smiled radiantly up at him, reassuring him that everything was all right; that from now on, between the two of them, everything always would be.

He flashed her an answering, heart-stopping grin. "We both have other reunions waiting for us in Tibet," he said, uncaring of his waiting audience. "The bearers are making their way there now."

"The same bearers that travelled with you to Kansu?" she asked incredulously, hardly daring to believe what might be coming next.

"Yes," he said, loving her with all his heart, knowing that he would love her till the day he died. "And Bucephalus and Ben are with them."

There was no time to say any more. His audience were growing impatient and the sooner he continued with his lecture the sooner it would be over, and the sooner he and Gianetta would be together in privacy.

As he turned away from her and towards the waiting sea of faces, Gianetta wondered how she could possibly contain joy so perfect and complete. She was reunited with the only man she would ever love; she would soon be reunited with Ben; and she was again to travel into the heart of remotest Asia. Each and every one of her dreams had come true.

Suddenly her eyebrows rose slightly. Not *every* dream

had quite come true. She still hadn't seen a blue Moon-flower. A deep and dazzling smile curved her lips. One day, she would. And when she did, her husband would be at her side.